GW00702126

Top Meadow

A MEDIEVAL
COMING OF AGE NOVEL

To Janet

With every good wish

by

John Hook

This first edition published in 2018
by John Hook
61 Bowyer Crescent
Wokingham RG40 1TF

minnow.novel@gmail.com
Blog – www.topmeadowbook.co.uk

All rights reserved
Copyright © John Hook, 2018
Map Copyright © John Hook, 2018

Cover Photo Copyright © Steve Aylward
showing a Suffolk Wildlife Trust reserve
reproduced with permission.

The right of John Hook to be identified as author of this work has
been asserted in accordance with Section 77 of the Copyright, Design and
Patents Act 1988.

All rights reserved. No part of this publication may be reproduced,
stored in a retrieval system, or transmitted, in any form or by any means,
electronic, mechanical, photocopying, recording or otherwise, without the
prior written permission of the publisher.

This book is sold subject to the condition that it shall not, by way of
trade or otherwise, be lent, re-sold, hired out or otherwise circulated
without the publisher's prior written consent in any form of biding or
cover other than that in which it is published and without a similar
condition including this condition being imposed on the subsequent
purchaser.

ISBN No. 978-1-9993420-0-5

Dedicated to
Heather, my wife,
for her patience
and to
all who strive to
promote our heritage and
make it appropriate for today.

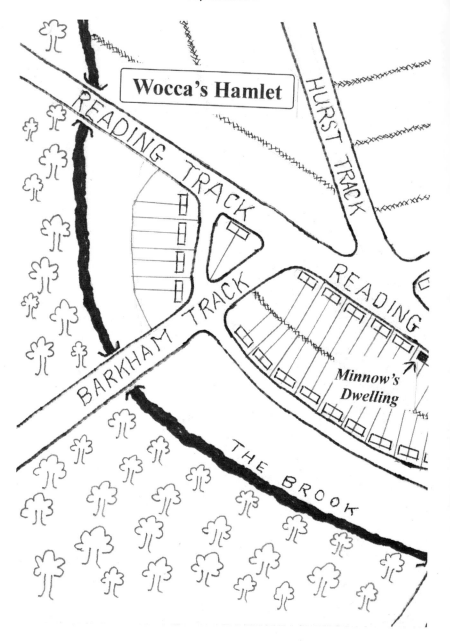

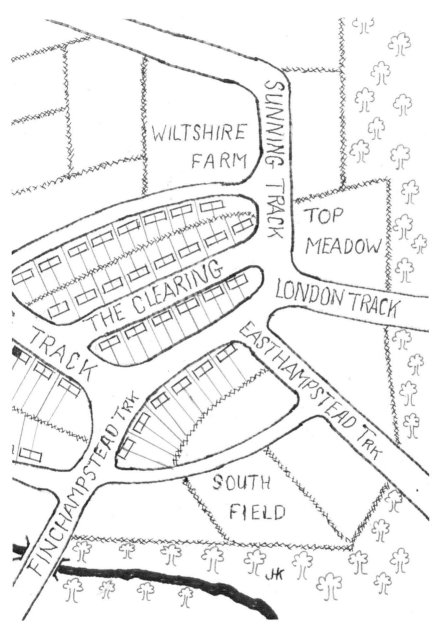

Contents

Preface

Wocca's Hamlet has been chosen as a Saxon style name for the current Wokingham in Berkshire. The ancient Wocca tribe established themselves in, and spread widely around, the current Woking in Surrey. At some stage Wokingham also had an alternative name of Oakingham reflecting the importance of the oaks of Royal Windsor Great Forest that surrounded the town. Wocca's Hamlet could have been shortened to Wocca's-ham and then eventually to Wokingham. This is a work of fiction centred around a chosen time in history.

The medieval Bishops of Salisbury had a palace at Sonning-on-Thames as a base for collecting tolls from users of the River Thames. Sonning-on-Thames had the Saxon name of Sunning and the parish was unusually a detached part of Wiltshire. The parish of Wokingham is in the Sonning Deanery to this day but neither place is part of Wiltshire or is overseen by the Bishop of Salisbury. Within the Diocese of Oxford the Bishop of Reading now has Sonning as one of a collection of deaneries.

The Clearing was the early name for an area of developed scrub land that is now known as Rose Street in Wokingham. It runs at a tangent to what would have been the track to Reading. The London track would have been parallel to and south of The Clearing. There were many tracks that led out of Wocca's Hamlet through the king's forest in several directions to places listed in the Domesday Book. Wokingham was not listed in 1086 which suggests it was an insignificant part of Berkshire.

There's no evidence that any of the events in this novel took place within the time period suggested. Circumstantial evidence is employed to coincide with some known facts about the reign of Henry II.

Chapter One – Strangers

There was the most peculiar activity on Top Meadow. This large space was the enclosed grazing at the end of the area known as The Clearing. A gathering of onlookers were making guesses as to the reason for the activity. They had their own work to do but a few minutes wouldn't be missed. The danger was that those few minutes were now increasing, that would lead to trouble.

It clearly wasn't the rounding up of the sheep and their recently born lambs, nor a Wocca's Hamlet gathering, market or fayre, as could sometimes happen in that area. The strangers were busy, hammering wooden posts into the ground, making a great deal of noise.

No one had any information that activity was expected on Top Meadow. The sudden arrival of the strangers, who set about their measuring, pacing out and marking, was excitement compared with the daily routine. Adding to the mystery were the language and communication difficulties.

The Wiltshire Farm manager was there, struggling to be understood. The men were only communicating in that foreign language from across the Narrow Sea. Their language, still regularly used by the lords, knights and earls since the invasion at Hastings over a century ago.

Horses, along with their baggage ponies, had been tethered to the rails either side of the gate within the meadow. Three displayed elaborate finery that wasn't from Wocca's Hamlet, Reading or Sunning.

Several Wocca's Hamlet children were also gathered. Any distraction from their daily tasks, of collecting water, foraging for food and wood from the forest that surrounded Wocca's Hamlet, was in the nature of children. They excitedly chatted making their own guesses.

The adult suggestions included stables to meet the needs of the increased traffic from Reading onward to London. Travelling over Loddon Bridge was the preferred route, avoiding the unpredictable river fords north of Wocca's Hamlet. It could even be a manor house for a lord.

No one was sure who'd suggested that the strangers were king's men but they were definitely not locals. One of them had surprisingly dark skin and clearly wasn't a Saxon or regular Norman.

Only king's men however would assume the right to access the land that King Henry now managed. He personally took all the taxes from the Sunning Deanery. No money was now going to the Church since the forced resignation of the Bishop Josceline de Bohon of Salisbury in 1184 as the bishop hadn't been replaced.

King Henry II was known to have recently been close at Winchester, Basingstoke and Salisbury. He was notorious for being frequently on the move both in England and across the Narrow Sea.

His wife, Queen Eleanor, had been confined to house arrest in Salisbury for some time following her part in rebellions against her own husband. Her children, including the deceased Young King Henry and the recently deceased Geoffrey, were also part of the insurrections but they had been pardoned due to still being youths.

No indication had been given by the travelling minstrels who brought their songs and stories regularly while linking the large towns with the interspersed market towns, villages and hamlets. They regularly visited Windsor with its castle, Reading its abbey - still under construction, Winchester and Salisbury with their castles and cathedrals as well as the many manor lands linking them all. News both good and disturbing was carried regularly by them and gave the excuse to the men of Wocca's Hamlet to gather in the alehouses of an evening. The name, Wocca's Hamlet, had remained, despite the size of the area having become an established village.

Knights from the many surrounding manors had been in constant demand fighting in the battles of King Stephen. They'd been engaged either in putting down usurpers or making claims to their own right for land, often joining with some other former lords, raiding as outlaws.

Most people had been affected by Stephen's tyranny. It was a very unsettled time. Stephen's constant tax demands were well known, especially by those who had to serve the manors and their farms.

For many years the Bishops of Salisbury had a smart residence, officially a palace, at Sunning by the River Thames. Sunning Deanery included Wiltshire Farm that administered this locally detached part of Wiltshire. The rest of Wocca's Hamlet was in the county of Berkshire.

Squires, from well-connected families in the surrounding area, serving the former Bishop and the knights, were also a source of gossip and tales amongst the children. They used Wiltshire Farm as a training base.

Horse skills were taught, not just being able to ride and fight in battle but also how to care for the animals. Even the youngest local children would watch their training and be willing to fetch and carry for the squires. They expected to be rewarded with some tasty items of food from the lunch provided for the trainees.

Kitchen, laundry workers and farm hands were another source of the latest gossip. Even the lowliest would know what was going on, not only locally but also around the country and sometimes about events abroad. The current activity on Top Meadow remained a mystery.

The farm manager was indicating the sheep that were showing signs of panic. They were crowding from one corner to another around the meadow. A shrug of the shoulders was the only communication from the strangers who continued their noisy activity.

A decision had to be made to move the sheep to another part of the farm. The adults decided it was now time to return to their own tasks.

They didn't have time to help herd sheep who could be the most stupid of animals at the best of times.

Most of the children wanted to help so some were selected to find the shepherd. He could have been anywhere on the farm's many pastures around Wocca's Hamlet. The rest were told nothing would be done without the shepherd. A small group continue to watch, it was more interesting than searching for kindling.

The hammering of posts continued, marking out a large square aligned carefully north, south, east and west. The strangers, shouting to each other across the square shape, added to the noise. All the while the heavy maul relentlessly upset the sheep.

These sheep were used to their own quiet existence. They produced the wool that kept so many of Wocca's Hamlet folk busy spinning, dyeing and weaving. The lambs were still to be separated and sorted. The female stock would be kept for breeding and milking, as well as for their wool.

The males would mostly be castrated and be gradually reduced in number over the next few months. This was designed to prevent injury should they developed the urge to become dominant. A couple of the strongest could be valuable for breeding but they'd have to be kept separate. They should become a source of revenue for the farm.

Chapter Two – It's a Mystery

Minnow had been the child that found the shepherd. He was lower down the hill, past the farm, by the small stream that was surrounded by further meadows. Like Top Meadow, the land had been claimed from the forest many years ago and was now pasture thanks to the animal droppings that everyone understood gave life to the soil.

More land from the forest was slowly being added as arable and pasture land. Pigs were used to work around the roots of the felled trees. Later oxen were used, with ropes, to haul the tree debris away. Peas, beans or wheat would be grown initially and then the land became pasture for a year. There was a three year cycle, every third year the land would lie fallow and recover from producing crops.

The shepherd was helping the herdsman deliver a cow of its offspring. The animal was quite capable, despite it being its first calf. The concern was that there may have been twins to deliver. Minnow was told to move away and find another place to play.

Minnow was regularly regarded as a nuisance by adults, particularly with his constant questions. Often he asked the same question but put in different ways. More frequently was the most annoying question 'why'? Few had time for him, he must have things he should be doing, why did he need to get under the feet of busy people all the time?

"But you're needed on Top Meadow," Minnow said insistently.

"You can see I'm busy, go away."

"I was sent to find you and say you're needed."

"And who in their right mind would send you to find me? Top Meadow is secure, I checked the fences and hedges early this morning, the sheep are fine." The shepherd started to sound annoyed.

"Farm manager sent loads of us off to try and find you. There are men, strangers, upsetting the sheep and their lambs. You're needed quick!" He hoped the urgency in his voice had started to be convincing.

"Why should I believe you of all the churls? You and the other children are always making mischief, playing your little games, having your laugh and running off. You can see we're busy, where are the rest hiding, having their snigger, watching your game?"

"Master, it's true, you're needed." Minnow could see he had to be even more insistent. "You can hold on to me if you think I'm not being truthful. I've never played a trick on you. I know I need to keep trying to understand things."

"You're a pain, hanging around, watching and full of all your questions. Just move back and give me some space. Anyone would think you've not seen a cow give birth before."

This was true, Minnow had seen lots of births in his few number of years. Dogs, cats, sheep, cows and even his Mama give birth. He had to imagine a horse giving birth as access to the stables of the farm wasn't easy.

Horses were often better looked after than most people, dropping a foal was done behind closed doors. Ducks, geese and chicken laid eggs like the other birds. Their young needed to hatch from an egg shell having been kept warm in a nest.

Minnow knew all this as he'd seen it. It was people he found difficult to understand. You could never tell how they'd behave or what they may say. The shepherd should have just gone to Top Meadow when he was told he was needed.

He began to wonder if making a fuss was all part of being an adult. Having thought that, the children of Wocca's Hamlet could be equally difficult in the way they treated him. Some had friends amongst each other but no-one chose to be his friend.

They'd steal the wood he'd collected, push him over when he was carrying a full water bucket, chase him, call him names, hold their noses when he went by. Others suffered as well but they seemed to especially enjoy picking on him. The ill treatment wasn't so bad now he'd given up crying when hurt, it was the crying they appeared to enjoy the most.

Minnow was small for his age and that's why he had his nickname. His given name was Will but he couldn't remember when anyone, other than his Grandpapa, had called him that. His parents would just tell him what to do without using his name. With no brothers or sisters he was the only one they would be talking to.

His Mama had three other children but they'd all died. He was the second born and could recall the most recent birth, a baby girl who'd lived just four days.

Minnow's Papa did labouring work on the farm, when there was work to do. He'd sometimes help with the felling and hauling of timber from the forest. At other times he'd fetch and carry items to and from Reading as a carter's assistant.

The bridge over the River Loddon from Reading made it a busy route but the cart track was very worn. Keeping the carts moving was where labour was most needed. The job sometimes brought a little extra with it, where things had fallen off the back of the cart. Minnow couldn't understand why they weren't just put back on the cart but perhaps it was because it was too full.

The shepherd eventually made his way up the track with Minnow following. The sound of the hammering became clearer as they approached Top Meadow. The shepherd started shouting at the farm manager when he saw the distress of his sheep but there were only gestures in return from him.

Nothing was stopping the progress of the strangers in their task. He had to think of the nearest place of safety for his flock and immediately looked to Minnow to help. He was sent back off down the lane to open the gate just past the farm buildings on the left.

Minnow opened the gate outwards onto the lane and it acted as a barrier so that animals would move naturally into the small enclosure. It was going to be a holding area while other plans were made. There was little grass for the flock in there. The sheep and their lambs soon followed and were quickly settled.

The other children had also returned from their searching for the shepherd and had been involved in helping to move the flock. With the sheep quickly settled, despite the small space for them, Minnow desired to return to Top Meadow. He hopeful he could make some sense of the activity.

It was now clear, that in addition to the large square, some smaller squares, inside the main shape, were the focus of the strangers. Additionally a couple of tents were being erected. They were being fitted out for night occupation by a newly arrived a group that included squires. An older man had also arrived, lit a small fire and was arranging cooking pots around the fire area.

The pack ponies had an area for grazing. Their loads were being stored in the tents. This looked as if it was going to be a long term project. The layout of the posts still gave no clues to an eventual purpose.

It was getting on in the day and Minnow still hadn't collected any hearth wood. He knew of a source but it involved quite a walk so he decided he'd better get a move on. He slipped away quietly so as not to attract the attention of the other children who may also have a similar task to complete before dark. He didn't need competition.

There was a lot of forest around Wocca's Hamlet but the fringes had been cleared of easily transportable firewood and knowing of sources became increasingly harder by the day. Minnow welcomed storms and wild winds that brought down dead timber and he'd often hide collections of wood within green bushes, away from the eyes of other children, for transporting later.

Now was the time to raid one of his hidden collections. He hoped it would not be taken off him as he returned.

Chapter Three – Foundations

Minnow had eaten his rough oats porridge before being sent off to fetch fresh water from the nearest well. The leather bucket only had one side handle which was fine going to the well. It was a struggle to bring back the full amount. He was used to having wet clothes but still turned the sacking he wore around his shoulders back to front to stop the slopping going through his shirt to his skin.

The sacking had also worked as a sling to transport the hearth wood the previous evening. Thankfully it hadn't been discovered. Minnow had it well hidden in a bramble bush. He'd told his Mama of the strangers up on Top Meadow, the upsetting of the sheep, finding the shepherd and relocating the animals.

She knew nothing to solve the mystery and didn't seem particularly interested. His Mama had had her own day of work and wasn't in a good mood. Nothing new there then he thought. The lack of hearth wood was definitely her focus.

He avoided Top Meadow and the distractions that would prevent him gathering a good supply of hearth wood today. He didn't experience any other children and guessed they were still gathered at Top Meadow watching the activities there. Late afternoon his Papa arrived home covered in mud.

He'd slipped while easing the ox cart through a sticky area of wet clay. Minnow was sent for extra water. His stack of wood was soon reduced as the water was given a little warmth. Slowly the warm water helped ease the dirt Papa accumulated on himself and most of his clothes.

The next morning Minnow placed the full bucket of water in the usual shady place. He put the heavy earthen plate as a cover and placed the large stone on the very top. Too often his efforts had necessitated being repeated when a local dog found it too far to make their own way to the stream or a nearby puddle for a drink.

Again his main task for the day was to fetch still more firewood. The kindling pile was very low and it was his fault. This was another thing he didn't understand, it was his fault. He didn't burn the wood, there was very little in the way of hot food for him to eat, it was late spring and the days were warmer so where did the firewood go? However it was easier to keep fetching wood than be in trouble, reluctantly he set off in search of kindling.

His choice of route today had to take him past Top Meadow, the encampment of tents and strangers. He noticed there was a freshly ridden horse tethered by the gate. Heat from the animal suggested it had been ridden hard over a good distance. The elderly knight, from the Bishop's Palace at Sunning, was talking with the farm manager.

Minnow had perfected, over time, a slow amble as if he were trying to find something he'd dropped. It often enabled him to overhear conversations. He slowly moved towards the two men. He could now hear some of their conversation. Avoid eye contact, he told himself, look all around at the ground, keep moving slowly as if on a search.

"You should have let me know," suggested the angry farm manager.

"I apologise and regret work started without your knowledge. I was journeying back from an audience with the King and had to go to Reading Abbey. I'd instructions to deliver for their part in the construction. The abbot there engaged me in a lot of discussion about the plans, his plans and difficulties sourcing materials".

"As you're aware the abbey is still under construction itself and the extra burden on the abbot was unexpected," he continued. "I was kept there for the best part of the week being shown every detail. I didn't believe the king's men would make a start so soon. You did well to send the message that things were happening here on Top Meadow." The knight spoke calmly, clearly having explained his own position.

"You can recognise how much of a fool I appeared," responded the farm manager, "when I knew nothing about the work. I had no way to talk with the men from across the Narrow Sea. You, as a knight, have the language but no one here understood a word they were saying."

"It was fortunate the sheep had already dropped their lambs," continued the farm manager. "We could have lost many with all the noise and upset. The king's men will have needs such as food and drink, I don't know where to start or how much they'll require. Who is to pay for their supplies? Have you any idea how long they are staying?"

There was still some anger in his voice but he'd recognised it wasn't the fault of the knight. He'd obviously ridden hard to try and calm the situation as soon as he could. Minnow continued his circling at a distance. The two men were so intent on their exchange he felt sure he wasn't being noticed.

"My instructions," replied the knight, "are to fulfil their needs, both bodily and with labour from Wocca's Hamlet. You will have noticed they have their own cook and yes he will need supplies. I have already spoken with the king's steward about their need for provisions, most of it will have to come from the farm. The steward will make payment arrangements with you."

"You will also need to supply tools, which to start with will be digging implements. You will be aware of who in Wocca's Hamlet could provide some labour. Work in return for food should be enough for most at the start."

"I'll have to make arrangements for payments as soon as I can," continued the knight. "There will be no particular skills required other than digging at this stage. A cart is on its way from Sunning, laden with basics for the king's men and their tasks. It should be here before the end of the day."

A slightly calmer farm manager recognised what he next needed to do.

"I'll start then with finding some labour and tools from the farm. I can only spare three men at this stage. Fortunately the sheep have all lambed so the men were set to ditch clearing. Digging here on Top Meadow will only be a little different. They should be with you within the hour."

Calm having been restored the knight knew some appreciation would be welcome.

"Thanks for that, there's still a lot more marking out to be done and setting up the rest of the encampment. When I see the men with their digging tools they can be set to work on some of the pits."

The farm manager set off down the lane to the farm. Slowly Minnow drifted away, back through the gate. He skirted around the meadow where it made a slope down towards the farm and the lower pastures. There were three woven split hazel hurdles marking off a small area the other side of the thick thorn hedge. Hurdles like this were often used to separate a single sheep or patch a hole in a hedge. The slight smell from the enclosure suggested it was a screened latrine for the encampment.

So, thought Minnow, they were going to be here some time, there was a cart due and that would bring items too big for a pack pony. Men will be set to digging pits. They have brought their own cook. There was a small smoky fire, the pots and pans confirmed there would be some cooking expected.

His next thought was that they'd need firewood. He'd still have to glean wood for the family but if he was the first to offer his services they may even give him some help and protection while collecting. He still had some firewood sources hidden. Taking along the cook and a pack pony would make the task easy.

What could he be given in exchange? Would there be spare food that he could take home? Minnow was bubbling with excitement at the thoughts rushing through his head. What did he need to do first?

He couldn't dare to talk with the knight. There would be no reason to talk with the farm manager who would eventually supply and then charge the King. Could he get the shepherd to support him after his being so helpful with moving the sheep yesterday? Would the cook only speak that strange language? And, with everyone else, he still had no idea what the king's men were doing.

With all these thoughts spinning around in his head he knew he needed to get the first load of firewood for home. His lack of effort, the day before yesterday, was obvious despite all his tales of the events. It wasn't the first time he'd been called useless. The message was very clear, get lots of wood today without getting caught up in any other events.

Turning right before he reached the farm and well within the forest he dragged out a couple of long branches that were quite dry. Putting them side by side and lashing them a little distance apart Minnow made a simple dragging litter. The bramble stalks were still flexible enough to bind the cross timber. Now he'd be able to start loading.

Stripping off the thorns of the bramble was a trick he'd seen woodsmen use. They'd run the stem through the base of a branch where it joined the trunk of a tree. The narrow v shape stripped off the thorns as it was pulled through.

As he wasn't very tall sometimes he'd use a small flattish log on the ground with the bramble stem placed across it. With another flattish log on top, steadied with the foot, he could strip the thorns. It was important to have the thorns facing forward towards the logs to help them catch and be pulled off.

The use of some more bramble stalks helped to hold the load in place. He made his way along the pathway, through the forest and towards the London cart track. This well used track was frequented by the horses, riders and carters going towards Windsor and the city having passed through Wocca's Hamlet. Royalty had also passed this way on occasions, especially if the River Thames was in flood.

He held the two branches, one under each arm and slowly dragged his load. The cart track was very rutted, like most tracks around the area and there were some deep wet patches he carefully avoided. His chosen route would take him past one edge of Top Meadow. The hedge had been intertwined during the winter to thicken it. It was high enough to keep the sheep in but low enough to be seen going past with his load.

His plan was to be noticed, he decided to sing. It was only a simple children's song that he'd heard his Mama use when he was much younger but it would have to do. Dragging his firewood had been hard work but he still had enough breath to sing. He decided to take it particularly slowly, perhaps take a short rest when alongside where the cook was working at his fire.

He could see, as he approached, that the cart had arrived and a trestle table had been set up near the fire for the cook. There were other trestles and benches outside of the tents and digging tools were in a heap near the marked out area. There were parchments on a trestle table outside one of the tents, their corners held down with large stones. Everyone looked to be very busy.

The three farm workers were being given instructions by the knight who kept checking that they understood. The scene was so busy Minnow almost forgot he needed to sing and be noticed. Just as he passed the fire pit, on the other side of the hedge, the cook was emptying some waste water over the thorn bushes. Minnow had been noticed, and, he'd nearly been covered with the contents of the bowl.

"Hold still there lad," said the cook in understandable English, "where are you going with all that firewood?"

"I have to get it home or I'll be in big trouble." At least the cook didn't speak that language from across the Narrow Sea. Minnow started to move on home but was told again to stop.

"I have need for firewood boy. You could let me have some off your load, it would make it easier for you. What do you say?"

Minnow made as if to give it some thought and then replied, "I must get this home, Mama and I will be in trouble if there's no wood when my Papa gets home. My Mama has no one else to help her and we have so little."

Minnow let the picture he'd described sink in. Before the cook could respond he offered some hope for him.

"If my Mama's happy with this load I can come back later and show you where to find firewood. It's not easy as every dwelling needs it and all the nearby firewood's been gathered."

The cook wasn't sure how it would be viewed if he helped himself to some firewood while the knight was still on the meadow. He promised Minnow something to eat when he came back hoping it would be enough to encourage him to return.

He was a cook, not a gatherer of firewood. The king's men had no thought for what he needed to prepare them a meal. What little they'd brought with them had quickly been used.

Minnow made for home with a big smile on his face. He broke up the firewood as well as he could, stacked it and then made his way back to Top Meadow.

Chapter Four – Doing What?

The three farm workers were busy digging in separate areas. Minnow started to make his way towards the cooking fire at the far end of the tents. As he passed the first farm worker he stopped, looked at him and the work he was doing.

"What are you doing?" he asked.

"Digging a hole, stand back unless you want a face full of dirt." The dirt was going in all directions and a point was made to spread it out all around the hole. Most people, thought Minnow, when digging a hole made a single heap of the dirt. Then it could be easily loaded on a cart and moved away.

"You could put a whole tree trunk in there with lots of space round it," Minnow added. There was no response other than dirt aimed in his direction.

Minnow stopped to ask the second farm worker, "Why are you digging a hole?"

"We have to dig foundations and I don't have time to waste answering your questions. Move out the way, I need space." Minnow had never heard of foundations but it was clear he wasn't going to find out any more from this person either.

Minnow thought about what he should ask the third worker. His question used the word foundation but he wasn't sure he'd used it correctly. "What's the foundation for? Is it something they do over the Narrow Sea?"

His questions brought a smile from the farm worker. He was glad to have a break from digging while he considered Minnow and his curiosity.

"It's a bit like digging a well, we've to dig deep and keep the sides straight, in a circle and keep it even. Here on Top Meadow it is unlikely that we will find any water but I may need a ladder or rope to get out. When the hole is deep enough carts will bring rock and stones to pack into it. That will then be a foundation."

Minnow thought about the answer but it still didn't make any sense. Digging a hole, just to fill it up again. Another of these adult mysteries that he couldn't understand.

"What needs such big foundations? Is it a castle?"

"We are building a church."

Now here was another thing that confused Minnow. Wocca's Hamlet had a chapel-of-ease. Why was another religious building required? Yes, it's a small old building, some holy days it does get a bit full, most of the time it's empty and locked up. It was used for baptisms and funerals, at other times all people did there was pray and praying could be done anywhere. He'd heard the visiting priest say you didn't need to go to church to pray. He'd said it to gatherings of people at the open space where the main tracks merged in the centre of the village. This seemed like a lot of hard work just to build another place to pray in Wocca's Hamlet.

The few people who had big houses and farms could fit into the chapel easily. They were expected to do this on a Sunday afternoon, all dressed up in their fine clothes. The visiting priests came from other churches and each week they were different. The bishop had them sent in from the parishes around Wocca's Hamlet.

Rarely, the knight as the current deanery manager, or the bishop before him, expected everyone to gather at the chapel-of-ease. This was so they could make some announcement and not be reliant on rumour. It was there Minnow's Grandpapa heard about the death of King Stephen. When he arrived back at his dwelling he quietly said a prayer, 'Thank God'.

At big gatherings many were left outside, especially the children and any message would pass back out through the door to the rest of the gathered folk. Looking at the marking out of Top Meadow it suggested this was going to be a large church.

"These foundations are for pillars to hold up the roof," continued the farm worker. "The pillars will be made from blocks of stone and further out from here will be the stone walls to to make the outside of the church. The King's decided the old wooden chapel-of-ease is rotting away. He's having this new building constructed so that all the people of Wocca's Hamlet can gather together."

This was now the clearest explanation he'd been given. At the least he could tell his parents and Grandpapa what was being built. "Thanks, you gave me a clear answer, I think I can now start to make the picture in my head."

The farm worker was willing to continue to talk, enjoying the rest from digging.

"The knight had to take a long time to explain it to us. I've never had to work on anything as grand as this before. I have helped to build, dwellings, barns and stables but they have always been wooden. I know what I'm doing with wood."

This Minnow could understand. Almost everything that was built or put together in Wocca's Hamlet was made with wood. The Royal Windsor Forest surrounded the village and was the source of all building materials, with the permission of the King and his forest manager.

The farm was where materials were requested and the farm manager made the further arrangements. There were a lot of rules about the royal forest. Navy ships had been constructed using oak that grew around Wocca's Hamlet.

"Thanks for the explanation," added Minnow as he moved away. He made his way around the back of the tents to where the cook was resting on a small stool. The king's men had eaten some lunch and the cook was sorting the scraps into a large cook pot that was set near the edge of the fire. He handed Minnow a piece of bread which he took and put straight into his mouth.

"I thought you may have been ready to eat and would not say no."

Minnow nodded and smiled. The bread tasted freshly baked, not one day old which was what they could afford at home.

"So you can now guide me to some firewood young churl."

Minnow asked if he'd any rope and if they could use a pack pony to bring back a good supply. The cook liked his thinking and went off to make the arrangements.

The Sunning steward and the cart had left the meadow. The knight eyed Minnow and then nodded to the cook. He recalled seeing the youngster laden with firewood earlier in the day. He remembered him singing a cheerful song which he recognised from his own childhood many, many years ago.

There wasn't much stature to the boy but he'd shown he was a worker by dragging such a large load. As a knight he'd not even considered the need for firewood. That should have been on the steward's list of supplies for the king's men and their encampment.

"We have the use of a pony and there are some lengths of rope in the store tent," said the cook. "I shall be glad to have a break from the smoke of the fire. Some of the wood I found yesterday was damp and still a bit green, it gives off too much smoke and little heat."

Minnow recognised the description of some hearth fires at home. A few times the whole space had been filled with eye-watering smoke. Those times had made it difficult for any of them to breathe.

Minnow carried the rope while the cook led the pony. Minnow chose the London cart track out of Wocca's Hamlet where it climbed gently into the forest. The tall oaks shut out much of the bright sunlight along the way except for one spot where an apple tree was full of blossom. In the autumn it was always laden with rich red apples and was an alternative source of tasty food.

Deeper either side of the track there were pockets of bright sunshine. Spaces left by trees that had been felled and where the undergrowth had reclaimed the ground. It was in such pockets Minnow collected and stored firewood.

Well before they reached the top of the slope Minnow indicated a narrow path that led off to the right. His best collections were on the left and he'd no intention of giving away his hard work. They continued some distance along the side path before discovering a lot of freshly fallen dead timber. The cook was delighted.

"We must not take any wood that is bigger around that the King's wrist. The forest is his and permission is needed from him if anything larger is taken out," explained Minnow. "There are very severe punishments, even for children, if the rule is broken. Some have been hanged for trying to bring out larger pieces."

They both set about gathering two substantial branches. The cook checked their size against his own wrist. The branches were easily more than Minnow would normally have been able to to manage on his own. They were attached either side of the pony to form the outside frame of their dragged litter. It provided a good base for adding kindling size material on the top. Rope made it so much easier to bind the huge bundle together.

The cook checked it was attached firmly behind the pony ready to be drawn towards the cart track. The width of the path made it difficult in places and pieces of good dry wood were being broken off as they wove between the trees and shrubs.

The pony was led by the cook so Minnow was able to kick the broken off pieces into the bushes. He'd gather them himself later, they'd make a good bundle that he'd bind together using his sacking shoulder cover. Perhaps he could beg some old pieces of rope to increase the size of the bundle he could hold together.

Back on Top Meadow a start had been made on additional round holes with three more men added to the original three. The king's men were sitting drinking wine and talking while studying one of the larger parchments. The knight was looking on and appeared to be asking questions.

Cook, Minnow and the pony made their way past the group with their collection. The knight stopped his talking and watched with his mouth wide open. The lad obviously knew the local area well and there was fuel for several days. He'd ordered the steward to supply some well-seasoned logs for the fire along with other supplies. If it had to come from Sunning who could guess when it would arrive.

The knight accepted the whole project had been poorly organised. The king's men were only interested in their building plans. They were giving no thought to the supply of initial materials or their longer term comfort.

Some food items had been delivered and were under a cloth on the cook's trestle table. He'd no idea what to expect so while Minnow undid the ropes he gingerly lifted a corner of the cloth.

There were a varied assortment of foods which included a jug of milk, butter and cheese that he would need to keep cool. The large hind leg of lamb he would start to roast now that he had some fire wood.

The selection of root vegetables, some mixed herbs in a linen bag, coarse flour and a skin of wine were a good set of basic ingredients. At the far end of the trestle board there were two large loaves of bread, some honey, a jar of preserved fruits, apples and some pastries that gave no clue as to their content, other than a sweet smell. Well, he thought, it was a start and they'd eat well tonight.

Minnow helped the cook to build up the fire and set the leg of lamb to roast. He'd never seen such a large piece of meat and was surprised that a sheep could produce one leg of such proportions. Lamb and mutton did sometimes cross their hearth at home but they only ever had small portions and it usually ended in the pot as a stew, packed out with root vegetables. After each meal more vegetables were added to the pot the next day. There would be no meat flavour left after a few days. The addition of flour added thickness but also made it more like a vegetable pottage that easily stuck to the base of the pot.

The cook next proceeded to dig a small hole in the shade of his tent. Into the hole he put the jug of milk with a platter over the top. Onto the platter he placed the butter and cheese then placed a large dish upside down over them.

A damp linen cloth was placed over everything with the edges hanging into the hole. A bowl of water was then placed on the top of the stack and a wetted second cloth was placed into the top bowl. The edges of this second cloth went outside the bowl onto the main cloth and kept it wet.

Minnow watched fascinated by the elaborate performance. Was it some sort of offering to God?

"The top bowl just needs to be kept topped up with fresh water," explained the cook, "it will keep the milk, butter and cheese cool."

"We keep milk in the shade," said Minnow, "but in the summer it is still bad by the next morning."

"This trick," concluded the cook, "comes from over the sea where the weather can be much hotter." Minnow assumed then that the cook must have been on many journeys with knights and other king's men. Perhaps he'd been on a crusade.

The cook put a simple fence around the hole using some of the sticks from the firewood pile and then turned his attention to the slowly cooking leg of lamb. Minnow wanted to stay longer but knew he could make one more trip back into the forest, collect the broken off bits he'd hidden earlier and get them home.

The cook allowed him to place a couple of lengths of well worn rope under his shirt around his waist. It was thought best not to be seen taking things away from the building site. The ropes were old and of little further use by the cook, other than for helping to light a fire.

Once he was away from Top Meadow he could attach them to the front of his shoulder cloak and make the collecting of a bundle larger and more secure. If he was careful the ends would hang down under the cloak and he'd tuck them down his underwear. They'd only be seen when holding the firewood together and he could bypass Top Meadow later by another track that led to his dwelling. The alternative route followed the main brook through the forest.

"I must get some more wood for home," Minnow explained as he turned to leave.

"You can have this loaf end if you keep it out of sight going past the king's men and the knight. You've been a great help to me. Come back in a couple of days and I may have some more tasks for you." The cook had really appreciated the firewood and considered the small reward had been well earned.

Minnow tucked the large piece of the loaf into his shirt and hugged one of his arms about him as he made his way out of Top Meadow. He'd have to take the bread home first and then collect the firewood. It had been a good day so far.

His Mama was preparing some vegetables for the pot and was pleased to see the large hunk of bread. Spread with some mutton fat it would make a good addition to the meal. Minnow told her why he'd been given it and that also pleased her having seen earlier the good collection of firewood he'd already stacked.

31

He said he was off to get some more wood. She'd never seen him so willing to collect. Perhaps he was growing up at last even though he was still small for his age. Unfortunately he'd not find work at the farm despite the shortage of men who had been lost in the many battles of King Stephen over the years.

The other children were a lot bigger and they were being given the jobs. Maybe he'd be useful in some ways to the group building the new church as long as he did his family chores.

Back along the path, he and the cook had taken earlier, Minnow started to collect up the useful sized bits that had been broken off as the pony dragged the bundle. He used a pointed stick to open up a hole in the edge of his shoulder sacking and threaded through an unravelled strand of one of the pieces of rope. This he repeated on an opposite edge and secured each piece of rope with a firm knot.

With the sacking now laid out on the ground he started to load the kindling pieces. Soon he'd built up quite a load and secured it firmly with the pieces of rope. He had a bundle he could just about carry and made his way home beside the brook with a spring in his step.

Chapter Five – Special Delivery

After fetching wood from yet another area of the forest the following morning, Minnow made his way to Top Meadow. He was curious to see the progress the men had made.

Sitting on the ground, within the large marked out square, were several of the young children from around the village. Each was busy picking out stones from the soil dug from the holes. Every stone was loaded onto their individual square of cloth. There was a general collecting area at one side of the main shape where they added their individual collection. The resulting pile was starting to look quite large.

"What are you getting for doing this?" he asked the child he knew who lived near to his dwelling. He was a bit younger than Minnow but like many children was also a lot taller.

"We get to take some bread home if we keep sorting."

Minnow counted twelve large circular holes within the marked out square. Six were as deep as a man and a rope would have been needed to help the men out. The other holes were still being dug so the stone and pebble sorting was being done away from them. There would be no space for him to work and he guessed several other children had been sent away. Sticks that he'd collected with the cook were being used to turn over the soil and reveal the stones that were being collected. It looked as if there would be at least a cart full of stones piled up by the end of the day.

A plain, but large, tent had been added to the encampment since yesterday. It had also been fenced off with several woven hurdles which suggested it was for more secure storage. Minnow went towards the fire looking for the cook. The knight was in discussion with just one of the king's men and gave him a nod. Minnow smiled as he'd been recognised and not chased off. The cook appeared from the new tent looking hot and not in a good mood.

"I've no collecting for you today," he huffed, "I said the wood could last a couple of days. I had a delivery of logs from the farm last evening so there's less urgency but thanks for your help."

"Is there not a pot to stir or veg to clean that I could help with? I've done my chores at home. My Mama is off washing clothes at the brook, the other side of Wocca's Hamlet. I just get in her way when she's doing that. For some reason the clothes end up muddier when I help than when we started."

"Tell you what, I could use some help in this store tent, if you're strong enough. We are due some sacks of lime and sand that need to be kept dry. There's just been a second cartful of long logs delivered. They'll keep some trestle boards off the ground. You could help me arrange the logs and help put out the boards. The sacks, when they arrive, will then be away from the damp of the ground. Are you strong enough to help?"

"I'm able to handle logs so just show me how to lay them out."

"Keep your hands off any of the other things in the store and don't ask any questions," warned the cook. "We need to try and be quiet."

At the far end of the tent Minnow noticed a man under a blanket, asleep on a pallet. His shield and sword were within his easy reach. Minnow guessed he could have been the night watch. A large dog was keeping half an eye on Minnow and the cook.

The logs, each one as long as Minnow was tall, were in a heap behind the tent. He could manage to drag a couple at a time. Soon he had them laid out in the empty area at one end of the space inside the tent. They were laid out the length of two of Minnow's strides apart, had a one stride gap around before the next set. Each pair of logs supported two trestle boards that they quietly laid on the logs. Some of the boards had seen better days but still had enough strength to be walked on without breaking. The weight of the cook did make them bend until they almost touched the ground but he seemed happy with the arrangement.

It was Minnow's Papa who arrived assisting the carter. They were guiding the ox with its load of sacks. Also escorting the cart was one of the king's men and a young squire. Both rode horses and were armed with sword and shield.

Cook told Minnow to stay out of the way while the farm workers had a change from their digging and took the sacks into the store. The load only covered a couple of the trestle boards. Then a second cart, with knight and two squire escorts, arrived with more sacks. This fresh cart was much larger and had two horses pulling the load.

Soon six more boards were loaded with the sacks of dry lime and sand. Minnow was keen to chat to his Papa. He was interested to learn where the lime and sand had come from. Had he finished for the day?

Papa explained the sacks had arrived at Reading, by boat, having been carried on the River Thames. The vessel had tied on the River Kennet, at the mooring built for Reading Abbey. The sacks had been loaded straight onto the carts.

The ground around the wharf was a bit soft till they reached the Reading to London cart track that crossed over Loddon Bridge. It was quite easy going up towards Wocca's Hamlet after that. The next two days they were expected to meet other boats with shipments of stone blocks that were needed on the site.

Minnow's Papa had heard that the builders at Reading Abbey were not happy. They complained that some of their building materials were being taken to other sites. They were glad of the support of the armed king's men and the squires.

Construction at the abbey had almost stopped while King Stephen had been on the throne. When King Henry's Grandsire had been buried at Reading Abbey, in front of the altar, the building was still under construction then. Progress since had been slow due to lack of money and the unrest throughout the country.

The king's men had arranged, that the following day, the boats, with their stone, were moored on the River Thames, by the mouth of the River Kennet. The distance to Wocca's Hamlet was slightly shorter from there and it was away from the abbey's wharf.

The abbey, thought Minnow, could not be that desperate for stone as they'd been ordered to demolish the castle keep within the abbey grounds by King Henry II. He'd ordered many castles to be demolished since he came to power as they'd been used as bases for opposition to the former King Stephen. Henry did not want that challenge to his reign.

Times did seem to be much more peaceful since King Stephen's death. Disputes in particular were being heard by courts that had twelve men hearing the arguments. These courts had been set up in the name of the King.

Money was being widely used to pay for labour but was also expected in return to pay rents, taxes and levies. There still existed the labour demanded in return for use of a dwelling and some land. This labour was at set times of the year in relation to the needs of the farm.

There was time for each family to manage plots of land to feed themselves. Finding additional work was a bonus when it gave you money. Most families also grew things that could be sold such as wheat and corn. Hemp and flax were also cash crops that was made into rope by the ropemaker at his rope-walk in Wocca's Hamlet.

Minnow's Papa had finished for the day. They both made their way home together to spend a little time on their plot, thinning out some of the young vegetable plants. When there were too many for their patch of ground they'd give them to neighbours. In return they would pass on things that they'd have to spare.

The Papa of Minnow's Mama lived in the adjacent dwelling. He could no longer manage his own plot. In return for his having some of the produce grown there Minnow's parents had the use of that plot as well. Six large apple trees grew on the border of the two plots. Additional fruit trees bordered the other neighbours plots. The fruit made a very drinkable cyder that kept well through the year.

The bushes today around their plot of land were strewn with items of damp clothes and linen. Minnow's Mama had finished the laundry and had put the items to dry in the sunshine. During the winter it was very difficult to plan a wash day when there was always a chance of rain. It did give an extra rinse but the items would not dry.

She'd done two loads today. One big load would have been too heavy to bring back from the brook when it was damp with the water. All the drying space was covered and some small items had ended up on top of the wood pile. If the wood had been dry when he collected it some pieces would now be damp. Minnow hoped some kindling had been put indoors to keep it dry.

As a family they set about thinning out pea, cabbage and bean plants. Some were transferred to Grandpapa's land and others taken around to other near neighbours. Their dwellings sat alongside the track to Reading, facing The Clearing and were almost in the centre of the village.

Top Meadow was in a straight line along The Clearing from their home. Each side of The Clearing had similar dwellings to theirs and included land behind each home. The Clearing still had signs of being a scrub land and some areas struggled to provide much for the dwellers there. A few more years of pigs contributing muck and rooting around would make the land more productive.

Minnow planted some spare seedlings at the home of an elderly widow who mostly grew herbs. She had a wide understanding of the way herbs could be used to help cure and ease illnesses. She'd passed on her knowledge to her daughters who now lived with their own families at various places around Wocca's Hamlet. They were the ones called on when women gave birth anywhere around the area.

It was always advisable to be generous to them as you never knew when you may need their help. The widow would occasionally spend some of her time with Minnow's Grandpapa when he was unwell. She would advise his Mama on how he could best be helped. When the weather was particularly foul his Grandpapa would move in with the family and share the warmth of the hearth. Mostly he preferred his own company and did what he could to look after himself.

Before all the daylight turned to darkness the damp washing was taken into the home and hung on cord lines. There was restricted space to move around the hanging washing. Smoke from the hearth became embedded in the fabric. It would dry very little but was ready to be taken out again the next day, if there was no sign of rain.

The stew pot had earlier been hung over the rekindled hearth to warm through with the addition of some cooked chicken legs and wings that had been given by a neighbour in exchange for the plants. Minnow's Mama ensured the pot had simmered for a good time before dishing out individual bowls full of stew and breaking up the hunk of bread. Everyone was hungry after such a full day and thankful for the nourishment offered by their chicken enhanced meal.

Chapter Six – Mortar

It was an early start for his Papa, to go with the ox cart, to the boats on the River Thames. Minnow set about his own tasks, helping to spread the laundry items in the early sunshine, fetching the fresh water and collecting wood.

Before he'd gone for the water the Tanner had arrived to collect their pail of body waste. His Mama kept a separate pail that Minnow and his Papa used first thing in the morning to collect their wee. She used it when washing some of the linens to try and lift out the grey colour.

The pail for the Tanner stank badly enough but their cart stank even more and the four open barrels were wafting their stench all along the cart track. Minnow could not understand how anyone could get used to such a smell, it made him want to vomit. He'd heard that the Tanners actually trod backwards and forwards in the waste forcing the liquid into the sheep and other animal skins that would become leather. Who would have thought such a process could produce such a strong and valuable product.

Their site was well down stream and a good distance from Wocca's Hamlet. Even animals could not drink from the brook after the Tanners had used it. Other streams did join later as it flowed towards the river but the smell lingered all the way.

Having fetched the fresh water, added more kindling to the wood pile, Minnow drifted back towards Top Meadow and the activity there. The first change he noticed was the arrival of two large open top wine casks full of water. They were like the Tanners barrels but these had a faint smell of wine.

Two of the king's men, with squires, had gone with the carts to bring back the blocks of stone. The knight was explaining to the team of six workmen what they'd be doing next. Working in teams of two, one would be down in one of the round pits, the other would be making up mortar with the lime, water and sand. They'd hand down the stone blocks and bowls of mortar. The blocks would be built up as a circular wall as if it was the inside of a well.

There was just enough room down the hole for the smaller of the two men to stand and build up the wall without standing on the laid blocks. Each team had one man smaller than the other which Minnow thought was well planned. Boards were set out beside three of the holes ready for mixing the mortar. Just then the ox cart arrived with the first load of blocks.

Each block was a rough cube, each side the size of a man's outspread hand. They'd made a heavy load for the poor ox who greedily drank from a dish of water brought over by the cook. Minnow's Papa had also been working hard helping to turn the wheels of the cart through some of the softer parts of the cart track up to Wocca's Hamlet from Loddon Bridge.

All three men and the young squire were given some ale, bread and cheese. The workers shared out the load of blocks into three piles. Each pile placed near the boards by the three holes in the ground.

The knight and a king's man carefully supervised the mixing of the mortar ensuring the correct mix of ingredients. Minnow was surprised by the spluttering sound that came from the mixture when the water was slowly added, it looked like smoke rising from the mix.

The cook, also watching the mixing, explained to Minnow the lime was a crushed white rock called limestone. It was then roasted to make it very dry. As it was so dry it became excited by the return of water and gave back the heat it had been given in the roasting. It was this that made the water boil and hiss.

The sand and the lime became a new wet rock that would become hard as it dried. This mortar would hold the blocks together and make a strong wall. Minnow now realized the cook knew more than just how to provide cooked food to the knight, the king's men and their young squires.

The workmen made a start on laying the blocks at the base of the holes with the mortar between the blocks. The next layer had the blocks sitting over the join of the under blocks. The king's man supervised the work in each of the pits and had to call the knight to explain the blocks needed to be as tight as possible against its neighbour.

The mortar, although strong, was still the weakest part of the foundations but also needed to cover every part of the block that met the adjacent block. Everyone soon recognised the Non, non, non as "No!" and waited for further guidance from the knight after discussion with the king's man.

The cook wandered back to his cooking and Minnow followed him hopeful of a scrap of bread and maybe a taste of cheese. He wasn't disappointed as there was some left from the ox delivery team and more had been set aside for the team accompanying the horse cart that was expected very soon.

As it was Friday, fish was to be sent up from the farm for the evening meal of the encampment. The fishmonger visited Wocca's Hamlet every Friday having travelled from Sunning. He supplied the villages and hamlets around the two river fords near the River Thames and the farms on the way. He'd have been to Wiltshire Farm and they'd have had extra to be able to supply those on Top Meadow.

There would be little left for those in Wocca's Hamlet. Any chance of fish scraps being available for the likes of his Mama who could sometime buy a few remaining pieces at a low price were today unlikely. That would mean a vegetable pottage for their meal.

The priests made it punishable to be found to be eating meat on a Friday. Yet another thing that Minnow didn't understand. It was all to do with rules but who made the rules and why? No one had been able to explain it to him other than it's just what we have to do, or not do, as it was in this case.

The cook interrupted his thoughts before he could start to ask his list of questions.

"While you're here you could make yourself useful and take this bowl of waste to the latrine. Make sure you put a thin layer of dirt over every bit. The sheep droppings attract enough flies without more breeding at the latrine."

The first latrine pit had already been filled and covered by the turf that had been set to one side. The new pit had been made longer and deeper but it was still safe to straddle each side and perform as was needed. There was a small wooden scoop for sprinkling earth over any deposit. Minnow tipped the contents of the bowl into a corner and covered it with some of the earth.

He used the privacy to empty his bladder before returning with the empty bowl to the cook. He'd a feeling of being naughty but important using the latrine of such high class masters.

The cook took some water from a barrel and cleaned out the wooden bowl, tipping the dirty water onto the hedge. He then used some wood ash on a cloth to rub around the bowl and then rinsed that away, tipping the water over another part of the hedge. The bowl was then left to dry in the light of the sun.

"I don't dry bowls face down," he explained, "the sunlight is needed to finish the cleaning. I have seen too many people have sickness from damp bowls that have not been dried in the light of the sun. It happens mostly during the winter when there's little sunlight. Often there's been a rush to not clean the bowls in very hot water."

"My Mama uses wood ash mixed with hard melted fat when she washes our clothes. She was taught by her Mama how to make soap. She tries to use it on my face sometimes but it makes my eyes red. I don't understand how something as dirty as wood ash can be used to make things clean. There's lots I do not understand."

"You've still a lot of growing up to do," commented the cook, "so don't expect to know everything all at once. We all learn in our own way, sometimes by doing and other times by asking the right questions. I can't explain why wood ash makes a good cleaner. I do know it's a pure powder made more pure by fire."

"Fat is melted off animal parts, again by the heat of fire," he continued. "Dirt is removed from some things if hot water is used, fire heats the water. But, fire alone is no good for us as we can burn in its heat. We have to use fire to provide the things we need such as poached fish. I can see some trout being delivered which I'm looking forward to preparing and cooking for this evening."

A girl, carrying a basket covered with a cloth, was approaching past the kings men and the knight. Minnow had never seen her before and didn't recognise her as living in the village. She wasn't one of the fishmongers regular helpers so he wondered if she lived at the farm.

"Thanks Mary," said the cook, "do you know this youngster?"

Mary smiled at Minnow, shook her head and handed over her basket. The cook took the basket to the store and quickly returned with the empty basket. "See you tomorrow Mary with the fresh bread. Careful how you go around all the materials scattered over the ground. Bye"

"Bye," added Minnow. Mary gave another smile and moved off.

"Thanks for the bread and cheese," added Minnow. "I see you've a good supply of logs from the farm so I guess you don't need any kindling wood. Is your fire burning day and night?"

"The night watch keeps an eye on the fire for me and sets a pot to heat ready for the dawn. You've been a good help to me so if you keep looking in I may have a few small jobs for you."

"Thanks. Bye," said Minnow a little reluctantly. He enjoyed chatting with the cook who certainly had lots to talk about and seemed to enjoy Minnow's company.

Chapter Seven - Treasure

Minnow wandered back across the meadow just as the horses and their laden wagon came through the gateway. The two horses looked just as exhausted as the ox had earlier. The cart was manoeuvred close to the work teams.

The horses were released from the cart and led to two bowls of water. Each horse was then put on a long tether. They were allowed feed on the remaining grass untouched by the building activity.

The squires each had a cloth and were rubbing down the huge horses, each horse seemed to enjoy the experience. There was no kicking out to send the lads running. Their own horses had been tied to the fence along with those of the king's men and the knight.

Minnow's Papa had gone with the ox cart back to the farm to help with repairs. The unusual load had shown up a weakness in part of the underframe and rope had been needed to hold the cart together. It would be a job for a carpenter who would first have to measure and then make the replacements for the damaged parts.

The carter and his Papa would make the cart useable as well as they could. The carpenter would need a whole day to make the full repair once he'd made the parts. With so much work the carter was annoyed he'd not checked his cart more fully over the winter. Repairs could then have been done at leisure. It could also mean that Minnow's Papa would need to find other work for a day. Still there was much to do on their plots of land and Papa could manage that.

Back at home his Mama was turning the washing to let the underside benefit from the rest of the day's sunshine. The washing had dried well, the gentle wind and the sunshine had been just what was needed. The door to the dwelling was held wide open letting the fresh spring air waft around the dark inside.

The chickens had been let out for the last few weeks during the daytime and were scratching at their fenced patch of ground. They'd be taken in for the night, as usual, to keep them safe from the foxes. The hens had been laying well recently and the eggs had been useful in exchange for replacement shoes for Minnow's growing feet. His feet were the only thing about him that did seem to be growing. The shoes were not new but still had some useful life left in them.

The pig was also rooting at the ground in its pen doing a good job of turning over the soil. In a few days it would be moved to another area and the churned ground would be planted. They'd managed to keep this pig over the winter and it was growing well on the vegetable scraps and occasional clean-out of the stew pot.

A fresh pot was always started when recently bought meat was available. They managed to buy a piece of meat about once a week. To provide food when there was less work and money, the pig was normally slaughtered at the end of harvest.

The pork would be salted, packed in a barrel and used over the winter and spring months. Often there would be more than enough for a small family and this was another thing that could be exchanged with neighbours.

Warm clothing was equally prized during the winter. Wool cloth from the sheep was converted this way by several households. If they didn't have the skills of spinning and weaving they could fashion the material into clothing.

Minnow set off as normal to collect some water. Some families had two water buckets that they carried using a wooden shaped yoke. It sat across the back of their neck and curved over their shoulders. Minnow had tried taking the laundry that way using a curved branch but it twisted and the weight was all on the back of his neck. One bucket of water, a couple times a day, was normally enough for the three of them, four if you included Grandpapa. Going now would avoid the bigger kids who would still be working.

He always kept a look out in case he needed to find an alternative route. Like today, there were sheep on the move so, he took a side path rather than wait for them to pass by. He knew the path but hadn't used it in a long while. He was walking towards the sun which was getting lower in the sky. Something shiny on the edge of the path caught his eye. He looked around to see if anyone was following him. There was no one around.

He picked up the object to discover it was part of a broken blade, it could even have been a bit of a sword. It was a little longer than his hand at full stretch. Most of it was beginning to rust and only a small part was still bright.

Minnow could hardly contain his excitement. He'd dreamed of having a knife. He pictured binding on a simple wooden handle from a couple of sticks. He thought he could even use the blade to shape the sticks to make a comfortable fit.

Now was the time to hide it, it was too valuable to have it taken off him. He found some broad leaves and wrapped the metal inside. He wound one bit of the rope that hung down inside his shoulder cover around the small bundle and used a twisted loop with the rope to stop it unravelling. He could not remember even collecting the water and getting it home even though his shirt was damp. His thoughts had been elsewhere.

Chapter Eight – A Safe Place

Having completed his tasks, very quickly, the next morning Minnow headed for a simple den he'd made in one part of the forest. The location was well hidden by holly and brambles. There was a narrow tunnel just at the base of the holly that gave him access. The tunnel was also used by a family of foxes that had their den well inside the bramble part.

His den was spacious but well screened from any people moving through the surrounding trees. Minnow untied his hidden bundle and started to closely examine the length of blade. He could now see it was a broken piece of sword.

There was a sharpened edge on both sides. One of the sides had numerous nicks and blunting, suggesting it had been well used in real fighting with another swordsman. The part that he held in his hand must have been the tip as it came to a badly worn point. There must have been enough left of the main blade for its owner to have it made into a short sword.

The broken part had been left for Minnow to find. Carefully he took the sharpest edge to a small branch of the holly bush. He couldn't make a cut as the other edge was still too sharp and hurt his hand as he applied pressure. He would definitely have to make a handle to be able to control the blade.

There was no easy way to even start. Sticks on either side, bound together with bramble stalks would be too wobbly. The blade could cut through the binding, as well as slide out of the back so more thought was required. The blade was again wrapped into the large leaves and then hidden under a stone in his den.

He could hear voices approaching and recognised one of them as his Papa. Papa was with the king's forester, the dark skinned king's man and the knight. They were studying some of the taller oaks.

The forest was the property of the King. Only the King could hunt and take meat from it. If a wild boar came out of the forest and killed a lamb, or even a person, once it went back into the forest it could not be hunted. Minnow decided to stay still and hidden in his den. There was an oak of particular interest close to the edge of the bramble thicket.

"So this will be another one we will be needing," said the knight having consulted with the king's man. "It's a good height and should produce several useful lengths of strong solid timber."

"These are the most valuable of the oaks locally," said the forester. "The King has suggested they may be needed for a fleet of ships. I'll need confirmation from his majesty that they can be used by you." The forester didn't sound happy. "Do they have to be oaks?"

"We have our instructions and the king's men are very experienced in building for his majesty. They know the materials they need and the timber will have to be seasoned before being used to form the roof. That will take a full three years of storage, protected from the weather. They need the timber to convert urgently."

"You saw the start being made on the foundations when you came to Top Meadow. The build will take that number of years and the roof timbers will be needed when the oak has seasoned. Would the King have sent his team if he didn't intend the building to be completed?" concluded the knight.

"With no bishop at Sunning I have lost touch of who is in charge. I know the King is in charge but he has not told me who is the current overseeing tenant." The forester sounded as if he was looking for an excuse for his reluctant behaviour and for preserving his best trees.

"Then take a good look at me," said the knight, "I'm the tenant and have oversight of the lands of Sunning by order of his majesty. Let's get this tree marked."

Minnow's Papa took four wedge cuts out of the lower part of the trunk. It wasn't enough to damage the tree but acted as a marker. The group moved on, keeping a similar distance from Wocca's Hamlet most of the time. The less distance into the forest, the less distance the timber would have to be dragged.

Minnow waited until the voices were well in the distance before emerging from the centre of the bramble den. He made his way back towards Top Meadow to study the progress on the foundations for the pillars.

The cook and the remaining two king's men were the only ones left on site. Minnow caught the cook's attention over the hedge and asked why there was no work being done.

"All the collected stones have been loaded onto a cart and taken to the stream to be washed."

"How are they going to wash them," asked Minnow. "The stream will just carry them away."

"They'll be using wicker laundry baskets. Fill the basket with stones, slosh it around in the stream to shift off the dirt and then load them back onto the clean cart. They should be back soon."

It seemed like a lot of effort just to have clean stones that would be going back into the ground. "Why do the stones need to be clean?"

"I have a pot to stir. Come round and chat and I'll try and explain." With that the cook went back to his fire and the simmering pot.

Minnow made his way through the gate and studied the circular arrangements of blocks that came about halfway up the twelve pits. The ground at the very bottom was well trodden but he could understand why the circle of blocks hadn't been made any higher. The men would have found it too restrictive to build above their armpits. It must have been difficult for them to get out as it was.

The cook was adding a little water to his cook pot and checked the thickness as he stirred. "Grab a log and sit by the fire."

Minnow positioned a large log near the fire, out the way of any smoke. Cook took a taste from the pot, disappeared into the store tent and returned with a small handful of mixed herbs. These he stirred into the contents of the pot. Minnow was starting to feel hungry just from imagining how it may taste.

"So, what was your question?"

Minnow asked again, "Why do the stones need to be clean? Aren't they just going back into the ground again?"

"The stones will be mixed with mortar to make something called limecrete. Dirt will make the mixture weak. The limecrete will be put inside the circle of blocks. When it has set, which could take a couple of weeks, the next circle of blocks will be built up. More stones will be needed to fill the core and may need to be brought in from Reading. We will have a fresh delivery of lime and sand by then."

"How did you learn all this? Have you been a builder? I thought you were the cook for the group." Minnow felt he was full of questions for this stranger who seemed happy to sit and chat.

"It's a long story but being a cook is the best part so far. As a young man I had an ordered, sheltered life. I had the chance to travel and came back with many experiences. Then as a traveller I kept my eyes and ears open. There were many things I understood just by being in the right place at the right time. Some things I learnt by being in the wrong place at the wrong time. I have had a lot of life experiences."

The cook looked far into the distance. He was obviously deep in thought. For some reason it made Minnow feel uncomfortable. There were voices moving back down the track from the forest. Minnow recognised his Papa's voice asking questions of the knight.

The cook returned to the present and went into the store tent. He emerged with a skin of wine which he took to the king's men's trestle table. He returned to collect some cheese and bread.

"Sorry lad, I need to get back to work. Pop in again some other time if you've nothing to do. I'm surprised you don't have regular work. Perhaps though you're a still a bit small."

Minnow stood up and made his way to be near his Papa. He was handing the axe to the forester and requesting permission to leave. The knight made sure he understood his tasks for the next day and let him leave the site. Minnow walked alongside him and asked what he'd been given to do.

With some excitement in his voice Papa explained he was to fell some of the great oaks in the King's forest. The wood was needed for the roof of the new church. He was being asked to help build the church. He'd be paid well by the knight but it would be hard work. It could take a whole day to fell just one of the trees. The tree would then need further work before it could be moved to the farm for sawing and seasoning.

The forester was going to provide three axes and a skilled blade sharpener. Oak trees are tough and blunt an axe very quickly. He hoped there was a good meal waiting for him at home, he was going to need all his strength these next few weeks. Minnow had never known his Papa so happy.

As they passed out through the gateway, to their right, the ox, with its cart of washed stones, was making its way back up to Top Meadow. Two of the children were each wearing a large laundry basket like a large hat that hung down their backs. Everyone looked quite wet but the warmth of the sun was slowly drying their clothing. More happy faces. There was a lift in the spirits of many of the members of Wocca's Hamlet.

Chapter Nine – Timber

Minnow's Papa was awake early and left home just after daybreak for his work in the forest. Minnow knew he had his tasks to complete before he could go searching for him. His Mama, had today, requested extra firewood that she could exchange for cheese. Papa would need the extra food as a lunch, he was unused to having such physical work. So, two extra trips, in addition to the normal kindling requirement for home.

A nearby family kept two cows but had no pig. They rented some grazing from the farm and milked the cows twice a day. Some of their milk was sold, most was made into butter and cheese.

Papa had already taken some diluted cyder for drinking. The sun was high in the sky by the time Minnow had collected the cheese. With a hunk of yesterday's bread and some extra drink Minnow set out to locate his Papa. The food was securely wrapped in a clean cloth, which he held in one hand and carried the skin of cyder in the other.

As he made his way past Top Meadow he saw the mixing of the clean stones with the mortar. The mixture was then being put into each of the twelve holes. It was being pummelled down using the end of large poles.

He walked up the London cart track, listening all the time for the sound of axe blows. Off to his left, level with the apple tree and its dazzling blossom, he could make out the steady sound of axe on wood. Following the narrow path towards the sound he soon came upon the small group watching his Papa working.

Already there was a very large wedge shape taken out of one side at the base of the tree. It wasn't half way through but had weakened the support for that side of the tree. Papa stopped his cutting of the other side and exchanged the axe with the axe sharpener.

It was then he spotted Minnow carrying his lunch. He went to the cyder skin that had come from home earlier that day and took a long drink. Minnow was made to stand well back from the cutting. It was cool in the forest but his Papa looked very hot despite having taken off his shirt.

The rhythm of cutting began again, working around the opposite side of the main wedge shape, moving evenly round one way and then back again. Each stroke cutting deeper and deeper into the mighty oak. The forester was watching the top of the tree looking for any signs of movement or sway.

The initial open wedge was designed to make the tree fall in one direction but that wasn't an exact theory. The weight of the crown and how it was balanced was the main factor in which direction it would eventually fall. Once again the axe was exchanged for a freshly sharpened one. Minnow's Papa had made just two new cuts and the order was shouted, "RUN!"

His Papa didn't need to be told twice. Looking up at the slowly tilting top of the oak he ran to the left and well back from where he'd been cutting. The rest of the group ran to the right and kept running as the mighty tree demolished surrounding lesser trees with a shattering crash. The oak hadn't only fallen but had kicked back and where Minnow's Papa had been working there was now the huge base of the tree, ten strides back from the splintered stump.

The forester made the decision to have a break and eat. He made his way back to his horse. It took a little time to steady the animal, which was jittery from the sudden explosion of noise, before he could take his food out of one of the saddle bags. This he shared with the axe sharpener who had just managed to grab the two spare axes before he ran from the falling tree. Minnow's Papa brought over the axe he'd been using and then opened the bundle of food Minnow had brought him.

"I hope you watched closely to everything that happened there," said his Papa, "never cut a tree down on your own. You need someone watching for the tilt, then you run clear of the fall and the kick back."

Minnow was impressed. He'd never seen a tree being felled before and marvelled at the size of the cut end. Where the axe had left its cut there was an obvious pattern of circles. The middle of the trunk was badly splintered but he guessed the circular ring pattern went all the way to the centre.

"Did you bring any lunch for yourself?" asked his Papa.

"I only brought yours, I hope you've enough." Minnow was hopeful for some bits.

"Just about, thanks. You can let your Mama know I'll be extremely hungry when I get home. This is hard work."

"What needs to be done next, is it on to another tree?"

"No, all the limbs need trimming off. The worst part is that the tree can roll while you're balancing on it using the axe. You need to be ready to jump clear very quickly and not damage yourself with the axe at the same time. You learn to react very quickly. I'm glad of this break, I shall sleep well tonight."

"Snoring as loudly as ever no doubt," added Minnow who then quickly ducked to avoid being clipped around the head.

Minnow took the empty cyder skin and started to make his way home. Back at Top Meadow the two carts had arrived with more stone blocks. The ox cart was now sagging very badly under the load suggesting the repair had still not been made. He made a quick wave to the cook, who was busy skinning a large hare, and continued his wander home.

The empty cyder skin he left for his Mama. She was busy cutting a freshly plucked chicken into pieces for the pot. Minnow found himself some bread and spread it with some pork fat.

Mama had placed all the discarded feathers into a sack. The collection would be spread out to dry in the summer sun later in the year, on a day when there was no chance of wind to carry them off. Eventually they'd be added to the large mattress that lay on top of their pallet.

Next door his Grandpapa was cleaning off some carrots ready to be added to the stew pot. It had been a good season for carrots but only a few were now left in the ground. The young carrot plants were doing well and there should be another good crop this next year. Minnow sat himself down on the bench beside his Grandpapa and leaned back against the wall of the dwelling. It was good to relax and soak up the warmth of the sun.

Minnow gave an account of his trip into the forest, the felling of the oak and an update of all the activity on Top Meadow. His Grandpapa listened to his chatter and nodded his understanding.

Grandpapa didn't say much. He often struggled for breath so it was easier not to talk. He'd been one of the sawyers for the farm. Once trees had been felled they needed converting into useful boards and lengths of timber. This involved the use of a two handled saw with a sawyer at each end.

On the farm there was a saw pit where logs were cut into lengths of even thickness. One of the sawyers stood on the log, the other was down in the pit. During the sawing the pitman would be covered in sawdust. The top man had the job of lifting the saw up through the cut and guiding the direction of the saw on the downstroke to keep the thickness even.

Underneath the main work was done by pulling downwards and extending the cut. The top man would have wedges that kept the cut open and helped the saw blade not to stick or jam. The most experienced worker was the top man. Old age would eventually give the top position to the lower pitman and a new sawyer would then be trained for their pitman role.

Grandpapa was the pitman for a great many years. Sawyers were valued craftsmen. They were excused the enforced fighting service of the majority of manor and farm workers. His only son had been a general farm worker. He'd been killed fighting with King Stephen.

Minnow's Mama was the eldest of three daughters, the other two had married and were in other parts of Berkshire. They lived a little less than a day's journey away so only rarely met in Reading at a holiday fayre. Grandpapa now became too exhausted to even think about such a journey.

Pottering on his patch of land suited him well with his eldest daughter looking after his needs. Now that Minnow was more independent and could hold a conversation, Grandpapa was starting to enjoy his company.

Minnow heard his Mama calling.

"Well it was a good rest while it lasted. Shall I take the carrots for the pot?" asked Minnow.

"Thank you, you're a good lad Will." Grandpapa was the only one who used his given name. Perhaps it was because his own son had also been called Will.

Back at the hearth the pot was warming over the fire. Mama put the carrots into the mix and then asked Minnow to fetch Grandpapa's large spare cooking pot.

"Your Papa will be in need of a warm water wash when he gets back so I need to warm a second pot of water for him. When you've brought the pot the bucket will need filling. You can then bring in some of the large logs from the wood store."

Just a few jobs then thought Minnow as he set off back to his Grandpapa's dwelling.

"Back so soon, so what does my daughter need?"

Minnow soon explained and quickly went into his dwelling to collect the pot. It was a lot bigger than any of theirs but then his family had also been a lot larger. The inside of Grandpapa's dwelling was relatively empty. There was no fire on the central hearth, his pallet was opposite the door on the far side of the hearth.

Just inside the door was a trestle and board along with a couple of stools. At one end of the space were the remains of some wattle fencing that would have sectioned off the animal's area. At the other end were a few clothes hanging against the wall from nails. His collection of pots and dishes were stacked in a corner and food storage pots were arranged in the other corner. Minnow knew one of the pots contained salted pork and another held oats.

Many of the smaller containers and the bags hanging from the beams had the seeds he'd gathered from the garden in the autumn. He tried to gather twice as many as he'd use in a single year in case there was a poor harvest. Grandpapa had taught Minnow's Papa the skill of seed harvesting but still liked to gather his own collection. He said it was good to have something to exchange for the herbs and care he often needed in the worst of the winter.

The pot was heavy and had signs of handle repairs. There was no crack in it so it still worked as a cook pot. It was special in that it had three feet that held it above the fire without a tripod and chain like his Mama's pots. When it was full it was too difficult to move so liquids were dipped out as required.

Grandpapa's pot was positioned at the edge, but just inside, the hearth and the water that remained in the bucket was emptied in. Minnow set off to fetch more water. After the second full bucket was added he needed to fetch just one more bucket full that would be kept for general use. His Mama had moved a hot log under the pot and was still waiting for the logs from the wood store. She was also keeping the food pot stirred so that there was some body to the meal and not a thin porridge with a burnt bottom. Minnow found two dry logs and they were added to the fire to give extra heat to Grandpapa's large pot.

Chapter Ten – Wet Activity

The next day the rain was steady and wetting but work was expected to continue. His Papa was off to make a start on the trimming and splitting of the huge oak trunk. The whole trunk was too heavy to haul out of the forest even with a team of six heavy horses. Eventually the oak trunk would be split in two along the whole length by his Papa using wedges.

A team of men would then be needed to roll each half using long poles and then the whole splitting process would start again to quarter the trunk. Each of the four quarters would then be of a manageable size to be hauled through the forest to the farm for sawing and seasoning.

The sawn timbers would be stacked with sticks separating each length to allow air to circulate through the stack which would be kept dry under a thatched shelter for three years. Every six months every piece would be turned and be moved from the centre to the outside to even out the drying. The sawyers would be in charge of the care of the oak beams and would have to adjust the stack to prevent twisting and curving.

The wet of the day restricted what Minnow could do outside. He did take a spade to clear the shallow ditch around their dwellings that took away the water that ran off the thatch. It was designed to flow into their garden plots and creating flowing channels was fun for a wet day.

He was given an old leather coat that was his Mama's. It had been well rubbed with fat so it did have a smell but it kept the wet off him as he played with the water. The pig was enjoying the mud by rolling side to side and digging its snout into the softened earth. The hens however were sheltering under a fruit bush making the occasional dash for a worm that floated on the surface of the drenched ground.

Minnow checked his Mama had no more jobs for him and made his way to Top Meadow. He was quite surprised to see simple tents covering the pits. The cook was sitting under a shelter beside the fire and was preparing vegetables.

There was no sign of any work being done on the build. The trestles had been dismantled or moved into tents. Minnow went directly to stand by the cook under covering. The smoke from the fire was collecting at his standing height so he squatted and checked he wasn't in the way.

"You could have brought some sunshine with you," muttered the cook. "you will find a small stool in the store, make sure you close the flap after you. The lime needs to be kept dry remember."

Minnow fetched the stool and sat near the warmth of the fire.

"There was no sunshine at home to bring you, sorry about that. Where is everyone? I didn't think a little bit of wet would stop work. Everyone on the farm works in the wet and dry. My Papa is splitting the oak tree he felled yesterday despite the rain. Is there nothing to do here?"

The cook thought for a little time before answering.

"You will have noticed the covers over the pillar foundations. Mortar only becomes strong if it has the chance to dry. Water raining down on the new mortar will weaken it and the wet ground will not help it dry either. Channels have been cut to drain the water away but there will be no work until there have been seven continuous dry days. There would be no advantage in digging the trenches for the outside walls either as they'd fill with water and that would seep back to weaken the pillar foundations. Building on the top of a gentle hill helps water run away from the site so hopefully work will start again as soon as we have had some dry weather."

Minnow was again impressed by the knowledge of the cook, the way he was able to explain it to him made it fully understandable.

"Do you have children?" asked Minnow. "You explain things so well to me, it is as if you've had a lot of experience explaining to children."

"No, I've no children or wife," said the cook pensively, "but I've done some teaching, even if it was a long time ago."

Chapter Eleven – The Cook's Tale

The cook started to give Minnow some details of of his adventures. Minnow sat protected by the shelter, absorbing every word.

'I am the second son of a baron who holds a large manor. My Papa put me into an abbey to become a monk. He knew, as I was not the firstborn son, I would have no inheritance of land. The abbey was a safe place for me to grow and learn. I was good at study, can read and write Latin and did some teaching of young novices. My life was very easy but at times boring.

I looked around for some kind of excitement and asked permission to join a crusade. The abbot was keen to impress King Stephen so agreed I went on a crusade with one of Stephen's lords. I would go as a monk and provide spiritual support. I should organise the morning services while we were travelling and a special service for the Sundays when we were resting.

I've already mentioned I have crossed the Narrow Sea but I didn't say how bad it was for all of us. Reflecting on it now, it was probably partly to do with the food we had before we set off. It was a Friday so we had fish. It should have been wholesome and fresh as we were beside the sea. However the river that flowed into the sea had a bad smell to it. If the fish were caught anywhere near the entrance to the river we could have been eating anything.

A lot of us drank quite a bit of wine that evening before going on board. Sometimes drink makes you feel extra courageous. On this occasion it made us feel very much worse before we landed in Normandy the next morning.

The sea was rough. None of us had slept, we were all being sick over the side of the boat. The first time I was sick I was facing into the wind. I was feeling in need of lots of air. That was a mistake, my sick came back into my face. Someone dipped a bucket of water out of the sea and threw it over me. I was cold and wet but no longer smelling of vomit.

I found a place out of the wind but could not get warm. The sickness lasted all through the night. The headache the next morning was severe. It was the first of many bad memories of that crusade.

The knights and their squires travelled with their horses. Most of the horses on the crossing suffered as well. Some were bruised as they were thrown around by the uneven sea. It took the best part of a week for us all, including the horses, to recover enough to move on.

We travelled with a couple of wagons laden with tents and cooking equipment, each pulled by two horses. Each lord and knight had a pack pony for his personal items but the rest of us had to carry our own kit. They did find room on the wagons for weapons though most carried their pike staff as an aid to marching. As a monk I carried my bedding and a simple wood staff.

Each day was long and uninteresting. There was little talk amongst us, we kept our energy for our legs. After a few days we were more accustomed to the expectations and found we were becoming fitter. We started to exchange stories and that made the days start to feel shorter. Sometimes a knight would give us a tale of his worthy deeds. The lords kept to their own group and mostly boasted of the extent of their lands, each trying to sound more important than the others with much attention on their ancestry.

Food was quite often a problem. There was a lack of it sometimes and the standard of cooking was poor. The leaders hadn't appreciated that food needs time to be prepared. When passing through a settlement, groups of men were sent out to find and take what food the people had. Between communities it would be dry bread and salted pork before stocking up at the next set of dwellings.

If a group had been warned we were coming they'd leave their homes and take everything they could carry with them. We were not popular and were not the first to make a crusade through their country. We however believed ours was a just cause, Jerusalem needed protecting. The Christian Church had that responsibility. Successive popes had encouraged Christian leaders throughout the continent to join the fight.

We were making good progress south through the land and would soon be able to take another ship. That didn't encourage us but we were told the waters were much calmer, the winds gentler and we would not have to march each day. There would be opportunities to practise fighting for the soldiers, archery for the bowmen and time to rest before the battles ahead.

There was a good chance the food could be well prepared. We were promised a variety of dishes from the regions we would be encountering. This thought lifted our spirits especially when told there would be some good quality wines to sample. The whole area was the source of wine for the Pope in Rome and the rest of the countries bordering the sea.

That boat experience was so much easier than our first. We would stop at busy ports where we were presented with gifts of food and wine. These people all wanted to support our crusade and wish us God's speed. The threat of invasion by the Saracens moving beyond Jerusalem was a threat to their comfortable way of life. To have a supportive army from England deserved gifts.

Many of the foods were quite strange to our English tastes. Olives, figs, dates, spiced meats, flavoured breads were just a few we had on a regular basis. The wines were so different and smooth compared with those we had over the Narrow Sea. We all felt like lords at a banquet.

Some soldiers drank too much at first and suffered the next day. We soon learned to drink in moderation, to enjoy the flavour, quench our thirst but not to the extent of becoming drunk. That would have taken away the pleasure of the next day. Travelling in that area was the most enjoyable part of the crusade.

Too soon we were at our destination. It was a large sprawling camp on an island off the coast of Jerusalem. The camp was made up of many armies. Finding space for our group was the first problem. Some groups had spread themselves wide and spoiled the ground with their waste. It was left for others like ourselves to clear the ground before being able to settle and build our encampment.

This was where I became very ill. At one stage I was in such a fever I was tied to my pallet to prevent me raging about the camp attacking others. A young squire was directed to keep me cool with cloths soaked in water. I drifted in and out of consciousness, oblivious of day or night. There were times when I was shouting, would you believe it, in Latin, ordering people about and threatening to fight anyone. Sips of water made me worse so I was given juice from fruits. There was an orange fruit that gave lots of juice, it was slightly sharp but seemed to help me slowly recover.

Our group prepared their battle drills. They were then taken by small boats to the main land and marched to the battle site. I didn't get to see any of the Holy Land. The weakness following my illness sometimes made it difficult for me to stand for any length of time.

Those killed in the siege and battles were brought back by boat and I somehow managed to carry out their funerals. A lot of men were lost. Some had loss of limbs or other serious wounds that they didn't survive. My illness had changed me. I was losing faith with the Church and my support for the crusade. I felt very alone, especially with no other spiritual support. I prayed to be given strength to go beyond my doubts. I felt my prayers were not being heard. I carried out my duties mindlessly, it was easier that way, just going through a set performance.

The few men of our group that remained returned to have a break from the fighting. It was good to see some familiar faces and their stories began to lift me out of my gloom. They still believed in the cause despite the fatigue. They told of the evil performed by the Saracens that had made them more determined to defeat them. Our small band of men were to be joined with a Spanish group and would train together before returning to the battle.

Latin was the chosen language to share with the Spanish so I became involved in teaching some of the language to our group. It was mostly battle commands, directions and the names for weapons to be deployed. Simple conversations started between the two groups and I was in demand to help with everyday words.

Men started to exchange information about families they'd left behind, their way of life, skills and food preferences. This soon became another welcome part of the crusade for me. I began to feel my prayers had been heard and God did have his use for me in an unexpected way.

The battle with the joint force didn't go well. The commanders couldn't agree and the men started to treat any captives as the Saracens had treated our men. There was indiscipline and some deserters. I remained on the island to pray for the dead. The stories that came back from the fighting triggered my religious doubts once more.

Without warning we were on our way back home. I never did find out why the decision had been made. One rumour suggested there was no money left to continue, another that those in charge could not agree on a way forward. Certainly fewer armies had been joining the fight recently. The Spanish and ourselves shared the boat trip back to the south of France.

There was no welcome in the various ports that we used on the return journey. It was difficult to obtain supplies and payment was demanded in gold or silver. The Saracen threat was still very real for them and our lack of support was seen as running away, leaving them on their own. It was worst in Italy where the Pope implied there was a lack of loyalty to the Church.

I did register there was no sign of him leading an army into battle. I did my best to offer spiritual support with standard holy services and reciting prayers to the Spanish and English on our boat. The attitude of the Pope did confirm my feelings of doubt about my overall commitment to the Church. It was then I started to question my vow of obedience in particular. God did hear me the last time I had doubts so I expected to be guided again in the direction he wished me to go.

We arrived at a port in the south of France where we set off north on our march back to England. It was then I knew I was a burden as I could not walk for more than an hour. I hadn't fully recovered from my illness and I had extremely low energy levels. There was talk of leaving me at the Cathedral at Periguex in Aquitaine. We would pass through there but it was several days march away. Room was reluctantly made for me on one of the wagons. The wagoner started to teach me some of the skills of driving a pair of horses. That was great fun. It wasn't just the skill of starting and stopping. There was the need to keep looking ahead and guiding the horses around obstacle and soft ground where the wagon could become stuck or tip over.

The waggoner was also one of the cooks and often our talk would discuss the finer points of making meals while moving from place to place. At the overnight camps I'd try to assist with the meal and learned many cooking skills. The waggoner persuaded the leader of our group to let me continue back to England with them.

It wasn't long before I took control of the second wagon. That driver went missing one night. He'd been in the company of a local woman he met at an ale house. We had all been bought ale by the lord in charge to lift our spirits after our simple meal.

None of us had been given any pay for months. It was discovered that the silver plate and chalice used for our communion services went missing that same night. Two soldiers had been left to guard our camp but they were so weary they let sleep take over. It must have been an easy theft.

Having charge of the second wagon had some difficulties. It had been poorly maintained and needed patching frequently. Only essential work was carried out due to lack of coin. The village craftsmen only had access to poor quality, unseasoned, materials, joints quickly became loose. My driving skills now involved avoiding twisting the frame of the cart as well as moving forward. There was as much rope holding the cart together as there was timber.

Our memory of the first journey across the Narrow Sea made us apprehensive of the return journey. The weather this time was kind to us and we were soon comfortable in the castle grounds at Winchester. We still had to sleep in tents but would eat within the hall, sitting on benches at trestles laden with succulent foods. The wine didn't match the quality we had experienced on the crusade but it was good to have traditional English foods we knew and trusted.'

"Did you return to the life at the abbey after your crusade?" asked Minnow.

"That's another story for another time. Have you noticed it has stopped raining and the sky is clearing of clouds? I have charge of lifting the covers off the foundations. You could give me a hand."

Minnow willingly helped the cook remove and drape the covers onto the hedges to dry. The wooden frames, over the pillar bases, were left in case there was the threat of a shower. The drying of the limecrete could now continue for the next few weeks.

"What will the king's men be eating today?" enquired Minnow.

"The farm promised some beef." The cook gave a small smile and looked as if he was tasting it from his memory. "There was a year old bullock that wasn't up to breeding so the farm is passing some meat on to us. It depends which part of the animal we are given. Everything will stew well but some parts will fry and other parts benefit from roasting. When I see what we have I'll then decide the type of fire that is needed. A sack of charcoal was delivered yesterday so that will help if a roast is needed."

"There are charcoal burners that work the forest around Wocca's Hamlet," said Minnow. "They are always covered in black dust and usually take their charcoal to Reading to sell at the market. When they move site I can sometimes collect a few bits to take home and then I'm covered in black dust!" The cook smiled as he imagined how Minnow would have looked after gathering scraps of charcoal.

Another thing Minnow didn't understand was how did burning wood, inside a covering of turf, make the black remains burn hotter than logs? The blacksmith used charcoal to make metal red hot so he could shape it using his hammer on his anvil. There was a lot of skills that he'd love to learn but to learn the magic of the blacksmith took years.

The son of the blacksmith was learning the trade and the secrets were well guarded. To learn the trade Minnow's Papa would have to pay and work for the blacksmith himself. There was no chance to learn that.

"I don't think I would like to be a charcoal burner," added Minnow. "The smoke and dust make me cough when I get near them. My Grandpapa has difficulty breathing and he's worse when he has a fit of coughing. The smoke from our hearth fire is sometimes enough to start him gasping for air but he also needs the warmth especially in winter. He spends most of the winter on his pallet under his covers. It takes him a long time to get moving again now that it is spring."

"There are worse jobs," suggested the cook.

"Yes," said Minnow, "a tanner. Do you think their noses have died?"

"I was actually thinking of when I worked as a guard, at the dungeons of a castle. Perhaps I had better leave that story till you're much older. It would be enough to stop you sleeping. Even now I still have the occasional nightmare."

"That does not fit in with you being at an abbey or on a crusade." Minnow could not fit the stories together.

"Enough of me," said the cook, "I need to get started on the vegetables for the meal."

"And I need to see if I can find my Papa," suggested Minnow. "The hammering of wedges should be a good clue and I remember roughly where he was working yesterday."

Drips from the rain were still falling from the trees as Minnow made his way through the forest. It was slippery underfoot where the autumn leaves hadn't been penetrated by new ground growth. The path was well trodden and it looked as if a horse had been taken through to the site of the felled oak. In the distance he could hear some voices and the urging of a horse. The next thing he saw was the horse coming towards him hauling a huge limb from the top of the tree.

Minnow moved well to the side and watched as the powerful animal and its load moved towards the cart track. Small shrubs and bushes were being flattened as the horse trampled its new route through the forest. The major task was avoiding the load being jammed between standing trees.

The path to the activity was now very clear and surprisingly easy to walk. His Papa was still removing the top branches and the side limbs. No start had yet been made on the splitting of the trunk.

There was so much top growth that was not appreciated from ground level. Only now, lying on the ground, was the extent of the growth visible. His Papa had severed only a few of the major limbs. Now he was balanced on the main trunk clearing space around him to be able to start attacking the next large limb. The axe sharpener exchanged axes with him and his Papa set about his task.

He was about half way through when the trunk started to roll. The limb had been a support and as it was weakened it snapped and the weight of the rest of the top branches made the trunk turn. Minnow's Papa slipped on the wet surface and was thrown off his feet. He fell into the path of the rolling trunk and rolled himself quickly out of trouble. It was a very close thing to him being pinned under the trunk.

The axe was still under the trunk, the handle crushed and splintered. The head of the axe was just visible but no one was going near it. There was no knowing if the trunk had settled and stopped rolling.

Perhaps there were worse jobs than a charcoal burner or tanner.

Chapter Twelve – It's All About Money

The next day looked as if it was going to be dry. Minnow's Papa had gone to the forest to continue working on the felled oak. Last evening he'd been visibly shaken by the trunk rolling and nearly crushing him. He was more upset that Minnow had been a witness.

His Papa had worked hard to reassure him, and his Mama, that he was fine to continue working. He was still young and fit enough to look after himself as he'd proved. Mama went with him to see where he was working. Minnow set about his routine and checked on his Grandpapa.

When his Mama returned she was a little happier and set about her own tasks. His Papa had been given some payment for the cart work so she was off to buy more cheese and some meat for a treat. Minnow was going to help carry as there were lots of things that were needed.

The list included more oats, flour, some fats, salt, wicks for lamps and candles. These were all basics and some would keep for times when money was short again. Some things would be shared with Grandpapa so there would be plenty to carry.

The farm was the source of most basic food items. Stalls in Wocca's Hamlet provided most of the other things that people may need. There had been talk of applying to the bishop or the knight for a regular market. That would attract the sale of animals as well as more traders from around the area.

Currently, if you needed special items such as tools, you would need to go the three hour walk to Reading market. The blacksmith could make some items by special order. He did not have the materials to make an axe for example. It needed additionally special heat treatment to provide an edge that could be sharpened and stay sharp.

Both Minnow and his Mama enjoyed just looking through the items displayed on the stalls. His Mama had dreams about some of the fabrics she saw. Minnow would have loved a knife to be able to make items for the home. Simple pegs, flat food turners, cooking spoons and wedges were some of the ideas he had.

Knives cost a lot of coins so there was no chance of buying one. The broken blade could be his dream if it could have a safe handle. It was then that he thought the cook may be able to help him, he did seem to know a lot about many things.

Well laden they both returned from the farm and put the purchases away. The flour and the oats would have come from the water mill on the River Loddon and been delivered direct to the farm in large sacks. If you grew your own wheat or corn the miller would make it into flour but keep a bag for himself as payment. Buying small amounts at the farm did mean there was less chance of it spoiling which could happen to a large quantity kept over a longer time.

Also at the farm the butcher asked if Minnow's Papa was the one working in the forest felling the oaks. When she confirmed he was there, the butcher produced some beef and some beef bones at no charge.

"He will be needing his strength with that job. I'll have to charge you for the fat but it will be beef fat if that is acceptable?" Minnow's Mama thought it more than acceptable.

It wasn't often there was beef available let alone beef fat. It was much more useful than mutton fat and gave a good flavour to fried food. The beef bones with their core of marrow would add flavour to the pot. They'd be eating well for some time with a fresh bone added every other day.

Minnow took some oats next door to his Grandpapa and then he and his Mama set off to the stalls where the tracks converged. Some candles and wicks were still to be purchased. They were cheaper at this time of year as there was less demand due to the evenings getting longer. This bit of extra income could be invested in things that would keep and be used later in the year. Minnow's Grandpapa had taught these things to his Mama. He'd less money during the shorter winter months from his work as a sawyer.

The winter was when many items became more expensive as there was greater demand. She'd understood these lessons of real life as his Grandpapa called them. Minnow had sometimes thought if he'd a place to store dry firewood collected over the summer he might make money selling it through the winter. It was just a dream, collecting would be a lot of extra work and he'd no secure storage place.

He had thought to ask his Grandpapa if he could use the unused animal space in his dwelling. The one problem could be if rats made the protection of a large wood pile their home. They'd be difficult to remove. Keep thinking, Minnow told himself, there must be a solution somehow.

With the candles, wicks and other purchases safely in his shoulder bag he made his way home. His Mama stayed to look at other stalls and chat with friends and neighbours. Most of the chatter was about the building of the new church, the number of people who were having some extra work along with their normal jobs, the strangeness of the king's men, boats bringing materials, the condition of the cart tracks through Wocca's Hamlet and the big question who would be paying for this new church?

If it was the King's idea he ought to be paying. He no longer had the extravagant expenses of the Young King Henry. He'd died and had been buried in Rouen Cathedral in Normandy a couple of years ago. Another son, Geoffrey, had also died recently, having been trampled by a horse at a tournament.

Perhaps the money he was saving was going towards paying for their new church. Many doubted the King would pay for everything and they all guessed who would have to contribute eventually. Some of the group had thought further ahead. They suggested several benefits of having a large covered space where the community could gather.

One mother had moved to Wocca's Hamlet from a place where there was an established, large stone built, church. It was used during the week for markets and gatherings. She said how much it had brought people together and built a strong community.

She missed the varied events that had taken place in the church. It was the safe space to meet with friends. It was fine for the men to drift off to the alehouses but it wasn't so easy for the women who had care of children. Events during the day in the church, where children were tolerated, was part of her early married life that she missed.

A thick grey cloud started to dominate the sky and each made their way to their dwellings with their purchases. Minnow's Mama had bought some strong linen, thread and a strong needle. She intended to use them to make into a replacement shoulder bag.

The bag Minnow had carried home had been patched many times, it was still of use but with the couple of pennies that were left she'd chosen to spend them. She did have a hidden stock of coins, not many, but enough to cover any urgent need for food. Her spend would be of benefit.

Back at the dwelling there was a messenger from the farm waiting. Two of the family would be needed at the farm in the morning to help with planting grain. Farm duties were expected in return for the use of their dwelling and the plots of land.

Her Papa was excused the labour due to his poor health and having been a full time farm worker when he was younger. Many older people were still expected to attend and do what they could when their turn came. Normally Minnow's Mama and Papa would be the team. Mama now decided that Minnow could be the second worker and allow his Papa to continue with the felling work which would continue to bring in money.

Minnow was small but could guide a pony. It was likely she'd have to direct the light harrow following another person broadcasting the grain seed. Ploughing had been taking place for a few weeks now and the recent rain would be ideal for starting the seed in the warmed ground. The small harrow was needed to cover the grain seed and prevent the greedy pigeons from gorging themselves.

Sometimes a falconer would arrive at the farm to give lessons to the young squires. He'd thin out the pigeons and send them elsewhere for a short time but they soon came back. Some of the kitchen women at the farm would feed the pigeons when they were not being watched. Minnow thought the food would be better used to help the poor, not feeding pests who regularly reduced the crops.

It must have been her Papa who told her how good food was wasted at the farm. Still, she was grateful to the butcher for the meat they'd been able to obtain today. There was the chance that the meat was payment for the felling work and there may be no coins. They'd have to wait and see.

Chapter Thirteen – A Harrowing Time

Soon after sunrise Minnow and his Mama arrived at the farm for their day of work. They'd eaten a good breakfast and left Grandpapa to keep the stew pot on a low simmer for the day. Minnow had collected water late afternoon the previous day so Grandpapa had liquid to stop the pot going dry. He seemed glad to have a useful part to play while they were having their day of labour.

Minnow was asked to lead a pony from the stable to the farm manager to see how he handled it. The pony was very quiet and seemed to respond to Minnow talking softly to it as they walked across the yard. Minnow imagined he was talking to a younger brother, he'd no idea what he'd say to a younger brother but it seemed to work with the pony.

The stable had harnessed the pony for hitching to the light harrow and very soon the older woman, charged with broadcasting the seed, was leading the way to the first of the fields that had to be sown. Mama held the reins and guided the harrow along the rutted lane. Even here the affect of the harrow was obvious. The ruts were being filled in by the harrow taking the tops off the ridges.

On the field a heavy harrow had already levelled the ploughed soil ready for the seed. The much larger horse and its team were now working on the next field. The light harrow had been folded to allow it to move along the track. The two upper layers were folded out, one to each side, and a wide harrow could now match the width of the thrown seed.

The pony felt the difference and was reluctant to pull the frame so Minnow had to talk firmly and coax it forward. Eventually it got into its stride and they were working as a team. The sun was starting to warm up the air and quite soon they'd a thirst. At one end of the field a farm hand had arrived with a pitcher of watered cyder and a bucket of water for the pony. The short break was very welcome and having been refreshed, they resumed their task.

Lunch was provided; bread, cheese, an apple and more cyder. There was a sweet pastry that had an apple filling. This was more than they'd normally have had for lunch but they'd not have walked so many miles either.

"What have you been saying to the pony all morning?" asked his Mama.

"Just things. I told it about the new church, how the foundations were prepared, Papa's work with the carts and felling the oak. It was just chatter. I think it feels it is less hard work if I'm distracting it. It makes the time go quicker for me too. I'm enjoying this lunch. Do they always give food like this?"

"The pastry is an extra," replied his Mama, "it was possibly left over from some feast or maybe part of a batch they sent to the king's men."

"The cook did have some pastries sent from the farm the other day so you could well be correct. Those king's men are well looked after. Their own cook, a comfortable encampment and they have a good supply of wine."

There was no time to relax as the seed broadcaster had re-filled her bag and was eager to get started. Minnow led the pony around to be ready for the next pass along the field. His Mama took hold of the harrow handles and they were away.

Minnow continued his chatter to the pony telling it of the deeds of the cook on his crusade and talked a little about his Grandpapa. It was getting late in the day before they'd completed the two fields. The harrow had its sides folded in and they made their way back along the track to the farm.

The stable lad unhitched the pony and gathered up the straps and tackle. Minnow led the pony by its bridle back to the stall where he'd been given the pony. It was in need of a good rub down but that was the job of the stable lad.

As he made his way back to his Mama he saw Mary by the farm kitchen door. He gave her a wave and she waved back. Mama had been brushing down the harrow spikes and was handing back the brush. They were both ready to leave.

The walk back up the track took them past Top Meadow where Minnow spotted the cook serving food to the king's men. The fire was burning without smoke and there was a slight hint of roasted beef wafting on the air. The night watchman's dog was circling the trestle hoping to be fed bits.

There were signs of trenches being dug out beyond the pillar foundations, they were long straight lines about four men feet in width. None were as deep as the pillar foundations, but must have been level with the waist of anyone digging.

They both continued on their way home and were hit by the welcome smell of the stew pot. Grandpapa was dozing beside the embers of the fire.

"Had a good day, Papa?" she questioned.

"So, so," he replied without opening his eyes. "Bit boring pot stirring all day. Don't think it burned. I've used most of the bucket so we will need some more water."

Minnow picked up the bucket and set off to fetch the water. By the time he returned his own Papa had arrived home and was hungry for food. He reported that after a full day the trunk had been given its first split along the whole length. He seemed to have an admiration for the strength within the oak but didn't speak about it in quite that way.

Grandpapa knew all about the toughness of oaks, they'd blunted many a saw blade in his years.

"Thing is," he added, "oak lasts for at least a hundred years if properly seasoned. Elm is the worst to try and split, the grain gets so twisted. I have seen a strong metal wedge be split by elm. It will take sawing and is ideal for gate posts if you can get a fixing into the wood. It takes a long time to rot so is ideal for outdoor use."

The meal was special, even better than the lunch with its sweet pastry. It was the whole family together, enjoying the taste of beef, chatting about their day and listening to the tales of Grandpapa.

It was getting dark outside so moves were made to settle for the night. Minnow slept very soundly, as did both his parents. Grandpapa had slept a bit during the day so took a little time to fall asleep but then he dreamt of his family of daughters and his wife.

Chapter Fourteen – Knot a Problem

Minnow woke with some stiffness in his legs but it soon wore off once he started his daily chores. No wood had been collected the previous day so that was going to be a double task.

The lad, living a few doors away, had the light harrow and pony today. He was younger than Minnow but bigger so should have no problem with helping his parents. The Mama would be broadcasting the seed, his Papa guiding the harrow and the boy leading the pony. Minnow had enjoyed his day and felt he'd a bit of a bond with that pony. They'd spent a lot of time in each others company.

Wood collection, he decided, had to be across the brook to the south today. He'd stores in that area he had not visited for a time. It would be a chance to see also what had fallen recently that he could add to his hidden hearth wood stores. There was a bit of a hill up the other side of the brook and only dead wood fell from the trees. The hill gave protection from the main winds and full sunlight only arrived later in the year. Dwellings were sparse beyond the brook and little of the forest had been cleared. It was further to walk but the track south that went through the forest was a lot less busy than the London or Reading tracks.

The area was on the edge of the main part for coppicing and the charcoal burning. Once charcoal burners moved on from a site, the area they left soon sprouted brambles. Brambles gave Minnow lots of places for hiding wood.

The coppicing however did little to clear the forest. The long straight stems were cut almost to the base of the hazel plant. They were taken away to be split and made into the woven hurdles. The only bits left were the top trimmings that were green and took months to dry enough to burn without smoke.

The cutters would return again to the same plant in a few years and collect the newly grown straight stems. While the plant had to struggle for light the stems grew quickly and straight up. Some of the older coppiced hazel was left to become thicker stems that would be harvested as long straight handles for tools. These bushes also provided tasty nuts that could be gathered after the grain harvest.

Minnow crossed the wooden bridge and soon turned left a little way up the track. He kept within sight of the brook and looking across saw how Wocca's Hamlet was growing. The brook gave ready access to flowing water. The gentle slope up to the centre of the village had the benefit of the direct sun to help the growth on the plots of land attached to each dwelling.

It was away from the farm so there would be a bit of a walk to work on the harvest or make purchases. At the London end of the dwellings was South Field. The land was marked out in strips for people of the Hamlet to produce crops. There were several other fields that were used in the same way. Here today Minnow could see some women and children were broadcasting seed.

The choice of crop was theirs though many grew hemp or flax to sell to the ropemaker in the village. Every third year the field was left unused by families. At the end of the previous harvest, grass seed was sown and left to grow over the winter. In the spring these fields were used for grazing and the animal droppings gave back goodness to the soil. This part was managed by the farm and the rotation of healthy fields benefited the people of Wocca's Hamlet.

Looking around him, Minnow could name every type of tree that grew in the forest. His Grandpapa had walked with him a couple of years ago and helped with collecting wood. He became too breathless now but he'd helped Minnow recognise all the different tree types. It was easy in the summer with the variety of leaf shapes. The tree outline, bark and sometimes leaf litter were the clues to recognising trees in the winter.

Each tree was good for particular things. The oak was best for large buildings, elm for outdoor posts and fencing, beech for quality trestle boards, and ash was used for tool handles. Holly could also be used for tool handles, it only gave short lengths but was smooth to the hand.

Each type of tree also had their different qualities when burnt. Ash was very hot but burned quickly, oak and elm burned slowly giving a steady heat. It was a waste to burn beech as even the smallest piece would make something useful for helping with cooking.

There, nearby, was a freshly fallen branch from an ash tree. As it had fallen it had broken off part of a holly bush. The smaller parts of the ash branch had already been taken by another wood collector. The main branch was too big for Minnow to try and move. It was the broken part of the holly bush that interested him.

The prickly leaves had started to brown but no one had shown any interest in taking it away, it was still too green to burn without smoke. Minnow saw part of it as a possible handle for the broken piece of blade. Carefully Minnow started to pick off the spiked leaves. He'd have to take the whole piece as it was still too green to break.

Before returning home, over the little bridge near South Field, he remembered to gather together firewood from a nearby stash. His shoulder cloth and the attached ropes made it a large but useful load. The track took him towards Top Meadow but his dwelling was off to the left as he came to the London track.

Stacking his wood collection at his dwelling he took out the length of holly and put it up just under the roof cover of the store. The last thing he wanted was for it to be taken to be burnt, the smoke would be thick and penetrating.

There was no sign of his Mama and he could not hear her voice coming from Grandpapa's dwelling either. He decided to go and see how his Papa was doing with the trunk splitting. The London track was empty and he was soon following the trail of demolition left by the horse drawing out the top pieces of the oak.

Those crown pieces would be left to dry at the farm and eventually be logged. Nothing went to waste. The tree bark and the dust from the sawing would go to the tanners. Some would even go to the dyers of the sheep's wool.

Minnow's Papa was on the final stages of quartering one of the halves of the oak. All the wedges were deep inside the half trunk and a metal rod was forcing them deeper. A couple of hits with the heavy metal headed hammer, move to the next wedge and it was repeated. His Papa was working along the length little by little.

Papa's help had some long tongs to steady the rod. Papa had good aim but the young lad was taking no chances of having his hands crushed by the heavy metal maul. Then came a sound Minnow had never heard before. It was difficult to describe, a bit like the crash of a falling tree or wood slapping against wood but a very short loud sound.

The trunk had split in two to the yelps of all watching. Minnows Papa let his arms drop and sank to sit on the trunk. He looked exhausted, picking up his shirt he wiped his face. The axe sharpener handed him a skin of drink and then went around collecting up the metal wedges. One wedge, near where the top branches had been removed, had started to be split itself.

A knot in the wood had twisted the wedge and started a split in the metal.

"Another for the blacksmith," he said. "Who would have thought wood could be stronger than iron?" he asked Minnow.

"It was deep inside, where a branch grew out from the trunk," continued Papa. "It has to be strong to bear the weight of the top growth. Knots blunt a saw blade as well did you know? Yet, around the knot, there develops a weakness as the wood dries. Often the knot will shrink and drop out of a board after some years. That is why you pay a premium for straight grained, knot free timbers. Let's hope the other half will split easier."

Having felt it was safe to move beside his Papa Minnow went over and studied the split in detail. He expected it to be perfectly straight but there was a definite twist along the length.

"Why is it twisted?" he asked his Papa. "When it was growing the trunk looked perfectly straight. How does it get so twisted but look straight on the outside?"

"As the tree grows it searches for the best light," explained his Papa. "The gaps above change as the other trees grow above it. Eventually the crown is above the other trees and the trunk can straighten but inside it still has the twists put in by its early growth. To grow a truly straight tree it would have to grow in the middle of a meadow."

"Grandpapa explained to me about the knots. He said elm was the worst for knots and was almost impossible to split," volunteered Minnow.

"I have ruined many a good axe, in my younger years," said the axe sharpener. "Trying to trim the limbs off an elm frequently the axe head would be split and twist if it met a knot. Axes are tough but an old elm can be tougher."

Having recovered his breath Minnow's Papa made a start on splitting the last half. A simple but hefty blow with the axe made a small split start in the half trunk. A small wedge was placed into the opening split and hammered home. This released the axe and made the split a tiny bit longer. Another small wedge was inserted to extend the split and then a third. The first wedge had become loose so was used to extend the split further. A larger wedge was put in place of the first wedge and hammered in firmly. The second wedge being loose was replaced by a second large wedge.

Bit by bit the split went the whole length of the trunk. Even larger wedges were now being used going deeper and deeper into the trunk. The metal rod was used to reach down to the head of the wedges. Listening, Minnow could hear the sounds of splitting that gradually continued even when there was no hammering. The trunk was reluctantly yielding to the force of metal within the wood.

Chapter Fifteen – A Heavy Load

With his chores completed, Minnow made his way along The Clearing towards Top Meadow. He saw little was happening and could only see the cook at his fire. Minnow went to the gateway and wandered across to the cook.

"Are you busy?" he asked.

"No, things are quiet at the moment," answered the cook. "All the king's men have gone to inspect a special delivery that has arrived in Reading at the abbey wharf. There are twelve bases for the pillars that have come up the River Thames all the way from Normandy. The craftsmen in Normandy are long established experts in carving stone. Each base is carved and shaped from a single block. They are costing a lot so they have to be inspected before they arrive on site. It's going to take six journeys to fetch the twelve bases here."

"They must have worked very quickly to have them made in such a short time. Normandy is across the Narrow Sea," suggested Minnow.

"They would have already been made," the cook explained. "There are many new buildings, castles, churches and cathedrals being built over the sea in lots of countries. The masons make many bases of the same design to be able to sell and supply them quickly which is what builders need. The king's men would have had them ordered at the same time as the King instructed the building of this church."

"Are they very large?" asked Minnow.

"Large and strong," replied the cook. "When the building is finished most of the bases will be below the ground level as an extension to the support. The important part is that they are joined to the foundation you've seen being prepared, using mortar. They have to level so that any pillar built on top remains upright. The king's men have those skills. It is very different to constructions using timber."

"Have you been on many building sites?" enquired Minnow. "You know so much about what is to happen."

"This must be the sixth, all the others were over the Narrow Sea. It's the first time with this team of king's men. They are true Normans and are less familiar with Latin which was the language of the other teams I worked with. The King himself made me part of the team here as I could speak our English language. He didn't think about his chosen men needing to be able to speak English or Latin which I understood. The knight has had to do all the translation but he does have a young squire who is trying to use his understanding of some of the Norman language. It's part of a young squire's training."

"You're very patient with me," stated Minnow. "Most people say I ask too many questions. They send me off to play somewhere else, get out from under their feet or go and ask your Papa. My Grandpapa says I'm a thinker and has added that I could be dangerous. He also says I need to be careful about asking too many questions. I don't understand why. How can I know about the world if I don't ask questions?"

"Your Grandpapa is correct in some ways. People can start to ask why you're asking questions. Spies ask questions to obtain knowledge to use against those in charge. You could make a good spy being so small and like a young child."

"I have recognised you're naturally curious and your questions are those I would have asked as a youth. I enjoy returning to speak English after such a long time beyond the Narrow Sea. At the abbey I taught novices and they were eager to learn. I see the same eagerness for knowledge in you."

"Don't you feel you need to go back to being a monk?" asked Minnow. "You seemed to have enjoyed what you were doing."

"The teaching and instruction was a good way of life," reflected the cook. "Do you recall I became very ill during the crusade? I needed a lot of care from a young squire. He told me during those long days of support what was happening in the battle with the Saracens. How the crusaders were responding began to shock me. I made an effort to see for myself what was happening in the fighting. All I did see was rows of hung Saracens. I can't even start to tell you what happened to them before they were hung. It wasn't Christian behaviour."

"The crusade had turned good Christians into some type of savage animals. The Saracens were behaving no better. I prayed to be able to understand but no answer came from God. There was no sense in being forgiven of your sins by crusading if you ended up doing evil. I was glad when it came time to leave."

"My weakness after my illness didn't allow me to perform my full religious duties of leading every service or even sometimes leading prayers. Often prayers would stick in my throat after all that I had heard and seen. I had truly lost my faith in the role of the Church."

The cook stopped his tale and looked away. It seemed as if the memory was becoming too painful.

Minnow said, "I'm sorry, I didn't mean for you to become upset. I think I had best leave you to your work. My Grandpapa will have some tasks for me."

"Stay a little longer, if you've time. I have a need to finish my tale if you could bear it?" The cook took a big breath while he waited for Minnow to answer.

"I thought I had done something that made you upset and you wished you hadn't started your tale. My Grandpapa can start some stories and not be able to finish them. We just change the subject. I don't have to go if you're happy for me to stay. Are you sure?" asked Minnow.

"I have never spoken about this to anyone. I would like to finish my story if you don't mind."

"I told the abbot that during the crusade I had lost my faith in the Church. He persuaded me to stay six months to pray, read the Bible and hear his sermons to give God time to talk to me. I tried hard to look for signs that God was asking me to continue at the abbey. All I felt was that I was trapped and my nightmares continued."

"I could not talk to anyone there like I have been able to talk to you. They were all too tied up in their own fixed beliefs to look beyond into the real world. You listen. You ask questions for clarification, not unbelieving or critical. It has made such a difference to be able to talk. Thank you for just listening."

Minnow sat for a time thinking about what he'd been told. The cook was like his Grandpapa in his story telling. He'd listened to many tales of how life used to be for families, how there had been difficult times, including fighting that had slaughtered family members, when Kings had their battles.

This story was about volunteers going on a crusade with a belief in the rightness of the cause and the chance to be absolved of their sins. They had the support and encouragement of the Pope himself. Something had gone wrong for the cook and he was still finding it difficult. Minnow felt a little uneasy. He wanted to ask more questions but now he wasn't sure it was the right time.

"I think I have made you feel a bit uncomfortable," commented the cook. "I'm sorry, but you've been a very good listener. I apologise, I have used you to offload my bad experience."

The cook stood up and went into the store tent. He was blowing his nose. Minnow could hear him taking deep breaths, having a little cough and clearing his throat. He came back out with a couple of sweet pastries and offered one to Minnow.

Minnow willingly took the pastry and lingered over the smell that came from it. He nibbled the corner, the pastry was so light and crumbly that it melted in the mouth. When he came to the filling it was so sweet and spicy he wished the flavour would last for ever. It was mostly apple but had so many other sensations he thought his mouth might explode.

The cook took a beaker of drink from a jug on the trestle and offered a beaker to Minnow. He didn't wish to lose the flavours so declined the drink.

"Thanks for the pastry," said Minnow. "Do the king's men have things like that every day? Could I be a king's man?"

"Sorry, firstly you've to be born into a noble family." The cook thought for a short time then suggested, "next you've to have learning from a skilled tutor and that would cost your Papa a lot of money." He then added, "it helps if you remember all that you're taught and can apply it to tasks you're set. Finally you need to be apprenticed to a craftsperson that already works for the King."

"The pastries are made only for special occasions and special guests. The farm must have had an important visitor but I've not seen them come to Top Meadow."

"Sounds easy to be a king's man," said Minnow with a sarcastic smile. "Are you a king's man?"

"Yes and no is your answer young churl. I have told you I was born into a noble family but wasn't the firstborn male. My tutors were the abbot and the other monks for my role in the abbey as I have already told you. I was an educated monk, not a craft normally recognised as a role for a king's man."

"The King and the Church are separate and each has its own leader and ways of doing things. The King has rule of the land. The Pope has rule of the Church. They exist side by side but can sometimes disagree. I'm a cook chosen by the King for working with his teams of builders so in that respect I'm a king's man. I can hear your next question, how did I become a cook? That will have to wait for another day as I can hear a horse and wagon that sounds as if it has a heavy load."

Through the gateway came the three king's men, two young squires, the horse and wagon, a carter and two other helpers. The two blocks on the wagon were huge, much taller than Minnow expected and were shaped with eight straight, flat sides. The top above the flats was rounded and ended in a circle, a curved slope joining the flat sides up to a circular ring at the top.

Minnow had expected the pillars to be square blocks stacked on each other. Seeing the circular ring at the top of the shaped blocks suggested a round pillar was going to be used. He thought that was going to make a lot of extra work just to hold up a roof.

Taking the pillar bases off the wagon was no easy task. The wagon had been moved to the space between the first pair of foundations. The horse had been unharnessed, led to be watered and allowed to graze on a long tether.

The wheels of the wagon were fixed to the ground with wedges and pegs so it could not move. Logs formed a slope off the back of the wagon and a trestle board placed on the logs gave a smooth slope. One edge of a block was eased up using a large wide wooden wedge and a smooth log was placed under it. Other smooth logs were added and the block moved on its rollers towards the back of the wagon.

It took the cook, squires, driver and his two helpers to move the huge weight. Once it was on the slope gravity took over and the whole group had to try and slow the descent with ropes to avoid damage to the block as it hit the ground. With a series of grunts and shoves they moved the block to one side and worked in the same way with the second block.

The now unloaded wagon, with the rested horse re-harnessed, returned to the farm. The trestle board and all the rollers went with it. The performance would be repeated over the next few days with the rest of the blocks.

No doubt by then the carter would have arranged a load from Wocca's Hamlet that needed to be transported to Reading wharf where a lifting derrick would make loading and unloading easier. There would be no point in wasting a journey and the chance of additional payment.

Chapter Sixteen – Wood, Large and Small

It was yet another laundry day. Minnow carried the basket of washing to the brook for his mother then left her. She'd carried the soap in a cloth and the bucket of men's wee that she used to remove stains. There were sometimes a collection of rags that had signs of blood that needed washing. Minnow could not recall anyone being hurt or needing to mop up blood. When he asked his mother all she'd said was that it was a women's thing and nothing to worry about.

There were quite a number of women at the brook today and the noise of the chatter was building. There was eventually so much noise Minnow could not make out what was being said and was happy to be able to move away.

Having completed all his regular tasks, checked his Grandpapa had eaten his breakfast and didn't need anything, he went to the wood shelter to find his piece of holly branch. Looking along its length he chose a section he thought was the correct size and shape for a knife handle.

Taking the small hand axe that was used to to split logs he made the first cut. The holly was so tight the axe became stuck. Minnow had to work hard to ease it free. His second cut was at an angle to the first and a wedge of wood flew free. Turning the branch over he attacked the other side and was shocked to find he'd cut right through to the other cut. Well, he thought, that was easy.

Measuring with his hand and adding a little he aimed for the other end of his proposed handle. Once again the axe jammed. He knew what to do and soon had the handle length he needed. Using the axe he worked at one end to try and round the end as well as he could. He'd use a rough stone to finally smooth the end. The handle would need to be split as evenly in half as possible to sit over each side of the blade. This is where it could all go wrong.

Looking at the end, where he would start the split, the tight circles of growth looked fairly even. Closer inspection showed a very slight bulge to one side. He decide the cut would go through the centre of the bulge and make it even both sides. He carefully positioned the blade and tapped the axe and the holly together onto the chopping block. The axe struggled to even make a mark. He'd have to be braver and hit harder against the block. The axe this time made a mark but not deep enough to stay in the cut.

Several times he worked at splitting the holly and gradually the axe went a little deeper. At last it held itself in the split. Lifting axe and the holly together he brought them down hard onto the chopping block. Success, a nice clean split. Flat both sides as he hoped. All he'd need to do was bind the blade between the two halves.

He put the two halves into the shoulder bag along with a hunk of bread. He'd go and see his Papa at work and then slip away to find his hidden blade. Aiming towards the sound of the steady axe blows he left the London track. He soon came to the area where his Papa was working with the axe sharpener and the forest manager.

The new oak was near his den and his hidden blade. Papa gave him a wave while the axe was being exchanged. Minnow judged he could enter the hidden tunnel without being watched and crept off to find his piece of blade.

Some animal had left a mess just at the start of the tunnel. Using a stick he removed as much as possible to one side and carefully worked his way into the opening, avoiding any mess that was left. Under the rock he found the blade. It had lost even more of its shine and was now looking quite dull. He would never have spotted it on the ground with such a level of grime, even in the best of daylight.

The blade joined the handle pieces in his shoulder bag. Minnow started to make his way out of the tunnel remembering to avoid the animal mess. As he stood up he heard the shout. "RUN!".

He looked up and saw the crown of the oak starting to fall towards him. He knew he needed to run side ways as far and as fast as possible. Clutching his bag to him he ran, leapt and tumbled as far as he could from the falling oak. As the mighty crown finally met the ground he felt the sting of green twigs brush his leg. He'd fallen and was panting on the ground, gasping for breath like his Grandpapa on one of his bad days.

The axe sharpener had spotted him running and then lost sight of him. He was shouting to the others, that included his Papa, and they all came in his direction. It goes without saying his Papa was looking very angry.

Minnow just lay there gasping for breath. He knew better than to say anything. He wanted to say sorry but it seemed so little and inappropriate. If he could, he'd have run away and faced the issue later. It was the forest manager who knelt beside him and asked if he'd been hurt. Minnow could only shake his head.

His whole body was shaking, as was his Papa's. Minnow felt as if he wanted to be sick, he was feeling dizzy and knew if he tried to stand up he'd fall over. His Papa sat on the ground and wiped his face with his sleeve.

The axe sharpener had gone off to retrieve his axes and came back with a skin of cyder. Minnow's Papa took a long swig from the skin but stayed sitting on the ground. He was still shaking. Minnow was offered a drink but he just felt sick so pushed it away. The forest manager took a drink and stood up to assess the scene.

"Well," said the forester, "I think we need to have a break to recover. I could do with some food and I'm sure we all need some rest. Let's come back after noon. I think you need to get your son home."

Papa helped Minnow to his feet and supported him along the path to the track. Neither had said a word, there would be lots of time for that later. Now the urgency was to get Minnow home into the care of his Grandpapa. Minnow was very wobbly and needed the support of his Papa all the way home. Once there his Papa made him have a drink, an apple and some bread to eat. Papa had the same. They then went to talk with Grandpapa.

He was told what had happened, was asked if Minnow could rest on his floor and maybe have a little sleep. Some clean rushes were put by the wall and Minnow lay down on them covered with an old coat.

Minnow had no idea how long he'd slept but it was still daylight. His Mama was back with a clean bucket and the wet laundry. He'd registered that the bushes were covered with damp items as he made his way back to his own dwelling. The fire was warming the stew pot for the evening meal. There was no sign of his Papa so presumably he was still in the forest.

"So, how are you feeling?" asked his Mama.

"Still a bit unsteady," Minnow replied, hoping there would not be too many questions. "I'm sorry if I was a nuisance to Grandpapa. He was kind to look after me. I just felt so weak and very tired. I did run fast but I've run fast before and have never felt like this."

"These things happen. Just so long as you've not been hurt you will soon start to feel better. Once we've had our meal we'll need to talk about what happened but now isn't the time. Could you manage to fetch in a couple of fair sized logs for the hearth?"

Minnow made his way slowly to the wood shelter to find the logs. The day had started so well here with the holly branch as his blade handle. He'd put the remaining holly bits well aside so they didn't get put on the fire. Minnow found a couple of well dried logs and took them inside.

"Give the pot a stir will you? Don't burn yourself, stay awake and concentrate. I'm off to turn the washing."

Minnow sat on a stool and gave the pot several slow stirs. The contents were very liquid so there was little chance of it sticking and burning. His thoughts kept racing back to the sight of the tree falling towards him. He could still feel his heart pounding as he ran, and ran, and ran. He remembered falling and could still feel the brush of twigs against his leg. They'd left no mark, he was totally uninjured so could not understand why he felt so unwell.

His thoughts had made him start to shake again. Give the pot a stir, breathe slowly and tell yourself you're in a safe place. It had been a close thing. Just like Papa when the trunk rolled while he was trimming off the limbs. Papa wasn't hurt but he needed time to recover and could not face the chopping until he'd rested. Minnow convinced himself he also needed to become calm. Think about keeping the pot stirred. Did the fire need another log?

His shoulder bag! Where was it? Had he dropped it? Was it under the felled tree? He looked around the room and didn't see it. He could not remember what had happened to it. Minnow put his hand to his shoulder and felt the strap. He was still carrying it, it was hanging behind him all the time. He pulled it to the front and felt inside. There were the two pieces of holly and the cold of the metal blade.

There also were the crumbs of the piece of bread he'd taken for his lunch. The bread had been totally crushed by his fall.

"That was how I could have ended up, totally crushed!" He started to shake again, unable to remove the image of him being flattened beneath the crown of the oak.

Minnow's Mama came in and brought him back to his task of stirring the pot.

"You still don't look right," she commented, "are you sure you were not hurt?"

"I feel very shaky every time I think about what happened."

"Then put it out of your mind. If you're not hurt you will be fine. You just need a good night's sleep. As soon as your Papa comes home we can eat and then you can settle for a long rest."

"Papa will want to know why I was there. I didn't think I was that close to him and the felling. I was just glad I heard the yell to run."

Minnow was starting to shake again. His Mama came over and put her arms around him till he calmed down. The next thing he knew he was in tears. His face flooded and he sobbed so deeply he was gasping to get air.

"That's a lot of noise." Grandpapa had arrived in the doorway and just stood waiting for Minnow to finish his sobbing. "That was the best thing you could have done, young Will. Having a good cry is sometimes very important. Did I ever tell you how much I cried when I heard my son had been killed fighting for that King?"

"I was so angry and your Grandmama had to hold me back from going to kill the King himself. Then I just broke down and cried. I then knew there was no point in attacking the King, I would have just ended up in a dungeon some where, being hung and what good would that have done?"

"When your Grandmama died I also cried, she was the best friend any person could have had. Your Mama gave me a cuddle, just like she's giving to you, we both cried and I cried till there was nothing left. I don't know how it helped but it did."

Minnow was aware of Grandpapa, he half heard what was being said through his sobs and he slowly became quiet. He felt he'd gone back to being a baby, needing to be cuddled. He'd not cried in a long time, not since he understood it was the cause of the bullying. But here he was in his own home and felt it was safe to cry. It was just he didn't know why he needed to cry.

Minnow took some deep breaths and said he was starting to feel a bit better. Mama went to talk to Grandpapa and Minnow resumed the stirring of the pot. The smell of the food reminded him how hungry he was now feeling and he hoped his Papa would be home soon so they could eat. Minnow put another log on the fire, the warmth was also a comfort and he started to feel less upset.

Papa didn't take long to appear and was eager to eat. Grandpapa joined them, each with their bowl of stew and hunk of bread at the trestle. It wasn't long before Minnow heard the question he was dreading.

"What were you doing then so close to where you knew I was working?" asked his Papa. "I had no idea you were still around. You seemed to have disappeared and then, there you were, running with the rest of us."

"I thought I had seen a young fox under a bush. I was on my hands and knees searching for it and then I heard – 'RUN'. I hope the fox cub wasn't hurt by the tree falling."

"It would be one less to go after our chicken," said Grandpapa.

"You were very lucky you were able to outrun the oak," said Papa. "When they start to fall they move so quickly because of their weight. You were nearly hit by it."

"I did feel some twigs sting my leg. I do know I was glad I could run so fast," replied Minnow.

He gave some thought to the lie he'd made up without thinking about it. Where had that come from as a story? They'd all seemed to accept it and there had been no further questions.

"You seem a bit more relaxed since you've some food in you," said Mama. "Settle yourself down and have a sleep now. It will soon be dark anyway. Have you had enough to drink?"

Minnow nodded and made his way to the pallet. Tired, after such an eventful day, he was soon comfortable and drifted off to sleep easily. He slept surprisingly well with no nightmares.

Chapter Seventeen – We Will Handle It

Minnow rose full of energy after a restorative sleep. He was both hungry, thirsty and glad there was enough for him to eat after his Papa had gone off to work, back in the forest. He caught his Mama giving him a sideways look a few times but he just smiled back. He was eager to attach the blade into the handle he'd made.

His regular chores quickly completed, he told his Mama he'd stay well away from the felling. He set off to find a quiet spot where he could work safely and uninterrupted.

With his shoulder bag and its contents he set off down beyond the farm. He turned into the woods to the left of the track that led to Sunning. It was an area he visited little as bringing back firewood from here he needed to pass the farm. There were always people moving around the farm and they all wanted to ask questions and help themselves to his collection.

Following a narrow animal track, likely made by deer, he found a quiet spot with good light and emptied out his bag. He'd forgotten about all the bread crumbs. He brushed himself down.

Sitting on a convenient fallen tree he laid out the three parts he needed to combine together. The holly handle had split perfectly in half and sat back together exactly. He laid the blade over one half and placed the other half on top. Now things were not so perfect.

The thickness of the blade kept the two halves apart. He'd need to be able to bind the whole set very tightly together. Minnow looked around for a tough bramble. He needed to walk a little further along the path and found what he was looking for. Having quickly stripped off the thorns he took the length of binding back towards the log.

Before he reached his seat he stopped, almost unable to believe the scene in front of him. A red squirrel was enjoying the donation of bread crumbs, along side was a beautifully coloured jay. Other smaller birds were flitting in and out looking for their share and were obviously enjoying the gift of food in an unexpected place.

It didn't take them long to clear all the bread and quickly flew off to balance their diet with their normal foods. The squirrel sat in the sunshine and gave itself a clean. Quietly Minnow moved towards the log and sat himself down.

The squirrel had moved off a little way but continued with its self-cleaning in full view of Minnow. It was showing no sign of fear so Minnow began to bind the handle halves together. He started by making a tight 's' shape along the whole length of the handle with a little loop beyond one end. At the other end he bound round and round over the top of the 's' and the holly as tightly as he could. Working along the whole length he kept the binding as close together as possible.

When he arrived at the loop end he put the end of the binding through the loop and pulled at the single end at the other end of the handle. The loop disappeared down inside and under the binding. When he guessed he'd arrived at the half way point he'd two ends to trim off.

Kicking around the ground he found a couple of stones and used one against the other to break the fibres of the projecting bramble stem. The finished handle looked very smart and the blade was projecting at a useful length. Now to try it out. Minnow took his knife to a small twig growing out from a branch. If the blade was sharp enough it should cut easily without cutting his hand.

Disaster, the blade wobbled and wasn't held within the handle. The whole thing started to fall apart despite all his careful craft with the binding. He knew the binding was as tight as he could have made it. The bramble stem hadn't broken and was still neatly around the handle but the blade wasn't being held.

Minnow tried some thin packing inside the split holly handle at each side to make up for the thickness of the blade but there was no way to stop the blade sliding out of the top or bottom. Minnow had no further ideas of how he could solve the problem. But perhaps he knew a man who would. As he stood up the squirrel shot up the nearest tree and watched him leave.

Minnow passed the farm, went up the slight slope to Top Meadow and straight to the cook who was sitting beside his fire. Minnow asked if he was busy and if he could be given some advice.

"What is your problem young churl?" he asked. "I heard you had a near miss yesterday. Are you having nightmares? I don't think I can help you with that."

"Grandpapa and Mama sorted me out yesterday, thank you. I had a good sleep and I'm keeping away from the felling. My Papa had a bad shock from my behaviour. He could have been very angry with me but I think he was so tired he just needed to sleep himself after his meal. I know I was very lucky to not be seriously hurt or even killed. Those oaks are so huge and looking up at them you don't realise how big they really are."

"Glad to hear you've had no after affects. Many would not have been so lucky or recovered so quickly. Well done you." The cook seemed genuinely pleased.

"So what is your problem that you need my help? Have you discovered some food and you don't know how to cook it? Don't ask me about fungi, I don't have a clue."

"One of our neighbours knows all about fungi." said Minnow. "They use some to help Grandpapa with his tight chest and breathing problems. I think they collect the fungi secretly and keep the magic to themselves. The women pass the secrets to their daughters who pass them to their daughters, on through the generations. One thing I have noticed is that different fungi grow at different times of the year. I think the women must dry them and turn them into a powder but that is only a guess."

"That is something I've never thought about, you may well be correct. I'm glad you're fully recovered but you seem to have something on your mind. What's your problem?"

Minnow told the cook all about finding the broken blade, making the two halves of the handle and how despite a tight binding and further packing around the blade the whole thing fell apart. He handed the three parts over for inspection. The cook studied the piece of blade and then the pieces of holly.

"You made a neat job of splitting the holly. The problem is that the blade is too thick to sit flat in the handle. A chisel could be used to carve out some of the wood but I don't have a chisel." The cook thought for a moment then said, "it may be possible to burn out some of the inside of the handle. It will change the temper of the blade but we should be able to return the temper when we have finished."

"Sorry," said Minnow, "I haven't a clue about blades having a temper. I know what a blade is and I can recognise when someone has a temper. You don't make any sense to me."

The cook smiled and studied Minnow. The poor lad must think he's talking to a mad man.

"I'll explain it as we work on turning these bits into a working knife. My fire has some good hot embers that we can use to heat the metal. We don't need it red hot at this stage, just hot enough to leave a burn mark inside the handle parts."

The cook put the blade into the hottest part of the fire embers and then went to fetch his metal cooking tongs from the store tent. He made a small shallow trench in the ground and sat one half of the handle in it with the flat side upwards. The other half of the handle he placed next to the one in the trench but this part was flat side down. Minnow noticed the blade in the fire gradually become darker. He knew it was getting hot but he also knew not to try and touch it with his hands.

The cook made a charcoal mark about one third of the way from the rounded end of the half handle resting in the ground.

"We'll need to put the blade in the same position a few times as we gradually char the wood. Once we have done it a couple of times it will be obvious where the blade has to sit."

The blade was taken out of the fire using tongs and carefully positioned on the half handle. The other handle half was accurately placed on top and the cook stood on the three layers while smoke shot out in all directions. He was careful not to let his boot near the hot blade. Slowly the smoke died away and the cook released the pressure on the layers.

Despite all the smoke the blade had only lightly charred the surfaces inside the handle. The cook repeated the process several times, each time making sure the blade was lined up accurately and facing the same way. A few times he worked at the charred surface with his cooking knife and the blade shape slowly sank deeper into each half of the handle.

"We don't want to go too deep, just enough to stop the wobble and help the binding to squeeze the two handle halves together. I think we are nearly there."

The cook gave a final scrape with his knife and handed Minnow the two halves of the handle. The blade he'd dropped into a dish of water where it sizzled and cooled.

Minnow brought the three parts together and noticed at once how the blade sat within the handle and didn't wobble. Just with hand pressure the blade was firmly in place. He was ready to go and find some binding and finish his knife.

"You're forgetting about the tempering," said the cook. "It is very possible that the end of the sword broke off because it was poorly tempered. Very hard steel can be brittle, it can shatter like a thin baked clay pot. Your blade needs to be strong but not brittle. This is achieved by a heat process known as tempering"

Minnow looked at the blade and could see no real change in the metal other than it looked a little dirtier having been in the fire.

"I can't do any more today," added the cook, "I have a meal to prepare and the next step will need heat from charcoal. Do you want to take the bits with you or leave them with me?"

"They'll be safe with you I'm sure, I'm happy to let you look after them," said Minnow willingly. "When would be a good time to come back?"

"Mid morning is normally best. I'll have time to set some charcoal going and you can learn the art of tempering. Remember to keep away from trouble, I'll see you tomorrow."

Minnow made his way back across the former meadow. All the pillar bases were on site but none had yet been put in place. The king's men were working with long flexible tubes. The tubes looked like animal intestines and were full of water.

There was a central point marked on the ground with a flat stone. Around it was positioned a tripod that held one end of an intestine tube. The tube was being filled with water.

The other tube end was at one of the pillar foundations. That tube was being slowly lowered above the foundation until water started to dribble out. A measuring stick recorded the distance to the top of both tube ends. Another thing to ask the cook about. These king's men, he thought, certainly do some strange things.

Chapter Eighteen – Temper Control

Minnow woke to a warm, dry day and soon set about his daily tasks. He was keen to get back to the cook and the completion of his knife. He felt certain he was learning magic and was enjoying everything he was being taught.

Before the cook and the king's men arrived he learned most things by making mistakes and looking for alternatives. At times this could be quite dangerous when he took risks. Survival was often a question of luck, along with good food. He was lucky with food, there always seemed to be just about enough and the whole of Wocca's Hamlet rarely had to struggle through lack of food. Luck was less predictable but as he increased his understanding of life so he could start to measure risks.

It was mid-morning by the time he'd completed his chores and made his way to Top Meadow. How much longer would the area be known as Top Meadow he pondered? There was little now for the sheep to graze and a lot of fencing would be needed for the small area was left as grass.

Some extra markers were now in position around most of the pillar foundations. Work was progressing to raise the level of one foundation ready for the placing of the first pillar base.

A complicated system of ropes had been tied around the upper rim of the heavy base and poles were ready to lift it over the foundation. The cook and three others were standing ready to help with the lifting while a fourth was applying the last of the mortar. The king's men were watching the operation carefully and pointing to areas that needed attention.

Minnow watched as the block was lifted by all four of the team. Slowly it was positioned and gently lowered over the centre of the foundation. A check was made on the level using the surrounding markers and the team relaxed. A dish of water was placed on the top of the block to check it didn't slope.

Minnow could imagine a pillar being built on a sloping base, leaning and eventually falling over as it became taller. The king's men were happy and a worker was left to build up the stone around the lower part of the block extending the foundation upwards to give all round support.

The cook made his way to his kitchen area and Minnow followed. It was obvious why it needed skilled king's men to keep an eye on the building. There was a lot that needed experienced care at the start of such a construction as a stone built church.

Minnow was sure there was less need for such ability when wood was used for buildings. The local people had become expert in the use of wood, hundreds of years of knowledge, passed on through the community.

"They'll need me to lift again in a while so we need to get a start made. I'll fetch your bits from the store and a set of hand bellows."

Minnow looked at the fire and saw some blocks of charcoal within the smouldering logs. The cook's tongs were to one side of the fire and when he returned he handed the two handle parts back to Minnow. He also placed a shallow bowl of oil on the ground. The charcoal blocks were brought together into the centre of the fire and Minnow was handed the bellows.

"The blade will need to be made red hot before we can make it as hard as it will ever get. You remember I told you it will break as easily as a thin clay dish. Afterwards we will temper it to keep it hard enough to hold a sharp edge but not so hard as to shatter. Have you ever used bellows?"

"I have seen some used at the blacksmith's to get a fire very hot. At home I just flap the fire with a dish to add a draught and that gets the flames going."

"Bellows concentrate the draught and makes charcoal burn very hot," explained the cook. "I'll place your blade on the coals and you gently start to pump in the air. I need to keep the blade on the top to get the best from the heat. Watch it carefully and notice the changes of colour the blade goes through. Those colours will be important at the next stage. Start pumping."

Minnow started to pump in the air and the charcoal began to glow hotter and hotter. The cook told Minnow to pump faster but keep it steady. His blade started to change from black through to a blue colour, then a straw yellow and gradually through orange to red hot.

"That's enough air, take the bellows and stand behind me," ordered the cook. The next thing Minnow saw was the blade entering the dish of oil. Flames danced across the surface of the oil as the blade sank and began to splutter and cool.

The burning oil started to give off a black smoke until the cook covered the dish with a thick damp cloth. Even then some smoke started to seep through the cloth and Minnow feared the cloth would go up in flames. The cook waited for the smoke to stop and then lifted the cloth, pulling it away from the far side.

"Notice the method I used to take off the cloth? That was in case there were more flames and the cloth could be put back on without the flames jumping up to my face."

The oil was still giving off a slight smoke but it was no longer flaming. Minnow could see his blade at the bottom of the dish looking very black. The cook used his tongs to lift it out and wiped the blade with another old piece of cloth. Some surface black came off but his blade still looked fine despite all the treatment in the fire.

"That was the first part of the tempering, your blade is now at its most brittle," explained the cook. "The final stage needs great care and control.

We need to heat it again but this time gently and with more care. We will still need the heat from the charcoal but just a little extra air."

"Remember how I told you to watch the colours earlier, we need to stop the new process when we have gone past the blue and just start to see a dark straw colour. Then we slowly dip it into the oil with the sharp edge going in first. This time it should fix the colour without boiling the oil. Do you understand?"

"Gentle heating, watching the colours and slowly into the oil when it is just a dark straw colour, cutting edge first," echoed Minnow.

"I'm going to get you to decide when to take it off the heat and slowly lower the blade into the oil. If you drop it in you may cool the whole thing too quickly and that will mean we have to start again from the beginning. Use the tongs to pick it up at the handle end and it'll be easier to lower the cutting part of the blade into the oil."

"Let's do it," said Minnow despite his feeling anxious about being in charge of the final process. He placed the blade onto the charcoal and let the cook slowly and gently add the air that triggered the coals to produce the extra heat.

Almost without warning the blue colour started to appear and the cook eased off the work with the bellows. Slowly the dark straw colour became dominant. Minnow took the tongs and lifted the blade from the coals. He slowly dipped the cutting edge into the oil. The surface started to ripple and sizzle around the blade as he continued to slowly lower it deeper into the oil. The cook stood by with the cloth but it wasn't needed. There were no flames dancing on the surface of the oil this time.

"We can leave it to cool in the oil, it may give an oily coating that will slow down the rusting process. We seemed to have timed it about right. It looks as if I'm needed to help with the lifting of the next pillar base."

The cook walked away from the fire, Minnow and the bowl of oil. Minnow stood there with his mouth open having surprised himself by carrying out the final process. He was a magician. He'd learned a new skill thanks to the knowledge of the cook. This stranger, he'd met for only a short time, was willing to share his knowledge with him. What was he expecting in return?

Everyone expected something in return for something given. The cook would be no different surely. What did he, Minnow, have that the cook may need? He'd not asked for anything so far other than firewood when they first met.

The cook had given him some rope and a story about being a crusader. He was the son of wealthy man, had been educated in an abbey, knew Latin and was a king's chosen man to help the team build a church in Wocca's Hamlet. Minnow was sure he'd soon be asked for something in return for all the help he'd been given by this cook.

With the base securely in place the cook returned to the fire and asked if Minnow was feeling OK?

"You look as if you've had a bad shock," he suggested. "Are you sure you're feeling well."

"It has been a bit of a shock learning some magic. The thing I don't understand is why you're so willing to give me knowledge and the time to help me understand. Most people say I'm a nuisance, I keep asking too many questions, I get in peoples way and I'm annoying. You don't treat me like most people do, you're like a big brother to me. It has made me a bit confused, that's all."

"I suppose I do have a reason for treating you as you've described," replied the cook. "My best friend was a younger brother, that was before I was sent away from home. We got on very well and were involved in a lot of pranks together. When I left home he was the one I missed most. I had to learn to work with others who didn't share any sense of fun, life was very serious and work, work, work. You remind me of my lost younger brother with your curiosity and getting into trouble."

"He was killed in a riding accident," the cook continued, "while hunting in a forest with my father. No one thought to tell me. I only found out when I returned from the crusade experience. It was then I knew I could not return to work within any part of the Church. God was cruel and was giving me no message of hope."

"I was eventually released from my vows and became a travelling cook using the skills I had acquired on the return from the crusade. I started to enjoy my life again but have missed teaching the young novices at the abbey. I knew there was no way I could stay at the abbey but then you came along with your questions."

"I do have this need to share my experiences and knowledge. You've been my chance to pass on some of the things I know. You've been a great help to me and shown me a direction that I could go in the future. I'm not sure what I'll do next but you've shown me that perhaps tutoring is something I can work towards."

Minnow wasn't sure he fully understood the cook's explanation. But it didn't sound as if he'd be needing anything in return for passing on his knowledge. Minnow did feel he owed the cook something but at this stage he didn't know what or how.

The cook was then called to help lift the next base onto its foundation. Minnow went with him to watch more closely and found himself studying the way the ropes had been applied to the block. As the block was being lifted the ropes became tighter around the neck of the block. He realised there was still so much he could learn about so many everyday things he started to get giddy just thinking about it.

Returning to the fire, it was time to take the blade out of the oil. It was still slightly warm but had an even dark straw colour all over.

"It looks good to me," observed the cook. "I'll try to give it a sharpen with the stone I have in the store. Just wait here a moment."

He soon returned and started using the stone in a circular motion all along the edge of the blade. The straw colour was removed where the cook worked to put on a sharp edge. He seemed pleased that it was hard work.

"This suggests it will keep its edge before needing to be resharpened," he explained. "Now we just need to bind on the handle. Just wait here another moment." The cook returned with a strip of fine leather, like a boot lace and handed it to Minnow.

This was yet another thing he'd not expected. Minnow laid the 's' shape loop along the length of the handle and with the blade snugly sitting inside started binding tightly from the blade end towards the open loop at the other end. The end of the lace he threaded through the open loop and then pulled the loose end lying over the blade to close the loop and draw it down under the binding.

It was a struggle as he'd bound the parts together so tightly. The cook offered some drops of oil at the loop end and Minnow pulled steadily until the loop inside was roughly half way along the handle. The cook cut off the two trailing ends with his kitchen knife and Minnow's knife was completed.

Minnow took it to the wood pile and started to make some cuts. He was surprised at how easily the blade cut into the dry wood. He started to make shavings and collected them together to hand to the cook. "Kindling for the morning," he explained.

"Thank you young churl. You look pleased with the result. I'm glad I was able to help in some small way."

"It was more than a small way, you've been a great help. Thank you so much cook. Now I just need to look after it. After all this work I would hate to lose it."

"It is not a case of lose it but how to keep it safe from doing any harm. You put it in your shoulder bag and it will soon cut its way out. Searching around in your bag with your hand and you could easily be cut. You now have a potentially dangerous tool."

"My kitchen knives I store in a wooden box, if they are not in the box they are on the trestle or in my hand. You can't walk around all day with a knife in your hand. You need to give some thought about how it is to be kept safe."

"Thanks cook," said Minnow slowly, pondering the problem. He'd not thought beyond having a knife. The cook was correct and Minnow had to think about the future for his blade. He could hide it away at home but then when would he get to use it? "Could you please keep it for me until I can think of a plan?"

"That is not a problem," replied the cook, "if you think that's best for the moment. I do think you're being sensible and it will be good for you to put your mind to solving another problem."

"Talking of problems," recalled Minnow, "what were the king's men doing yesterday with the animal intestines and the water?"

"I'll give you a clue to see if you can think of your own answer. You noticed the bowl of water put on the pillar base to check it was sitting level. Ponds of water are flat and only flow out of a gap at the lowest point. One end of the tube you saw was fixed at a known central point and at a fixed height. What did you see happen at the other end of the tube?"

"The water stayed in the tube until it was lowered. When the water just started to flow out the height was marked on a post at the foundation. It was as if the two ends of the tube were at different positions in the same pond, just at the surface. Were the king's men were marking out levels?"

"Well done," said the cook, "you will go a long way if you put together what you see and add in the things you know. You now understand because you asked the question and had only a little help to answer your own question. The monks would enjoy teaching you but I'm not sure you would enjoy having to learn the few things they teach. Life is a much better teacher, especially if you're skilled with your persistent questions."

"Eventually you will ask the correct question. Don't be put off by those who have no time for you. Seek out those who are willing to share their knowledge, impress them with what you already understand and they'll be more willing to add to your knowledge. I need to stop my lecture, the next block needs to be put in to place and then I have a meal to prepare."

Minnow saw the knight arrive through the gateway and make his way to the block lifting. He spoke with the king's men in their language and spoke to the cook. Minnow felt it was time to leave and give some thought to how to keep his knife safe.

Chapter Nineteen – Work Experience

The next morning Minnow was told not to kindle the fire as his Mama was to make soap. She would be using the wood ash that needed to be cool. When collected together it would be put in a medium sized cooking pot. Minnow went about his regular tasks and used his time in the forest to ponder on how to keep his knife safe.

He wandered away from Wocca's Hamlet a lot further than usual and came upon an old fallen silver birch tree. He immediately set about stripping off the bark which he knew made the best fire-lighting material. His shoulder bag was full to overflowing and in his shoulder cover he carried as much as he could.

There was an oil in birch bark that took a spark from a flint and steel quickly. The top surface of the bark especially when old and dry would crumble between the fingers easily and need just a little draught with the spark to leap into flame.

Back at home he unloaded his collection into a particularly dry corner of the wood store. Indoors his Mama was ready for the fire to be relit and Minnow set about the task with confidence using a small amount from his birch bark stock.

Soon flames were licking around the kindling and he moved in some part burnt logs to warm. A few thicker sticks added to the heating of the logs and soon a good but small cooking fire was well established.

Mama hung the medium sized cooking pot on the tripod and started to add some of the hard fat she'd been able to get with the beef from the farm. She kept a very careful eye on the mixture. It was important not to overheat the fat, the fat needed to be absorbed by the wood ash as evenly as possible and then the mixture poured into a small, long wooden trough to let it cool.

In a linen bag were some pine needles she'd bought at a stall to try and disguise the beef smell. At other times of the year she'd include mint leaves from their plot of land in the linen bag to add a fresh smell to the mixture. She had to be careful not to burst the bag as she gently stirred the pot, there was nothing worse than having to wash off withered mint leaves or pine needles from clothes she'd washed with the bar of soap. Rose petals were the choice of the wealthy but a great number were needed to add an aroma. Growing food had a higher priority over growing roses.

There was little left for Minnow to do so he went to check on his Grandpapa. Grandpapa had only just risen from his sleep and was eating a little cold porridge. Mama had left him some fresh milk in a dish which helped to wash down the porridge.

It wasn't too long before Grandpapa was having a fit of coughing. He blamed the milk and was struggling for breath. Pushing aside his bowl he hunched away from the trestle and eventually produced an evil looking lump of phlegm which he spat on the floor.

"I needed to shift that," said his Grandpapa. "I shall be fine in a few moments. The only trouble is it is agony, my whole chest is so tight it is painful to just take breaths. I could do with a swig of cyder if you could bring some through for me from your Mama."

"Mama is making some soap so I'll have to pour it. Where is your tankard?"

Minnow looked around and saw it near the pallet. Taking it next door he told his Mama about his Grandpapa and how he'd asked for some cyder.

"I gave him some milk to drink earlier. Has he finished it?" asked his Mama.

"It was the milk he says made him cough so much. He needs to clean his throat with some cyder. He coughed up a lot of dark green phlegm," explained Minnow.

"Did you notice any blood in the phlegm?" asked his Mama.

"I didn't study it closely but none was obvious. I'm sure I would have noticed if there had been."

Mama nodded while continuing to watch and stir the mixture in the pot. Minnow rinsed the tankard with a little water and then poured in some cyder from a flagon. He returned to his Grandpapa and saw he was breathing a little easier. Grandpapa took a few small sips from the tankard, had a little cough and then thanked Will for sorting him out.

"What are you up to for the rest of the day young Will?" he asked.

"I expect I'll look in at Top Meadow and see what is happening. The cook likes to chat and he's helping me learn things while I look at what is going on. He persuades me to ask questions. I learnt yesterday how the church will be built level. The king's men used a central measuring point, the long intestines from a pig and filled the pipe with water." Minnow went on to explain the process but wasn't sure his Grandpapa fully understood.

"These Norman invaders have brought some strange ideas with them young Will. I don't see what is wrong with a good solid wooden building. It is easy to get the floor level after a drop of rain. You just notice which way the water flows and level it out. I can't see the need for animal intestines to make things complicated. Perhaps things are different with a stone building though."

"When you're feeling well enough you should take a gentle walk through The Clearing up to Top Meadow and see what has been going on," suggested Minnow. "There's been a lot of work done that is now covered up. They are called the foundations and they went into the ground as deep as a man is tall."

"Some barns I helped to build had stone foundations for the bottom part of the walls but they didn't go that deep. The main part of the building has always been timber on top of the low walls. It was just a way to stop the ends of the wood rotting in the ground."

"I have to accept that it is progress and I'm sure there will be some benefit. It may help a building last more than one hundred years, which if you think about it will be less work for builders. Wooden buildings constantly need repair and that gives people work. Keep your eyes and ears open. I enjoy hearing what you've been seeing and doing."

"Shall I take your dish of milk away if it makes you cough?"

"No, leave it. I may need a good cough again in a bit."

"Bye Grandpapa," said Minnow as he left aware he'd said nothing about his knife and the other learning he'd acquired. He checked his Mama didn't need him for anything and made his way to Top Meadow. There were still a couple of bases to be placed on their round foundation and the trenches for the outside walls were still being dug.

More cubes of stone had been delivered and were being laid out beside the trenches. The cook was supervising the off loading of more sacks of lime and sand that were being stored in the large tent. Minnow decided the site was the busiest he'd ever seen it so far. There were a lot of local men and the only strangers were the king's men.

Minnow caught the cook's eye and asked if there was anything he could do to help. The cook pointed to the shepherd who was organising the work team. "The shepherd knows what has to be done, he has little farm work at the moment, ask if you could help lay out the cubes of stone."

The shepherd was very happy to have an extra pair of hands. "Just do as you're told and don't ask any questions," he added after explaining what needed doing. One of the men was using a hand cart to bring the blocks from the pile where they'd been off loaded.

Minnow laid the blocks in a row by the side of the trench that was nearest to the London track. A full man's stride was needed to straddle the trench. He laid out the cubes of stone without gaps as instructed in a long double line. The team moved to the other side of the building and did exactly the same along the whole of that side.

Another wagon load of cubes was being delivered. The team added these cubes to the lines of cubes already laid out doubling the height beside each trench. Everyone's attention was then drawn to a clanging of a metal spoon on a plate.

By the fire a trestle had been set up and laid out with bread and various spreads. Minnow made his way with his team and lined up for their share of the food. Minnow put some soft meat paste onto his chunk of bread and found a clear patch of ground where he could sit and eat. Everyone was too busy eating to talk much.

A large cooking pot had been put on the trestle and the cook was ladling out cyder. There were only a few beakers so the queue was for the beaker and then a drink. The farm manager arrived and called everyone to be quiet.

"You've had a change from your regular jobs on the farm today to help with this important construction for our village. You will be paid as if you had done your day's work on the farm as normal, you've just been working here instead."

"The king's men have been watching what you've been doing and think a few of you can be offered regular work here on this site. I don't know at this stage how that will affect the running of the farm. It could be we all have to work that little bit harder or longer. If that is the case your pay will be increased to cover any extra you're asked to do."

"Those chosen to work on the site will be paid by the king's men and the knight, who cares for the lands of Sunning. Should you not be needed on site you will still have your jobs back on the farm. I'll come and talk with those who will have regular work here and the rest will be back on the farm in the morning as usual."

Minnow knew he was only helping out and when the men went back to work he went to join the cook.

"Can I help with the cleaning up?" he asked.

"If you could feed the fire I'll be needing some hot water soon," answered the cook. "It has been a very busy morning as you will have seen. Lots of things needed doing all at once, I've been rushed off my feet and I still have the evening meal to start. At least they found someone else to lift the final couple of blocks onto their foundations. The boards in the store are creaking under the weight of the sacks of lime and sand, I just hope they stay dry."

The cook went into the store and Minnow sorted the fire. He found some dry logs under an oiled sheet and set them to warm around the edge of the fire, just as he'd do at home. Once warm they'd start to burn when placed on the already hot embers. The cook returned with a pot of water and hung it on the tripod. Minnow adjusted one of the logs to give a more direct heat and looked to the trestle that had been used for lunch.

All the bread had gone, there were lots of crumbs and the pots of various pastes were in a mess. The cook counted and collected together his blades, these were not the sharp kitchen knives but blades used just for spreading.

"An honest group," he commented, "none missing."

"I'm sure they knew they'd be searched if any had gone missing and that would have lost them their job on the farm," suggested Minnow. "They all know how important regular work is for them and their families." Minnow knew that is how his Papa felt and his family benefited from him having regular work.

The cook collected together the dishes of spreads, consolidated the left over contents and put them in the store. When he came back out he asked Minnow to take one end of the trestle board and they both carried it towards the hedge.

"Put it upside down on the top of the hedge and give it a few bashes to knock off the crumbs. The small birds will find the crumbs when we move back. There are not enough bits to attract the rats."

With the board back on the trestle the cook brought out the base of a small cut down barrel, put in a few scrapings of soap and added some hot water. He used a hand brush to scrub the top of the board and remove any of the spreads and fats that had remained.

The set of blades were given a rinse and laid out to dry in the sun. The barrel base was moved to the ground and a couple of cloths were washed in the last of the soapy water. These the cook took to the hedge, spread them out and left them to dry.

"How good are you at preparing vegetables?" he asked Minnow.

"I'll need a sharp knife," he replied.

"I may well have one you could use," smiled the cook and he produced Minnow's own knife.

Minnow set about removing the outer surface of a swede as thinly as he could. His knife was so sharp and it was easy to to peel away the surface. The cook watched as he handled the blade, cutting away from himself, producing the thinnest of shavings.

"Did you need it chopping?" asked Minnow.

"Can you do that as well?" enquired the cook. "I would like thumb sized pieces if you can manage it but no thumbs thank you."

Minnow went to the trestle and set about the dicing. The cook brought him a longer knife that made the task easier and soon the whole swede was ready for the pot.

"I still have not solved how to keep my blade safe," said Minnow. "I know if I had some leather it would be an answer. I have seen that is what the knights and their squires use for their daggers. They have money to buy leather and can even pay to have the cover made."

"I have been thinking about using some green birch bark. The oil in the bark may stop the blade from rusting, I would need to bind around the outside to hold it together but still try and make it tight enough that the knife does not fall out."

"Good thinking," agreed the cook. "If you carried your knife carefully I'm sure you could find some bark quite quickly. Bring it back here I could try and help you make it. You will need some binding, I don't have any more leather lace."

Minnow took the peelings from the swede to the latrine pit, made himself comfortable and returned to the cook's area. The cook was talking with the farm manager so Minnow quietly put the empty dish on the trestle, carefully picked up his knife and went to walk to the forest.

"I have been looking for you," said the farm manager to Minnow. "Are you helping yourself to one of the cook's knives?"

"The knife is his," said the cook. "He has been helping prepare a swede."

"A useful looking blade," commented the farm manager. "I've been trying to find you after you did some work before lunch. You heard what I said to the farm workers earlier, there's work here for some. The king's men pointed you out as someone they could use. Do you have a regular job of work?"

"I have been told I need to grow bigger before anyone will give me work. I can't help being small, I have lived several summers but I don't know how many. I help my Mama every morning, I don't have any other work."

"The king's men need you to work after noon every day. Cook says you're a bright lad and we have seen you can do as you're told. The shepherd says you ask too many questions but that I think is something good if it helps you understand what you have to do. It is your Papa felling oaks for us is that right? Can we rely on you to turn up for work each day?"

"Yes, my Papa is felling oaks. Are you giving me work each day?"

"If you can show you're reliable, you've a job."

"Thank you, and I start each day after noon," clarified Minnow.

"You will have your pay each Saturday," added the farm manager. "Report to the cook who will know what you're to do. I need to talk to some others. Don't be late."

Minnow almost forgot he was off to find some green birch bark. The promise of work was something he'd not expected and had left him full of excitement and apprehension.

He decided he urgently needed to find the birch bark as he'd be busy every afternoon in the future. The cook had given him an old cloth to wrap around the knife to make it safer and less obvious what he was carrying.

It didn't take him long to find what he was looking for. He was careful not to scar the tree all the way around as that would kill it. Two strips a little longer and quite a bit wider than his knife were all he needed. Some easily cut lengths of bramble stem completed his collection. Having a knife made the collecting so much quicker.

Back at Top Meadow he checked with the cook that he could use his trestle. He started to trim one piece of bark to shape making it larger than the knife outline, especially at the handle end.

The second piece he placed under the first with the outsides of the bark on the very top and on the underside. The second piece was cut to match the first. He planned that the knife would slide inside and between the two pieces.

With both pieces the same shape he put some small nicks along the edges to stop the binding sliding up or down. It would also help keep the two parts lined up. Starting half way along Minnow tied a simple knot and started to wind the binding towards the closed, pointed end, finishing with another knot.

From the centre he worked towards the open end and made a knot that was easily adjustable. Minnow squeezed the edges to make the pocket open up. He was surprised at how difficult it was to prise the pocket apart. He found a stick and eased it into the pocket, pushing on the edges as the stick went deeper down. It needed a second thicker stick to make the shape become the pocket he needed. Having removed the sticks he gently eased his knife into the opening.

The blade slid in easily but the handle was too big to go in. Minnow eased off the binding a little and gently pushed the handle into the pocket. With half the handle covered he decided it was in deep enough and finished off the binding. He tried to shake the knife out, it was held in the pocket as he hoped. Holding the pocket he pulled on the handle of the knife and it slid out ready to be used.

The cook had been busy at the fire rearranging his cooking pots so hadn't seen what Minnow had been doing. Minnow replaced the knife in the pocket and went to show the cook. The cook tried to shake it out and then drew it out by the handle.

"A neat piece of work young churl," he said. "Can't call you churl any more, you will be a working man tomorrow. What should I call you?"

"If you would ask for Minnow everyone would know who you're looking for. My given name is Will but only my Grandpapa calls me that. I'm happy to be called Minnow."

"Minnow it is then, it sort of suits you and if that is how you're known then it is best to use that name. I'm not sure your knife pocket will last too long but you may soon be able to buy some strong leather. You've done a neat job with the birch bark and your knife will be safe in your shoulder bag in that pocket you've made. Who taught you how to do that?" the cook asked.

"I have never done anything like it before, I just thought it would work so I gave it a try," answered Minnow.

"Those nicks to stop the binding sliding made all the difference, you must have had the idea from somewhere."

"No, it just seemed to make sense," Minnow added thoughtfully. Where did the idea come from? He didn't think deeply about it, he just did it. Wasn't that how everyone did things? Tried it and hoped it worked.

"Well, I wouldn't have thought of it until after the bindings had slid off and I would had to have started again. You've a way of working that should take you far young ch.., young Minnow."

The men were starting to leave Top Meadow. Minnow took his leave of the cook, waved to the farm manager and made his way home. He was going to share the story of his knife with his family and how he was to start work after noon the next day.

The home had a smell of pine from the soap making. Oh, no, he thought. It will be a full body wash this evening for everyone. The pot would need washing out three times to get rid of the soap before it could be used again for cooking food.

Chapter Twenty – Being a Builder

Minnow had slept well as usual and soon had completed his morning routine. The family had been shocked, but very pleased, to hear he was to have a regular job. Papa particularly recognised the change from the boy to being an adult.

Minnow had shown Grandpapa his knife and told him the story of how it was put together with help from the cook. Grandpapa knew about tempering which they had to do to the saw blades. In his day it involved a much larger container for the oil as some blades were nearly twice the length of a man.

Minnow was keeping an eye on the sundial Grandpapa had in his garden. It had been a gift from the farm after he became too ill to work any longer. Someone suggested it would be something he could look at when he'd nothing else to do.

Grandpapa had been angry with it a few times and it had been kicked more than once. Minnow set it back up again after each kicking and made the adjustments so that it was able to give a guide to the actual time of day, when the sun shone.

The shadow had moved past eleven so Minnow suggested he needed to make his way to work. It sounded so grown up to be able to say that. Grandpapa smiled and told him to do as he was told and stay out of trouble.

Mama was away doing laundry with her fresh batch of soap and the clothes that were changed for clean ones after the whole body wash. Minnow admitted he did like to have clean hair but it wouldn't stay in place. He left his shoulder bag with his knife at home and set off to get his instructions from the cook.

He was to help with the mixing of the mortar. He was sent to fetch a bag of sand which was quite heavy but he managed it. Then he fetched a bucket of water from the barrel as he was told. Next he made his first mistake. He brought the bag of lime as instructed but placed it directly on the ground and not on the old trestle top.

"Non, non, non," yelled one of the king's men. He went on to say some other things in an angry way but Minnow only understood he'd made the mistake. He moved the bag quickly to the old trestle top and made sure the possible damp part was at the top ready to be used first.

The lad from the farm doing the mixing had himself only been working for a year. The farm manager had agreed to him being on Top Meadow as he'd not developed any particular skills on the farm. He could well have been Minnow's age but was much bigger.

This lad didn't enjoy working with the animals, they didn't do as they were told. Digging and clearing ditches was boring. He said he'd be happier off fighting if he had his chance. All that grabbing stuff after the fighting, you could gather a fortune if you were lucky.

Minnow just nodded. There's no way he'd fancy being a fighter. He needed to concentrate. He watched the mixing of the mortar, shovelled it into a bucket and carried it over to the trench by the London track where he tipped it onto a board for it to be used in the wall foundations.

The next bucket of mix was ready and he carried that to the other trench. He watched carefully the proportions used for each mix between fetching and carrying. It soon became a routine and his thoughts drifted back to how his life used to be.

He had to re-engaged with the task. He asked if he could swap jobs for a short time. The other lad agreed. He was getting bored and wanted the chance to have a chat with his farm mates. Minnow checked he was getting the proportions correct and made his first mix.

The other lad set off with the bucket and Minnow started the next mix which was ready before the lad returned. He needed to slow down a bit or the mortar would start to set before it was delivered. Too much chatting was slowing down the work. A mistake doing a job swap. He changed back again and soon restored the steady rhythm of delivery.

A few trips to the store for more bags and fetching water broke up the monotony a little. There was no time to chat with the cook. The cook did walk over once to ask how Minnow was doing but other than that it was all work.

The end of the working day soon arrived and Minnow was surprised how quickly it had gone despite the lack of variety. Cleaning up the tools, buckets and the board didn't take long and he made his way through the gateway with the others. All made their way to their dwellings along The Clearing.

Spread around the bushes in the garden were the freshly washed clothes. His Grandpapa was sitting outside breathing in the last of the warmth of the day. Mama must be tending to the cooking and there was no sign of Papa. He was quite often home only just before it started to get gloomy.

Grandpapa gave him a wave and Minnow went across to chat. He described his tasks, said it was a bit boring at times, explained how well the foundations for the walls were going and how he felt proud to be part of the team building the church.

"Work is often full of boring bits but I'm sure you will be offered some challenges along the way," said Grandpapa, "and you will have some pay in a couple of days. Have you any idea how you would spend it?"

"I would like a piece of leather to make into a knife pouch," said Minnow reflectively. "Mama will expect some of the money to buy food and some stronger clothes now that I'm working. I'm not sure I'll be able to save much. I know I need better shoes as well."

"Welcome to the world of work and expenses young man. What you're doing should have a lasting place in Wocca's Hamlet. You deserve to feel proud of that. Building a church could have benefits beyond the grave."

Young man! That is what the cook said, young man. This is a big change in my life and Grandpapa is correct, I'm helping to make an important building for our village.

"Minnow, I thought I heard your voice, can you turn the clothes for me. I need to swap the pots around on the hearth," called his Mama.

That was something he could do. As he turned the various items of clothing he was aware of how worn and old they looked. What would they have if they were expected to dress and go to church once the building was finished? They wouldn't be let in, not compared with the wealthy of the village who went to the old wooden chapel-of-ease on a Sunday. Maybe his earnings should go towards some fine clothes to wear. Stop, he thought, now he was getting too far into the future.

Inside his home Mama was stirring a pot that gave off a strong meaty smell. He was suddenly hungry and feeling a bit tired. Papa arrived through the door way and asked how the worker was. Minnow said he was fine but hungry and Papa said he was the same.

"Bring over the bowls, I can dish up," said Mama. "Take a bowl over to Grandpapa will you?" Minnow grabbed a hunk of bread with the bowl and delivered it to Grandpapa. He didn't stay, he was ready for his own food.

The stew had an extra flavour tonight. It was the marrow bones that had been simmering all day and added to the meat stew from previously. Could he also taste a hint of pine or soap? No, it was good strong meat.

Luxury, just what the workers needed. Minnow was glad, he felt he now deserved his share, it had been a busy day.

It was soon dark and Minnow had no problems sleeping. He did wonder if he'd snore like his Papa. He'd ask his Mama in the morning, if he remembered.

Chapter Twenty-One – Man Time

Saturday, pay day. Minnow's following few days had gone much the same as the first. Mortar mixing and distribution to those laying the wall foundations. At some stage during the morning more blocks had been delivered and laid out. The afternoons were when they were mortared into place.

The wall foundations were now just below ground level. Small clean stones had been added to the mortar to fill between the two lines of foundation blocks. The new blocks were much bigger than the foundation cubes. They were heavy and Minnow struggled to move them.

He was then glad he was on mortar mixing and delivery. The demand for mortar was slower than previously so he'd the job of both mixing and delivery. He also had to fetch the bags of sand and lime but the new filled water barrel had been put conveniently close by.

Those laying the large blocks were keenly supervised and had to keep the blocks close together and smooth the mortar flat where the blocks joined. After a couple of blocks had been laid back to back the next one was laid front to back. There was a pattern developing. A rectangle then two squares.

At this stage Minnow could see no reason for the pattern other than eventually it could look interesting. A call was made to finish up. Minnow returned the part used lime and sand to the store, cleaned off the mixing tools, cleaned out the buckets and returned everything to the store.

The king's men were sitting at a trestle with a parchment and a coin bag. The team of workers stood back and waited to be called forward. There were several called Will but had their job added to their name to be paid the correct amount. Will north foundation blocks, Will London track trench.

The job label wasn't needed in every case but it did help where the same name had been listed more than once. Minnow was called as Minnow and given his coins. There were less than for the whole day workers but to Minnow it was the most money he'd ever held of his own in his hand. He considered where he could get a coin bag to use the following week. He didn't wish to lose any of his hard earned coins.

Still clutching his money he went to see if the cook had time to talk. He'd missed his time learning things from him and wondered if he'd be welcome mid mornings if the cook wasn't too busy.

"Mid morning would be fine young Minnow. Have you found work hard? I noticed you stuck to your tasks and there was no sloping off or lengthy chatting."

"It was a bit repetitive at times, but it did mean I could notice some of the other things that were going on. Those king's men are the busiest of all. Escorting wagons to and from the river, checking on our work, studying and comparing with the plans, measuring and marking out, they hardly sit down."

"They have a great deal of experience and the King expects them to make a good job of building this church," added the cook. "They are a small team compared with those building beyond the Narrow Sea. Some of the managers there can number ten or more, but then spend a lot of time arguing amongst themselves."

"Here they each have their own special skills, know what needs doing and when. That is why your Papa is felling oaks. The dark skinned man knows all about the time needed to season the timber before it can be used. One is an experienced builder in the use of stone and the third is skilled at negotiating deals so that a fair price is paid for the materials. He's the one who had the pillar bases sent from Normandy".

"Well," said Minnow, "enjoy your day of rest. I know I will, I have some aches that need to recover. I hope to see you on Monday mid morning if that is convenient."

"Yes, see you Monday."

Minnow, still clutching his coins tightly, made his way towards home, meeting his Papa at the gateway to Top Meadow. He'd walked up from the farm having collected his pay for the week. Minnow opened up his hand and showed his collection of coins.

"Cover them up," said his Papa, "you need a pouch to carry your coins under your shirt. Perhaps your Mama will be able to make you one. Don't go around showing off coins, you will become a target."

Minnow pictured himself in the sights of a bowman, circles painted on his shirt. "Why would a bowman want to shoot me?" he asked his Papa.

"You could be a target for robbery," explained his Papa with a sigh. "Most workers go home in a group when they have been paid. A person on their own could easily be robbed of their pay."

"I was in a group as I came up from the farm. You then joined me, we are still part of a group so being robbed is less likely but you don't go showing coins. With your hand open, someone just bumping into you could scatter them on the ground, a couple of heavy treads would push coins into the mud and they could collect them later."

There was so much more to being a paid worker than Minnow realised. His Papa was being helpful, giving him advice. It was hard taking on all this learning, he'd need to remember it all and do his own thinking beyond these little bits of advice.

Minnow handed his coins to his Mama. She counted them and put them in her coin pouch. "We will collect enough to buy you some strong shoes. You will need good footwear for working. There's not enough here yet but there soon will be." Papa handed over his coins but Minnow noticed he kept a few for himself.

"After I have some shoes, will there be some coins left to buy a piece of leather from the tanners?" asked Minnow.

"Why would you be needing leather from the tanners?" asked his Papa.

"I need a strong pouch for the knife I made," Minnow reminded him. He knew his Papa had been impressed with the work that had gone into assembling the knife and its birch bark cover.

"We will have to see what other things are needed first," said his Mama. "You should be able to spend some of your coins but we need to buy important things that you need to be able to work safely. Before the winter arrives you will be needing warm and protective clothing so there's lots to plan for."

"I think I need to make a coin pouch for you soon. I did buy some material a few days ago for repairs and patching. There should be enough to make a pouch. I'll have to buy some cord so that it can be closed. It will then require a thicker cord that you can put it around your waist. Your coins will soon be spent but it's good that you have a job."

After their meal Papa suggested Minnow could go with him to the alehouse. Mama wasn't very pleased about the idea but Papa said it was time he heard the tales from the minstrels and learnt what was happening in the country. Mama suggested Papa could tell Minnow on Sunday and she could hear what was going on at the same time. Papa said it was part of his growing-up to go with him. He promised not to be back too late.

Minnow didn't know what to expect. He'd walked past the ale houses many times but they were almost empty during the day time. They had their own particular smell that his Papa had on him when he came home on a Saturday night. As they drew closer Minnow could hear the level of noise increase and the sound of a song with a chorus that he recognised.

The song was one his Grandpapa sometimes sang on a summer evening after he'd drunk quite a lot of cyder.

The inside of the alehouse was quite gloomy, there were a few lanterns, trestles and long benches. Mostly it was men holding tankards talking loudly at each other. The song had finished and men were gathered around the landlord having their tankards filled from a barrel.

The barrel was on a cradle on its side with a tap coming out from the lid. Coins were handed over for each tankard of ale. Minnow's Papa took a coin from his pouch and was given some of the liquid.

"Have a taste," he said to Minnow after having taken a good mouthful himself. Minnow took a sip and found it far more bitter and harsh than the cyder he normally drank. He wasn't keen to drink any more.

At one end of the room was the minstrel. He was adjusting the strings on his lute. Striking the strings loudly a few times, the noise level dropped and he started to sing.

It was a tale of a lord who had four sons, each of the sons demanded a share of his wealth. Each was given a share but they wanted more and fought each other to gain more for themselves. Two of the sons died and that left just two who still argued that each should still have more. The song ended with the lord still promising to share out his lands to his sons.

"Do you have any idea who the lord may have been in the song?" asked his Papa quietly.

"Would it be someone I'm supposed to know?" asked Minnow. "Is it not what lords do with their lands all the time? It could be any lord."

"That is the skill of the minstrel," said his Papa. "If he named the lord as a very important lord he'd be in trouble. We guess who his song is about even though no names are given. We know who had four sons, two have died, one quite recently and the remaining two are fighting for a share of the lands."

Some coins were being thrown into the lute case and there were calls for another song. This time he sang of the wish of a lord, murder in a cathedral, God sending punishments, monks thrashing a lord and the lord building churches to avoid purgatory. Again no names were mentioned but this time a lot more coins were added to the lute case.

"Is that why the King is having a church built here in Wocca's Hamlet?" asked Minnow.

"Keep your voice down," said his Papa. "What the King does is up to him. We just do as we are told. If he wants to pay to build a few churches that is up to him. You should be grateful he has provided us with jobs."

Papa offered Minnow another taste of ale which he tried again and then Papa finished the drink. "Time to go." he said to Minnow. "Some are drinking more than they can handle. There will be trouble later so it's best we go now."

Minnow was ready to go, he was feeling tired and he was up much later than normal. He guessed his Papa would be snoring deeply tonight. There was a day of rest from mixing mortar tomorrow but there would still be lots to do on the plots of land with their vegetables and crops.

Chapter Twenty-Two - The Lord and His Manager

Monday came around very quickly. It had been a full day on Sunday, lots needed doing to establish the young plants into the ground. Even Grandpapa had done his bit with advice as to what needed to go where.

He was good at plant recognition, a lot of the young plants all looked the same to Minnow so he was glad to be guided. Minnow was fetching water quite a bit of the time so soon had a wet shirt. Perhaps there would soon be enough money to get a bucket with two handles.

Having completed his chores for his Mama he made his way to Top Meadow and found the cook assembling the items for lunch. There were two trestles set up, one with benches for the king's men, the other with a large pot for the cyder. Freshly baked bread, recently delivered from the farm, was sitting under a clean cloth.

"Morning cook," said Minnow. "Anything I can do to help?"

"If you come with me into the store you can help carry a few things. Did you have a restful Sunday?" he asked.

"Busy with planting and watering. It was different to mixing mortar. My hands are less dry after my work last week," replied Minnow while carrying a platter of cheese.

"Yes, lime can do that to hands," answered the cook. "You should try some mutton fat rubbed into your hands before you start this afternoon. I have some that I was about to throw away that should help. It has a bit of a smell but it should help your skin."

"Thanks," said Minnow. "What else is needed on the trestles?"

"I just need to fetch another clean cloth and a skin of wine for the king's men. Find a stool and sit by the fire. I'll be with you shortly."

The fire had been left to die down but was ready to bring to life should it be needed.

"I have a question," said Minnow when the cook returned and sat with him. "What is purgatory?"

"Yes, so where did that question come from young Minnow?" asked the cook with astonishment. "Did you also go to the chapel on Sunday?"

"No," answered Minnow and then went on to tell of his visit with his Papa to the alehouse and the songs of the Minstrel. "Why is the …, why are people so keen to avoid purgatory?"

"The Church teaches that after life we all go to a place called purgatory. There we are left to think about our life and what we have done with it. Eventually we are judged and moved to heaven or hell."

"Purgatory is thought to be a very uncomfortable time, a bit like a repeating nightmare that never seems to end. Release from purgatory is welcome even if it ends in going to hell. The Church also teaches that some good actions in life can take you past purgatory. Building a church is one of those good actions."

"So, would my helping to build a church save me from purgatory?" asked Minnow.

"It may help, I must admit I'm not sure. It can't do any harm can it?" suggested the cook. "One thing I do know is that the word purgatory cannot be found in the Bible so who knows what is true."

"Is it true the King had a man murdered in a cathedral?" asked Minnow.

"Be very careful what you say and ask," advised the cook quietly. "There are stories where it is best not to use names. You could get yourself and me into trouble. Did someone tell you that the King did that? They could be in serious trouble if they did."

"No one said who it was, they just said it was a lord and didn't give a name. I just thought it may have been a very important lord like the ...," explained Minnow in hushed tones, being very careful about what he said.

"There are times when you need to be less clever young Minnow, you can't go around saying things about our King. The King has spies looking for people who may be saying things against him. He has enough problems as King without people saying things that make him unpopular."

"He's building a church here. The last thing he needs are people saying things that suggest he's a bad person. To answer to your question, no, he didn't have a man murdered in a cathedral. A man was murdered but the King didn't ask for it to happen."

"I guess the minstrel may have made up a story just to entertain people. It did seem to make some sort of sense and did suggest a reason for building a church. It just happens that it matched what is going on here," explained Minnow.

"Perhaps I need to tell you another story. It may be true or it may just be a story. Do you think you can listen without adding any names young Minnow?"

"I understand what you're saying. No names," added Minnow.

"A couple of lads from different families were brought up and taught by skilled tutors. They were both very clever and each tried to be better than the other but it was a friendly relationship. Eventually one became an important lord and asked the other to help him by looking after his money and lands. Let's call him a manager."

"The manager was so good at his job he also became wealthy. He liked to be seen as an important manager by wearing fine clothes and had servants to go before him and clear the way. The lord was very pleased with the work the manager was doing. They stayed very good friends."

"The lord had his own priest who started to argue with him so the lord told him to find a job elsewhere. He asked his manager to take on the job as priest as well as continue to manage his money and lands. The manager told the lord he could not do both jobs, being a priest involved a special duty to the rules of the Church. He wanted to just remain as a manager.

The lord thought making him a priest was just as important as being a manager. He accepted he could find others to manage his money and lands so insisted he became the priest. The lord felt there were things within the Church that his friend could change and that his friend would do as he asked."

"The newly appointed priest made it quite clear his new role involved loyalty to the Church and to the Pope. He gave away his fine clothes and wore the simple clothes of a priest. He'd been made a priest and that is what he'd do. The friendship started to break down."

"The lord did, one day, ask if there was anyone who could rid him of a troublesome priest. He didn't expect four knights to murder the priest in a religious building. The lord was told what had happened and was angry with the knights."

"The story of what had happened to the priest spread quickly and the Pope eventually made the dead priest a saint. There were reports of healing for those who visited the dead priest's tomb."

"The lord felt partly responsible for his friend's death and eventually allowed himself to be beaten by the monks who looked after the church where the murder took place. After that, when a couple of his sons died, he felt the need make his peace with God and started to carry out good works for the benefit of the lands that he controlled."

"This is just a story, no names have been given and that is how you should tell it to others if you need to. I don't think I can answer any questions. I hope the story fitted in with the song of the Minstrel."

Minnow was quiet for a time comparing the song and the story. They both told the same thing and it was easy to put a name to one of the characters. The name of the 'manager' wasn't so easy to guess. He didn't know the names of many saints. Perhaps he should go to the chapel-of-ease and learn about God and Jesus.

He knew about Jesus being born at Christmas and dying at Easter. It always made him think he must have had a short life of just a few months. His Grandpapa explained he lived several years in between. There were plays put on, in the area used by the stalls, that told those stories. The saints were a bit of a mystery.

Minnow noticed there was activity at the gateway with a king's man arriving with a wagon loaded with more stone blocks. This was followed by a second wagon and escorts. There were four squires also making up the group.

"Looks as if they'll soon be needing their lunch," suggested the cook. "Can you bring the pot off the trestle into the store and I can add some cyder to it?"

"Thanks for the story," said Minnow. "It has helped a little. I won't ask any questions for now. You will be needing some beakers."

"Good thinking, you may have distracted me. You're good at getting me to tell stories and I lose all track of what I should be doing. When the others have taken some lunch you can have some as well for helping me. I guess you won't say no. By the way, I've been told to tell you that you're back on the mortar mixing."

Lunch was unexpected but welcome. There was no surprise about the mortar mixing. He remembered to ask for the old mutton fat which he rubbed well into his hands. The cook was correct, it did smell but if it helped his hands not to go so dry it would be worth it.

Chapter Twenty-Three – Sanctuary Failure

Minnow was still thinking about the story of the lord and his manager as he made his way home at the end of the day. Grandpapa would be a good person to ask who the saint may have been. Working at the farm, as he did before he became ill, he'd have heard many things about the King and other things that were going on. He said a quick hello to his Mama then went straight to see Grandpapa.

"Can I ask you a question about a saint Grandpapa?" enquired Minnow.

"You can ask, I may not have an answer for you," was the reply.

"Do you know who was murdered in a cathedral and made a saint?"

"I'm glad you gave me an easy question. It was Thomas-a-Beckett. He was once chancellor to the King who made him Archbishop of Canterbury. Later he was murdered in the cathedral by four knights. The Pope made him a saint very quickly after people started being healed when they visited his tomb. Canterbury is too far away for me to go and try to be healed."

"Thanks Grandpapa."

"Why the interest in the saint?" asked Grandpapa.

"The minstrel sang about a murder in a cathedral at the alehouse and I just wondered who became a saint. The minstrel didn't give any names and made it sound as if it was just a made-up story. Is it true someone very important asked to be rid of a priest? No name was given."

"I'm glad no name was given, the minstrel would have been in a lot of trouble. Even I'm not going to say his name, I would like to live a bit longer. Perhaps that tells you how important that person could be. And no it is not your Papa young Will."

Minnow smiled, he knew who the important person now was. What a story. He didn't need to put the cook in danger by asking questions. He'd managed to put together the whole story with contributions from just three people, maybe four if you included his Papa taking him to the alehouse.

He also started to understand why no names were used. The outcome was no longer a mystery either. A new church building in exchange for avoiding purgatory. Not only that but it had given him his first experience of paid work.

"Thanks Grandpapa, all the bits of the story fit into place. Is there anything you need? Papa's not home yet."

"Just bring me a meal later thank you Will. I could do with some cyder as well if you could remember," added Grandpapa.

"Do you like ale, Grandpapa?" asked Minnow. "I had a taste at the alehouse but I don't think I like it. I prefer cyder."

"Ale you have to get used to, it is very different from cyder. The taste is a shock at first but the bitterness is refreshing and excites the mouth much more than cyder. Not every brew is the same so there's variety that cyder rarely offers."

"Don't rush to get a taste for ale. It can become a drink you feel you need more of and that can lead to loss of control. Some people easily get into fights after a lot of ale. I guess you and your Papa left before it became too noisy."

"Yes, I was glad to hear the minstrel's stories. He was good, clever too, not to mention names but still kept us interested. I'll go and check if Mama needs any help. See you soon with your meal, and some cyder."

Mama looked up from stirring the pot. "You were in a rush to see Grandpapa, what was so urgent?"

"He'd an answer about a saint that I needed. It helped to make sense of a story started by the minstrel at the alehouse." Minnow went on to explain the whole story, whispering the names and having her assurance she'd not use the names if she passed on the story.

"We women knew there must have been a reason the King was being so generous to Wocca's Hamlet. I would never have guessed that was the motive. Let's hope the money continues, you and your Papa are now dependent on the work at Top Meadow. You need a wash, there's a rank smell, I hope it is not on your clothes."

"Sorry Mama, it is old mutton fat on my hands to stop the lime dust drying out my skin."

"Take some warm water from the pot on the side of the hearth and use some soap. Make sure you wash out the dish afterwards, and do it away from the dwelling."

Minnow was also glad to be rid of the smell. More pleasing was that his hands were not dry and starting to crack. He would ask his Mama if she had mutton fat he could use in the future.

Papa arrived home and they went in together to put out the bowls and bread. Mama dished out the meal and Minnow poured the cyder. Grandpapa had suggested he was ready to eat but seemed more grateful for the drink which he downed in one long swallow. He asked for more to be brought when Minnow had finished his meal.

The discussion around the trestle was about the minstrel's songs and the only name mentioned was Thomas-a-Beckett. Papa had heard the story some time ago but had forgotten the name. He added there had always been arguments between the ruler of the land and the rulers of the Church.

Minnow then remembered Grandpapa had asked for a second drink which Mama poured adding some water to the cyder. She'd taken him a drink at lunch time. It had also been a warm day where he'd been sitting outside enjoying the warmth of the sun. He did breathe easier when the air was dry but it also made him thirsty.

The daylight was starting to go so things were cleared away quickly and soon everyone was settling to sleep. Minnow was sleeping long before his Papa started snoring. His dreams were a mix of murder, beatings and purgatory for the knights who knew they were on their way to hell.

A hint of daylight woke him as usual when he found he was covered in sweat. Not a good way to wake. He went and used the urine pot, gave his face a wipe on a cloth and then registered how warm the air was. He then knew it was building to a thunderstorm.

It was going to be a difficult day for work. Papa was going to be at risk in amongst the tall trees of the forest. He'd struggle to keep the lime dry before it needed mixing. If there was heavy rain it would wash out the mortar before it could set. No doubt the king's men would have a solution to any problem. One thing he did know, he was going to get wet.

After sorting his chores his Mama gave him an extra layer for his shoulders before he went off to chat with the cook. There was thunder far in the distance but the sky was still mostly clear of cloud.

Everything looked as normal on Top Meadow. Blocks were being laid out and trenches were being dug at each end of the square shape. They would soon be ready for the foundations there.

The cook was busy clearing away and cleaning down the trestle boards. Minnow noticed that the knight was talking to a king's man. Every so often the king's man threw his arms in the air and spoke very quickly, waved his arms wide to indicate the whole building site and then slumped his shoulders. There was obviously a problem. Minnow made his way to the cook, sat by the fire and waited.

"Don't ask, I have no idea what's going on," said the cook when he came to sit at the fire. "It does look like there's a problem but the Norman language is beyond my understanding. I guess you've heard the rumbles of thunder. It may pass us by but the air feels very unsettled. Now the farm manager is coming through the gateway. We've not seen him for quite a time. Whatever the problem I think it must be serious and I don't think it is the weather."

The meeting of the three top people moved into the king's men's tent. The laying out of blocks and digging of trenches continued as if there was no problem.

"Can I ask you about Thomas-a-Beckett?" enquired Minnow who was eager to get a full background to the minstrel's story.

"What do you need to know in particular?"

"Was he more than just a priest?"

"He was the head of the Church in England. He was known as the Archbishop of Canterbury. The Pope has to agree to him having the job and Thomas agreed to do as the Pope asked. You know land is the property of the King but the Church also has land in this country."

"For years they have agreed to each have their own land and rule it with their own set of rules. Sometimes the King does not agree with the rules of the Church and the Church does not agree with the rules of the King. Thomas wanted to judge priests who had done wrong by using the rules of the Church."

"The King however wants anyone who does wrong to be judged by his one set of rules that he has taken great care to try and make fair for everyone. Twelve men hear the complaint along with the arguments and suggest to the King's court what should happen. The King has the final say and orders any punishment. Without this system the King would be doing nothing other than hearing disputes."

"Thomas had the support of the Pope and the King has been trying to get the Church to see his side of the problem for a long time. He thinks the Church do not punish bad priests harshly enough. Even if they kill someone they are only beaten by the Church, moved to another area and made to say sorry."

"Did Thomas get murdered in his own cathedral?"

"Yes, by some knights. Any church building is considered a place of sanctuary where anyone can ask to be kept safe. Thomas didn't expect to be killed there and neither did anyone else expect such a crime to take place. Sanctuary has been agreed by both Church and kings for many years. Some kings have needed to ask for sanctuary when other lords have tried to take their life and lands."

"Have people been cured of serious sickness if they visit the tomb of Saint Thomas?"

"Cures had been happening before Thomas was made a Saint by the Pope. They are still happening but not for everyone. No one knows why some are cured and some not. If you're very unwell it is worth going there with the hope you may be cured."

Minnow looked up at the sky and the clouds were starting to gather.

"What needs to happen before we get some heavy rain?" he asked the cook.

"The mortar from yesterday needs covering. Go and grab the men quickly. Send them to me at the store tent. I'll get out the oiled sheets."

There was a flurry of activity with pairs of men running with the sheets covering the lines of blocks that were put into place the day before. The small tents that had covered the pillar foundations were also brought out and covered the few remaining gaps.

There was a huge clap of thunder that brought the farm manager and the knight from their tent. The king's man flew out as if shot from a bow and then stood looking at all the sheets covering the walls.

"Bon, bon, bon," he exclaimed. Minnow assumed he was pleased.

Bits of stone were being placed to hold the sheets down and prevent them blowing away as the wind increased. The first drops of rain were large and had everyone heading for the shelter of the store. The night watchman stirred in his sleep, his dog was alert and ready to pounce should anyone get too close. The cook was keeping an eye on his stock. Minnow was enjoying the lightning show with its sound of thunder as it rolled around Wocca's Hamlet.

Chapter Twenty-Four – An Unsettling Storm

The cook's fire didn't survive the downpour. The rain didn't last long but it was extremely heavy and the ground was sodden. Puddles, rivulets and mud. The clouds had cleared almost as quickly as they'd arrived and the sun was turning the wet canvas of the tents to wisps of steam.

The king's man gestured that the sheets be taken off and put along the hedges to dry. He inspected the mortar and was pleased that it had only suffered in a very few places.

The knight was talking with the cook and praising him for his swift actions. He decided it may be the right time to call the men together and explain about a problem that had taken them away from seeing the approaching storm.

"You've all acted swiftly and shown you're the men for the work on this site," started the knight. "We are pleased with everything you've been asked to do and you've shown a willingness to learn new skills. Thank you, all of you."

"Unfortunately there's a bit of a problem developing. The King has returned to his lands across the Narrow Sea. He has, thankfully, paid for all the materials which are going to be delivered to the site. This includes the stone for the pillars, the arches are coming from Normandy, the windows are also paid for so the building is well funded. Regrettably the King has not left money to pay you to carry on with your work."

"Sunning Deanery does have some funds for the work of the Church and I'll keep as much as possible going towards your pay. There may have to be a charge on the people of Wocca's Hamlet to meet the rest of your pay."

There was a murmur that went around the men as they considered the reaction to a charge on the people of the village. They hadn't asked for a new church, they had a chapel-of-ease. Only this part of Wocca's Hamlet was in the Sunning Deanery, the rest was part of Berkshire. Why should they pay for a stone church to be built? What did priests do anyway other than baptise or bury?

"Those who would feel they'd prefer to go back to farm work are free to do so," continued the knight. "The farm manager is here and you can talk with him now. Those who wish to continue building the church will, for a time, be paid as usual. I do not know how long funds will be available."

"We have sent word to the King asking that he increases the funds he gives to the Sunning Deanery to cover the added cost of your pay. A reply will take time and the King has new costs with his issues in Normandy. We hope and pray he will not forget this project in Wocca's Hamlet."

"You're a good team and have made impressive progress on this building. We hope you feel you will be able to continue on the journey of constructing a building for the future that many will enjoy using. God bless you and thank you."

Minnow was stunned. Here he was having only just started on his adult life as a paid worker and the future was uncertain. The building couldn't stop. All the materials were on their way and had been paid for. Would they just be piled up and left unused or pillaged?

Two wagons arrived through the gateway loaded with more stone blocks. The other two king's men were taken aside and given the news. Minnow could hear raised voices from the tent and saw the exit of the farm manager.

A couple of workers went to have a word with him. He nodded, suggesting they could return to work on the farm. One was the young man who wished to go and fight. Minnow wasn't surprised he wanted to leave the site, he'd be restless where ever he was, other than fighting and grabbing treasure.

The cook was beckoning to him and pointing to a stool by the soggy fire pit. There was still time before noon and everyone seemed to be in shock. The ground was very slippery and moving blocks would not be easy. The sun was shining and the air was much fresher but a gloom had settled over the site.

Minnow looked at the state of the fire pit, fetched a spade and cut a drainage channel to clear the moat of water around the soggy, charred logs. The next fire would have to be started on a raft of dry logs and the heat work its way down and dry out the pit. That's if there's any dry kindling. He noticed all the oiled sheets had been taken to cover the curing masonry, including from the wood stack.

"What is it with you young Minnow, you can't stop doing things to help?" said the cook who had reappeared from the store tent with a second stool. "So, what are your thoughts about the future?"

"Firstly, I don't have a job at the farm to go to. I'll still find it hard to get another job being much smaller than others of my years. I'm not sure I'll still have a job here. I can't lift those large blocks of stone like others can and that is what is needed at this stage. I'm just waiting to be told I don't have a job because they can't pay me."

"I can understand what you're saying," agreed the cook. "In your position I would be feeling the same but there's money for a few weeks, even a bit longer with a couple of men that look as if they are going back to farm work."

"The build will be slower but money will be found. I'm sure the deanery of Sunning is not that poor and will find ways to keep the build going. The king's men and I are not being paid by Sunning. The farm manager has his own pay arrangements for supplying the king's men."

"With a smaller work team and perhaps a small charge on the traders of the village the church will eventually be built. Are you able to help me sort out some lunch?"

The trestle was very clean after its rain wash and the sun had started to dry the surface. Minnow carried the spreading knives and loaves while the cook sorted the various spreads. There was a block of cheese but the contents of the pots of spread were getting low. The cooking pot was carried out with its cyder content and a clean cloth covered everything until it was time to eat.

Minnow asked if he could have a go at starting the fire. The cook gave a nod so Minnow set about with a layer of the driest logs he could find as a base. He put some birch bark from the store on top and built a small cone of fine birch twigs over the bark. The cook provided a flint and steel blade and watched as Minnow directed the sparks into the birch bark.

There was a wisp of smoke which he gently blew and soon the smoke changed to flames licking at the cone of twigs. Gently he added more small twigs directly onto the flames and then added small sticks. These were a bit damp and protested by giving off a lot of smoke before they eventually started to burn and give some real heat.

More sticks, gradually thicker and thicker produced the foundation to the fire. A small log was placed each side to warm through and soon they were adding to the heat of the fire. Four logs were added to the top, the fire produced a lot of smoke and then burst into flames.

"Expertly done young Minnow," marvelled the cook, "I couldn't have done it better myself. You need to start believing in yourself. You've a good set of skills and I have seen you learn things quickly."

The cook put a bowl of water out for the team to wash off their hands before eating. He'd sorted the table for the king's men well apart from the main trestle. He was sure there would be a lot for them to discuss, not that anyone would understand their talk.

The signal was given to have a break and some lunch. The mud covered the clothes of the workers and in some cases their faces where they'd tried to wipe away sweat. The sun was making it hot today.

After lunch Minnow mixed and distributed mortar. The ground was still a bit slippery but he managed to keep upright. Oiled sheets were put over the fresh mortar before everyone left for their homes. Everyone walked home in silence, deep in thought about the future of the build.

Minnow's parents listened to the news and Papa wasn't sure who he was working for. He was paid at the farm but his work recently was all for the roof timbers of the church. The carter had paid him when he assisted the carts, he did have some work on the farm but it was just odd days. He started to wonder if he was going to have regular work once the required number of oaks had been felled and quartered.

There was little more to talk about as they ate their meal. Minnow knew his spending plans would have to wait. Mama considered if replacement shoes for Minnow would be needed. Papa thought he should have worked at a skill to be sure of a regular job.

Grandpapa arrived at the doorway asking if he was going to be fed. A place was found for him at the trestle. Apologies made, they started to tell him the latest news from the building site.

"That's the way of kings," he sighed. "Full of big ideas until the next problem comes along. That then becomes their next big idea. We are lucky to have had this settled period of time. Back in Stephen's time there were always disputes to settle, money being collected and men sent to fight."

"Let's hope Henry can manage his battles over the sea with the men he has there and not need to take men from us here. It's nice to have some air I can breathe, the storm cleared the stuffiness but I did think I might be flooded. The ditches just about managed but a bit of a clear-out would be worth doing before another storm."

Minnow said he'd do it in the morning before he left for Top Meadow. He reminded Grandpapa he should take a gentle walk to the site and see for himself the shape of the new church.

"Is that before work stops and it all returns to a meadow?" he asked with a smile on his old face. Everyone else smiled, Grandpapa could always look beyond a crisis. With the light starting to fade things were cleared away quickly. Everyone settled to try and sleep despite the uncertainty in their minds.

Chapter Twenty-Five – Would a Knight's Bishop Help?

Minnow woke having had a good uninterrupted sleep. Clearing the ditches around both dwellings hadn't taken long and he was off to Top Meadow before Grandpapa had risen. His Mama had been sitting outside making good use of the light stitching two rectangles of strong cloth.

Inside on the trestle he'd noticed some lengths of cord. He assumed she was making him a money pouch. She at least thought he'd continue to have some work.

The Top Meadow had dried out well after the heavy storm. Blocks were being carried and stacked along the side of the walls. There was still only a single layer of blocks laid on the foundations so there was a lot left to do to complete the outer walls.

It looked as if there were four fewer men working at the site today. The cook was busy clearing the trestle that had been used by the king's men for their meal. It was having a soap scrub and was likely to be used for their parchment plans when it had dried.

There was just the one king's man on site as usual The others, along with the squires, would have ridden to escort the wagons back from the river. There was a routine to the days that Minnow enjoyed. He knew his role and had a pride in making the mortar mix exactly as instructed. Having a morning time chat with the cook was a bonus.

Minnow made his way to the smouldering fire where he pushed the logs a little closer to prevent the fire cooling too much. The cook returned with the pot of warm water and placed it back on the tripod over the fire. He added some more water to the pot and then returned with a second stool.

"Sorry," said Minnow, "I'm sitting on your stool. Shall I bring over a couple more logs to warm at the side of the fire?"

"You know how to keep a fire going without being wasteful, young Minnow" he remarked. "Just a couple will be fine."

"Have you noticed we are four men down today?" asked the cook. "There are still enough to keep things going and it means there are fewer to pay at the end of the week. Our knight says there's enough money to keep the build on track for a couple of months. By then he should have heard back from the King. So, Minnow, what is your question for today?"

"I was thinking about this bit of land being part of Sunning and the rest of Wocca's Hamlet being in Berkshire. It was something one of the men said yesterday about making a charge on the village. With most of the dwellings not being part of the Sunning Deanery, would that make things difficult?," asked Minnow.

"One day you will ask me an easy question. Where do I start?" The cook took a little time to think and then started his answer.

"There's not been a Bishop of Salisbury for several years. The old one was sacked for being a spy for the Queen. She is under house arrest having plotted with her sons against the King. The Bishop had a palace at Sunning as well as at Salisbury. The Church has lands in both places and the Church lands here include the farm."

"The King is administering the bishop's lands and adding the funds from Sunning towards running the country. He has appointed the knight to manage the Sunning lands. That is why the building is on the bishop's Sunning land."

"It is unlikely the Bishop of Winchester will be building a church in Wocca's Hamlet. The church will be for all the people of Wocca's Hamlet but a Bishop of Salisbury or the King will appoint the priest."

"The funding for the build must come through Sunning. The Bishop of Winchester could block any other outside funding. I hope that has made it complicated enough for you."

Minnow let the explanation sink in and he threw it around his mind while understanding why any charge on Wocca's Hamlet would not be supported. There being no Bishop made it difficult but also made it easy for the King to start the build. So it is dependent on the King to find the funds for the workers pay.

"Lets hope the King finds a way to pay us," concluded Minnow.

"You're a bright lad Minnow. I wasn't sure I had given you what you needed to know." The cook wondered if there was anything he needed to add but Minnow had drawn the only conclusion.

"It's now up to the knight to sort it out for all of us and the people of Wocca's Hamlet. Talking of the knight, he's on his way over here now," observed the cook.

Minnow looked up and saw the approaching figure. He made to leave but the knight indicated he sit back down.

"Cook tells me it was you who noticed the approaching storm yesterday and made it possible to cover the walls in time. The king's man felt he'd been distracted from keeping his eye on the weather. We had difficult things to discuss as you may be aware."

"I wanted to thank you and say that your job here is safe even though you didn't come as a farm worker. I know it is only half a day and I wish I could make it a full day but you know I have a funding problem."

"Thank you sir," acknowledged Minnow. "I hope having time with the cook is acceptable. He has helped me in many ways. He has a lot of knowledge."

"This part of the day is his time," said the knight. "If he's happy to share it with you there's no problem. I know he does wonders with preparing some excellent meals from an open fire. Is he teaching you how to cook?"

"Not yet sir," added Minnow, "he has been explaining how he has collected his other knowledge from his experiences over the sea."

"Yes, I understand he's widely travelled. The King himself selected him to support this build and we have been very pleased with his commitment. I must be going, other things to sort as always, but again thanks for being alert yesterday, you saved the day."

"Thank you sir." Minnow stood up as the knight moved away and took a deep breath. "You told them," he said to the cook.

"I may have mentioned it last evening. There was a discussion about who should be kept on the build. I hoped it would help you keep your job, sounds as if it worked. It was true, you were the one who noticed the storm was on its way."

"I was worried about my Papa up in the forest under all those trees. It's not the safest place in a thunderstorm. He was actually at the farm, they'd just pulled a quartered oak out and they took shelter just as it started to rain."

"There's less to sort for lunch today. There are fewer of us and there's only butter and cheese to go with the bread. You happy to give me a hand?" asked the cook.

"Will there be enough for me?" asked Minnow.

"At this stage the farm still provides the food so there's no problem. I'm happy to feed you if you help."

"Sounds like a good deal for me," said Minnow. "If there was time to help clear up afterwards before I needed to start on the build I would feel that was fairer but there's not that long for lunch."

"Don't worry about that, you're needed more on the build than before with fewer workers. Let's get sorted," added the cook.

After lunch Minnow applied some mutton fat to his hands from the small pot his Mama had given him and started on the mortar mix. The lime didn't fizz and react as normal so he called the cook over and explained the problem.

"Must have got damp with the rain yesterday. Get a fresh bag, I'll explain to the knight." The cook went to talk with the knight who came back with the cook as Minnow brought out a fresh bag of lime.

"Once again we have to be grateful to you young man," said the knight. "The mortar would have been useless if you had used the damp bag. Not everyone would have bothered to say anything and there would have been a weakness at the base of the structure. Well spotted lad, thanks again." As he went back to the king's men he patted the cook on the shoulder.

"Thought I'd done something wrong," stuttered Minnow. "What will happen to the old bag of lime?"

"I'll use it at the latrine, it will help rot down the waste that goes in there. It still has a use but not for mixing mortar. I'll let you get on. Men are waiting."

Minnow was soon back into the swing of production and the afternoon was going well. The men who were left on the build also knew what they were doing and there seemed to be little change in the rate of progress.

Now that the second layer of stone was being laid the pattern was now obvious. The front to back block sat across the two back to back blocks. The back to back blocks sat across the front to back block. Those going front to back were called the key and would hold the structure together as it became taller.

The next thing he noticed was a tap on his shoulder. He looked up and saw Grandpapa standing beside him leaning on his two long walking thumb sticks.

"What are you doing, Will?" he gasped.

Minnow explained about the mortar while he worked, Grandpapa listened and nodded along with the explanation. Minnow delivered the load and returned with two empty buckets.

"You've made a real mess of Top Meadow, I guess it will never be the same as before. I can see the main shape from the walls and those lumps must be for the things you called pillars. Did you say those lumps came all the way from Normandy?" he asked. "They are neat pieces of stone."

Minnow explained there were arches and windows made from stone being delivered at some stage. "It's going to be a big building when it is finished" added Minnow.

"If you finish it," suggested Grandpapa. "You said the King has gone off without leaving any money to pay you."

Minnow explained that the knight had a plan and was sure something was to be sorted. He went and fetched a stool from the cook for his Grandpapa. While Minnow worked, the cook came over and had a chat with Grandpapa. Minnow couldn't hear what was being said but they were both laughing at times.

The cook returned to preparing the evening meal and Grandpapa said he'd make his way slowly back home.

"You may even be back before me," he added as he left using both poles to carefully steady himself over the disturbed ground.

Grandpapa did make it home before Minnow. He was sitting in his usual seat outside in the sunshine breathing heavily and enjoying a tankard of cyder.

"The most exercise I have had for a long time but worth every bit," he gasped. "That cook is a character, had me laughing with his tales. I thought I had forgotten how to laugh like that. Today has done me a world of good. Thanks for suggesting I took a look at what was happening young Will. Sounds as if they like what you're doing as well."

Minnow hadn't seen Grandpapa so happy for a long time. Perhaps he should try taking a walk more often.

Chapter Twenty-Six – Ropes, Poles and Pillars

It was soon Saturday again, pay day. Mama had finished his pouch, threaded it on to a waist cord and threaded a second cord through that could be used to close the pouch.

It was also big enough to carry his pot of mutton fat with the wooden lid he'd carved. The fat had worked well for him and there was no sign of skin dryness or cracking. Some of the men laying the mortar had also started to bring their own mutton fat having spoken with Minnow. He did explain it was the cook who first suggested the solution.

The men were treating Minnow with a degree of respect and Minnow felt comfortable being part of the team. They'd chat and discuss all sorts of things during the short lunch break.

Minnow learnt quite a lot about the working of the farm. There was more than labouring in the fields. The animal side had such a lot of variety that he hadn't appreciated.

Thinking of that, there was a lot of bleating from the sheep today. Back at the farm they must have separated the lambs ready for shearing the main flock.

His Papa had always been involved in the clipping of the wool. It was one of those occasional jobs he had at the farm. He'd have to stop the tree work while the wool was being gathered.

Wool was the main source of income for the farm. It was a high value product and the village folk relied on the processing to bring in their share of income. Kings have always recognised the value by taking their share as a tax known as the clip.

Minnow gathered with the others to collect his pay. Today he noticed how all the others put their pay away into a pouch before tucking it under their shirt. He made his way towards home with the others to the gateway. Here he waited for his Papa.

He was kept waiting some time and wondered if his Papa had remembered to wait for him. Eventually a small group made their way up from the farm. His Papa was at the back of the group. Minnow joined him and asked why they were so late.

"Instructions for Monday," explained Papa, "I'm wool clipping for the week. I have an additional job of training up a youngster. It will slow us up a bit but will eventually give us an extra pair of hands."

"I hope it is not a certain one of the group who returned to the farm from Top Meadow," commented Minnow. "His aim is to go off and fight. He thinks he can pillage his fortune when they overcome an enemy."

"The one I'm to train has been a regular on the farm for a few years. He has proved to the farm manager he's reliable and keen to learn. You've done the same on Top Meadow but in only a few weeks. You've surprised me. I had my worries about how you would cope with work and, even if you would ever have a job."

"Thank you for such confidence. You, Mama and Grandpapa have all influenced me. I'm only what you've made me. I'm enjoying my work and having pay at the end of the week. At the start of the week I thought there was going to be no further work. We will just have to wait and see what happens."

Mama was sitting by the hearth stirring the pot. The smell was different tonight. Lots of herbs which was unusual. The meal was salted pork, the last of the pork kept over the winter. Mama explained with extra money each week she could buy more fresh ingredients and it seemed a waste not to use the last of the pork.

There were no objections, it had been a little time since they had the salted meat and the herbs added that extra flavour. It was more of a treat than a boring regular meal tolerated in the depth of winter. Grandpapa joined them for the meal and talked of his walk to Top Meadow and the time he'd spent with the cook.

Everyone felt good after a full meal, knowing there was money for things they needed at the moment. Papa felt too tired to visit the alehouse, he'd pick up on the tales on Monday at the clipping. Everyone went off to sleep feeling very comfortable.

Sunday brought a steady drizzle. It didn't stop the work that was needed on their plots of land. It did make digging a bit easier and little watering was needed.

Grandpapa supplied more seed, Papa drew the shallow trench, Minnow placed the seed thinly and Mama brought the soil back over. Sticks were placed at each end to indicate where seeds were planted and the process repeated several times throughout the morning.

After lunch they had the loan of the pony and light harrow. They broadcast flax seed on their ploughed strip of land. Papa suggested there would be an increase in the need for ropes as the church walls rose higher. He'd already been looking at potential poles from the forest that would carry platforms for the builders.

Papa had rarely talked so much about his work and now he was making plans for the future. Perhaps not being tied to regular work could be an advantage added to a little foresight.

Monday's return to work saw smaller blocks being delivered. These would make up the main structure, built on the carefully constructed lower walls. Minnow knew he could handle these blocks but continued with the mortar mixing. Everyone considered him the expert and he was quite happy.

The day was dry, the wool was dry and the clip could proceed. The sheep still called for their lambs. Once shorn they were reunited and gradually the bleating subsided.

Daily progress on the build saw the men happy in their work and the king's men visibly more relaxed. The farm regularly supplied the food and the cook did wonders with his simple fire, pots and ingredients.

Minnow had occasionally seen Mary leaving, having delivered the bread. He was given a smile each time he said hello. It had been a few weeks since they'd seen the knight but when he appeared he also looked relaxed and happy. He went first to talk with the kings men and then called the team together.

"You may have hoped that I have some good news from the King. Perhaps my face confirms that the news is good. He has agreed that I keep the King's revenue from the clip and use it to pay you. He has added some of the King's revenue from the clip at Salisbury as well to the total. The build is secure. He expects to be busy in Normandy for some little time but does look forward to being able to see the completed church in a few years time."

"God bless the King," said Minnow. "God bless the King," echoed the team. The knight beamed with pleasure and added his own "God bless the King."

The men were very soon working almost at their height limit. The smaller blocks were easier to handle. The inner space between the inner and outer blocks was filled with a mix of mortar and stones, the same as was used in the foundations of the pillars. The outside of the walls were flat and straight. A plumb line was regularly used to ensure the walls were vertical.

There were so many things the king's men checked and double checked. Only once did a section have to be pulled out and rebuilt. It was now obvious that some form of platform was going to be required to enable the build to go higher.

Papa had long ago finished the felling and quartering. He had returned to assisting carters with their journeys back and forth to the riverside. Minnow was quite surprised to see him arrive with a cart loaded with long straight poles freshly cut from the forest.

The dark skinned king's man was quickly directing him to the area he wanted the platform. There were a couple of trestle tops nearby and a pile of ropes.

Papa started to unload the poles and a couple of men were sent with him to assist constructing the poles into a platform. Six uprights, diagonal supporting poles and poles to form the base under the boards were assembled.

Two trestle boards were placed overlapping on the top and the platform was ready for use. Minnow was called over and made to jump around on the structure to check it was secure. Only after that did one of the men carefully climb up and move around to check it would hold his weight.

A pile of stone blocks were loaded onto the platform and soon the wall at this side started to grow in height. Papa constructed a platform at the other side of the wall and soon the blocks there were in place. The limecrete again filled the gap between the two rows of blocks.

Added to the outside of the walls were buttress structures, each with their own foundation. The knight explained that there would be a lot of weight going on the walls. When the roof was added it could force the walls outwards. The buttresses would support the walls between the windows and make the whole building strong and solid.

Minnow was busy with both mortar and limecrete mixing. He no longer delivered, men came with the empty buckets and took them filled with the needed mixture back to the platform.

Papa was now constructing a third and fourth platform structure, without the trestle boards. These were extensions to the first two platforms. The build would be moved sideways when the men could no longer reach to put in the limecrete infill.

Eight men were needed to lift and move the whole platform structure to extend even further the construction of the wall. Eventually more poles would be added on top and the platforms raised higher. Papa added more diagonal poles to stop the structure twisting. After a few months all the side walls were twice the height the tallest of the men on the site. It was now mid summer and there was yet another change in the items being delivered.

The round blocks for the pillars arrived, eight at a time on a large two horse wagon. The king's men had been missing recently and had been checking the dimensions of the solid cylinder shapes before they were delivered. The chalk had come from caves where it had been shaped while it was still soft. When it was exposed to the air, any dampness escaped and the chalk became hard.

Minnow noticed there were some lumps left about half way up each cylinder. That, he thought, must be a clue as to how they'd be lifted into place. Four men would be needed to lift a block but not above their heads. The king's men must have a system. Minnow was interested to know how it would be done. However, he'd have to wait a few days.

The first few pillar blocks were in place easily. Minnow's mortar mix was used to secure them in place, building up from their special, level, foundation block.

Minnow's Papa provided the materials for the next stage. He delivered three long straight, very strong, poles. They were the thickness of the top of a strong man's leg, top to bottom. Minnow had never seen such sized timber outside of the forest that had not been sawn to shape. The King must have granted special permission as they were well beyond the thickness of anyone's wrist.

It took two men to carry them and they were laid side by side on the ground with a small log keeping one end just off the ground. It was here the ropes were woven over, under, over, around and back again several times as tightly as possible at the one end.

Rope was then forced between the poles and wound around and around the woven binding. With the three poles securely bound together, the binding would become the top end of a strong but heavy tripod.

A massive double wheeled pulley block was secured to the middle of the binding. One end of an extremely thick rope was attached to the base of the top pulley block. A second double wheeled pulley was threaded to join with the secured pulley. One length of rope became five side by side lengths. A strong metal hook hung from the lower double block.

Minnow could picture the final position of the tripod over the already started pillar and how the next blocks would be raised into place. It was no wonder that the poles were so big and long. The next challenge was how to raise the tripod.

A fourth, standard sized, pole was brought in. A rope was attached between the top of the tripod that was still flat on the ground, across to one end of the single pole and then the rope trailed across the ground.

Everyone was to be involved in raising the tripod, even the king's men and the cook. Six would be needed to raise and separate the legs of the tripod, two to each leg, as it rose up. Two steadied the fourth pole and the rest had to haul on the rope.

It was a failure. The fourth pole fell to one side and was unable to lever the top of the tripod more than a little off the ground. An additional pole was added to the single pole to make a long legged X.

This time the X pole did act as the lever and the tripod became vertical. They struggled to separate the legs but it was eventually stable. Three cross poles were used at the base to keep the legs apart and were securely lashed into place.

It took the six men to manoeuvre the structure. One end of a base cross beam had to be released to allow the tripod to sit in position over the started first pillar. The next pillar block was brought in close, attached to the lower pulley block and was carefully raised, being pulled at the same time to one side as it rose to clear those already in place.

A hinged step ladder had been used to place some mortar on the top of the established pillar and the new block was gently lowered into place. Adjustment was made by raising the block and then lowering it again until the three king's men were happy. It had been a real team effort but that was just the first of many blocks.

Even with the tripod and pulleys it wasn't possible to reach the height required by the king's men. They'd ordered thinner blocks made that could be carried by a couple of men. These were raised as far as they could be by the tripod and pulleys and then taken the last distance by the men on the platform that surrounded the pillar.

Minnow's Papa was responsible for all the scaffolding structures. Some had even more additional poles on top of the first sets of poles to extend the platforms even higher as required for the men to work. At the base poles were set outwards, at a slant, to give increased stability to the towers of scaffolding.

Minnow was now putting in a full day's work. Two youngsters had been taken on to help with the increase in activities. It was left to Minnow to train them in the art of mixing the mortar and limecrete. Both mixtures were in demand and the two new lads were kept busy. Minnow was frequently checking the quality of the mix and giving advice.

His main job now was removing the lugs that had enabled the cylindrical blocks to be lifted into place. Starting at the lower levels wasn't a problem. Higher up, the scaffolding provided a good base from which he could work. He'd always climbed trees with confidence so his Papa's scaffolding was easy. The cook told him he'd been chosen as he was the smallest, lightest and most agile.

One of the king's men had worked with him for a week. He taught him how to use a saw for cutting stone and files to take off the lugs. As if that didn't have to be careful enough, the final work with a rag, block of flat wood, oil and fine sand to produce the smoothest circular finish was crucial.

Every area had to be inspected as it was completed, he could not move on until the king's man was happy. After a couple of weeks, Minnow was able to complete a whole pillar before it needed inspection. Minnow loved the white of the chalk that seemed to glow in the sunlight. Fortunately the highest blocks had no lugs.

The very top block was of another type of stone. They were shaped with some fancy carvings and had been brought from Normandy. These were not chalk and had a warmth of colour that matched the blocks at the base of the pillar.

Chapter Twenty-Seven – Relationships

While doing a full days work, Minnow had started to take notice of a regular visitor to the site. Mary daily delivered the freshly baked bread. Sometimes, while platforms were being adjusted to give better access to the lugs, he had the chance to chat after she'd made her delivery.

She was very shy. At first she said very little other than that she helped in the farm kitchens. She mostly did cleaning, laundry and vegetable preparation. Mary eventually told him a little more about herself.

She'd been brought up at the farm after her mother had died giving birth to her. Her mother had been several months pregnant when the father, that Mary never knew, had been killed fighting for King Stephen. Both her parents had been employed at the farm.

She kept away from the farm workers and had been warned they could be rough with her. It was only since the building of the church was she allowed off the farm to deliver the bread to the cook. The cook at the farm kitchen considered the short walk would be safe for her when everyone else would be busy working.

Minnow was aware his voice had deepened over the last year. He carried men's hair on his lower body and he could be judged to be of marriageable age. Nothing had been discussed on the subject by his parents. Families made arrangements with another family to agree suitable marriages for their children. Another thing to raise for discussion at some stage at home.

It was a Saturday evening and Papa had gone to the alehouse as usual. Minnow thought it would be a good time for just him and his Mama to have a talk.

"Are there any arrangements for me to marry?" he asked.

Mama was taken aback by the question that seemed to have come from nowhere. After a time to assemble her thoughts Mama responded.

"I have tried to find a family that would take you as a husband for their daughter but there have been difficulties about your small size. I have been made to feel small myself when I have tried to suggest a joining of families and don't know what to do for the best."

"It has even been suggested you become a monk in a monastery so that you do not have to marry. We don't believe you should be shut away just because of your size. I'm sorry, but I don't think we will be able to find a family that will consider you for their daughter."

Minnow hadn't known what to expect as an answer. Since he'd worked on the church build he had given his small size little thought. The rest of the team accepted him as a fellow worker and his size wasn't an issue. They knew the deepness of the voice and the start of face hair made him a man. They expected him to perform as a man along with them.

His Mama's response was difficult to accept. He'd not been prepared for such a statement but he felt she was being genuine and honest. Perhaps there was one good thing about the situation, he wasn't going to be married off to a stranger. There was obviously no rush. He decided there would be time to build a relationship and try to obtain approval.

"What brought about the question?" his Mama asked. "Have you met a girl that you like?"

"I have been talking with a girl from the farm. She has no Mama or Papa. She must belong to the farm manager's family as they look after her. I think she's their kitchen servant. She has been warned about keeping away from men. Perhaps she thinks I'm just a child and it is acceptable to talk with me."

"I'm not sure if she likes me or is just glad to have someone different to talk with. The cook says he thinks she must like me, she has never spoken to him, she only smiles. We did wonder at one stage if she could talk."

"So, what have you been talking about?"

"I just chatter on about the work I'm doing and she tells me about her work. When I mentioned I had a Grandpapa, she then told me about her Mama. We don't get long to talk, its usually while I'm waiting for Papa to adjust a platform."

"Mary has told me she's the first one up in the morning, sets water to heat and lights the bundles of twigs in the bread oven. She says she's good at lighting and rekindling fires. She mostly washes things, prepares vegetables and cleans."

"The cook at the farm has not taught her how to make meals but she says she watches and is learning that way. Mary knows all about the problems caused by the King going back to Normandy and how the farm manager has to provide for the team on Top Meadow as well as run the farm."

"She says he often mentions the loss of good grazing for the sheep and how long it takes to clear replacement land from the forest. The kitchen team dread when he visits them as they get shouted at and then the cook shouts at everyone again," finished Minnow.

At least she has a name, thought Mama. It sounds as if they have been chatting over some period of time. She is also is very aware of what is going on around her, a simple person would just ignore complicated issues.

"When I go to buy from the farm, perhaps I should keep an eye out for her," suggested his Mama. "She sounds bright enough. A good time would be perhaps to walk back with her after she has delivered the bread to Top Meadow. How does that sound? Do you want to know if she has feelings for you?"

"I'm not sure, I do enjoy talking with her but I expect the farm manager has some plans for her future. If she's not being taught to cook she will not take over from the present cook."

"It will have cost him to keep her," continued Minnow, "after her Mama died, so she thinks she has to work to repay his kindness. He has made it clear that he'd not keep her if she had a child. That is why she keeps away from men. Even around the farm she will not go near the stables."

"Delivering the bread to Top Meadow has been the first time she been away from the kitchen on her own. Even that, she says, she finds a bit frightening."

"It will do no harm to have a short chat with her," said Mama. "I'll be needing some things from the farm on Monday so I'll try and choose the right time. Maybe I could see what has happened with the build before the bread is delivered and then walk back with her."

"Mary normally delivers a bit before mid morning. The cook will have finished clearing after breakfast and having his morning break. I'm sure you could chat with him and he can show you what has happened since you last looked at the build. He enjoys talking and does like a change of company. Mary will leave the bread on the trestle board and go unless she notices I'm able to chat."

"That sounds like a plan," said Mama. "Has Papa noticed you chatting with Mary? What has he had to say?"

"All he has said is be careful, she could be a man eater. I didn't understand and was going to ask the cook what Papa was trying to say. I know Papa was having some sort of fun but I didn't know how to respond without showing he'd confused me," explained Minnow.

"You're right, Papa was having some fun with you. It is a man's way of saying don't trust a stranger when they show an interest in you. Be wary and be sure you're being given truthful answers to your questions. If possible find out what they really want from you."

"With Mary," continued Mama, "she may just enjoy having someone safe to talk with but she's being very careful too. Relationships are a difficult game to play which is why sets of parents get to know each other before suggesting marriage between their children."

"I remember," said Minnow, "having the same thoughts about the cook at Top Meadow. I asked myself what did he want from me, why was he being so friendly? It turned out that I reminded him of his youngest brother that he missed after he was sent away from his family."

"The young brother was his best friend and the cook apologised for using me as a substitute. I told him I had been looking to find answers to life and its little problems so we both were able to meet each other's needs. I also used Grandpapa and he has taught me a lot about life's little ways that have confused me."

Papa arrived back from the alehouse.

"No minstrel tonight, not much gossip. Saved me buying two drinks. People were actually asking me about the situation with the King and if he was likely to return soon. I couldn't give an answer as no one knows the mind of our King."

Mama said nothing about the conversation with Minnow and soon all were settled to sleep.

Monday and Minnow was working up a pillar when he spotted his Mama come through the gateway and go towards the cook's fire. The cook was returning from the latrine with an empty bowl. Looking towards the latrine reminded Minnow of a thought he'd had a couple of times. The screening was effective at ground level but did little to block the views of anyone working at height. He wondered if latrine users had even considered their lack of privacy.

"Hello cook, I'm Minnow's Mama. He said you may have a bit of time to show me around the build."

"Pleased to meet you. Most people just have a wander and come to their own conclusions. Minnow is a good worker and I understand he'd not take time away from his work to show his Mama around. Is there anything you would like to know in particular?"

"There look to be more poles here than in the forest. Is it all safe?" asked Mama.

"It had better be, it's Minnow's Papa that's in charge of all the platforms. Have you spotted Minnow up on that third pillar on the far side?"

"How did he get up there? I don't see a ladder. I hope he's tied on. I'm not sure I should have come, I shall worry all day now."

"Minnow is nimble and uses ropes to help him climb the poles. The same rope is used by him to haul up the tools he needs. He's removing lugs, sticking out bits, from the chalk blocks. The king's man has confidence in his newly acquired skill and only needs to check his work when the whole pillar is finished."

"Minnow is a quick learner and has the sense to ask questions when a task is not clear. You would be surprised how many men say they understand a task and then go on to make a disaster of a job."

"I can see the outside walls are getting quite tall as well. Why are there such large gaps just above head height?"

"The church will have windows that use glass to let light into the building. Windows will make the building less draughty and wooden shutters will not be needed. Glass is now frequently used in castles and manor houses. It is becoming less expensive and the king's men have experience in constructing buildings that use glass."

"Thanks Mary," added the cook, "just put it on the trestle as usual."

"Thanks for your time cook. I need to go to the farm for some bits. I could walk with this young lady if that is where she's going."

"Nice to have met you, please come again if you can and we could have a longer chat. Careful how you go over the rough ground. Bye."

"Hello, I'm Minnow's Mama," she said to Mary." Are you going back to the farm?"

Mary looked for Minnow and saw he was busy so she nodded her head. They both carefully picked their way to the gateway.

"Minnow has told us you bring the bread every day from the farm. I have not seen you there when I go to buy things. Have you been there long?"

"I work in the kitchen," said Mary.

That is a good start thought Mama, at least I have a spoken answer. "I'm after bread today, would you be able to bring me some?"

"You would have to ask the farm manager's wife. She's in charge of selling. I just clean in the kitchen."

"Minnow has mentioned he's occasionally spoken with you," added Mama.

"He's easy to talk to and Top Meadow is a safe place where we can sometimes talk. If he tried to hurt me, I'm sure he wouldn't, I could fight him off and there would be people to help me. The farm manager does not want me to get involved with men. Minnow is a bit different, I know he has grown from a boy to a young man but he's not like other men. Sorry, I do not wish to sound rude about your boy. Yes, I do like him and he seems kind."

"I must let you get back to your work while I buy the bread. It's been good to have met you and you've not been rude about Minnow. He is different, but very likeable."

Shame the walk back to the farm was so short thought Mama. However there was enough time to obtain some measure of the girl. She has been very sheltered and lacks confidence but is bright enough and knows how she'd look after herself. What a strange situation she has found herself in. The next question is how to move forward from here.

Chapter Twenty-Eight – No Time to be Idle

Autumn was on its way. The summer had been kind to the build with very few downpours and only the occasional drizzly day. Everyone was now on a three day week to enable the harvest to be gathered both on the farm and on each householder's plots.

There was never enough time to achieve everything without working well into the evening. They were long days but necessary if the efforts of the growing year were to be gathered and stored to see them through the winter months. Three day's pay wasn't a lot but the harvest was equally important and had its own longer term value.

The dark skinned king's man was the only one left to oversee the work on the site. The other two, according to the cook, had gone to Normandy to check on the parts for the windows and the arches.

They'd taken their drawings with them. They needed to mark and identify all the pieces that would go together to make up a window or arch. Things, thought Minnow, had started to become complicated. He did recognise that such large items could not come ready assembled. He also had no idea how the team would have to work to construct the arches.

Minnow's Papa had the first clue. The knight called him to the king's man's tent and showed him a parchment illustrating an arch made of stone. Below the arch was a second drawing of a wooden frame that was needed to support the stone arch as it was being put together.

The knight explained that once all the stone pieces were secured with mortar the wooden frame could be removed and used for the next arch. Papa had to construct the wooden frame to the exact sizes given on the drawing. He'd never used measurements.

He was able to make things to fit a space when he could see the limits of the space. An arch, way up above the ground, that wasn't there to fit a wooden frame to, was going to be a challenge. The knight persuaded him that the king's man was an expert and would guide him all the way.

Since Minnow had started to work full time there had been few opportunities to talk with the cook. He'd missed their chats and with the agreement of his Papa had invited the cook to their home regularly on a Sunday morning. The cook had helped them with work on the land while still having time to chat. Grandpapa also enjoyed his company and the cook often brought something for their lunch.

During some of these times Minnow had learnt more of the justice system the King had introduced. He started to understand how vast the lands were that he ruled. The cook explained how power was shared through the lords, barons and earls including the role of knights and their squires.

Then there were the troubles the King had with his sons and the Queen, the King of France and his sons, the King of Scotland, the rulers of Wales and his trying to manage Ireland. Added to all this Henry tried to have his say about the appointment of bishops and frequently fell out with a succession of Popes.

It was no wonder that the King was always on the move, managing his kingdom. The cook held the King in high regard and Minnow understood why he felt that way. Grandpapa agreed the country was more peaceful than during Stephen's reign.

However he held an additional view. He blamed King Stephen for the death of his son, thought all kings were just land grabbers and tax imposers. He could see Henry's sons being as bad as Stephen. They had already shown the signs by the way they'd fought their own sire.

Grandpapa saw the Normans, and their changes, destroyers of the English way of life. It had once been simple, where everyone knew their place. He'd been fortunate with his life on the farm having a secure occupation. That was how life had been for many generations, passing on skills, playing their part in the scheme of things.

He felt the church building was all for show. Grandpapa couldn't see the need for such a large building and why did it need to be so tall?

Minnow's occasional visits to the alehouse had added information to the knowledge from the cook. Minnow enjoyed the background to the stories but also knew not to name names. He'd started to get a taste for ale. The alternative to cyder was refreshing, sometimes there was a dark ale which was sweeter and this became his favourite of the ales.

He noticed his Papa didn't give time to the wenches that sometimes brought drinks to the tables. He certainly didn't touch them like some of the men. When he asked about the women Papa told him they were looking to earn extra money from the men by spending the night with them. Papa didn't need such company as he'd Minnow's Mama.

This raised lots of thoughts in Minnow's mind. They were soon dismissed as he could not see any girl being interested in him, they'd be put off by his height. Mary was a friend he could talk with but the farm manager must have his own plans for her future. She was a good looking girl and the farm manager could recover some of her upbringing costs by finding the right husband who may be willing to pay for her as a wife.

After the harvest the weather became too difficult for work on Top Meadow. There was little work for Papa on the farm. The occasional cart now had other helpers.

Mama had been careful with the money. She used the savings to buy the extras for the pot that didn't come from their land. There were still some winter crops that they could rely on. When the pig was slaughtered and packed in brine it would see them through the months of winter.

The knight had arranged for a small guard to look after the build day and night and they were fed by the farm. The king's men and the cook had packed up and moved to the Bishop's Palace at Sunning for the winter months.

Wocca's Hamlet had their Winter Festival with a gathering and meal in a large tent on the remaining part of Top Meadow. The Church had celebrated Christmas with a mummers performance and mulled wine outside an alehouse. The chapel-of-ease did have a special Christmas service but there wasn't room for everyone.

The winter months were ideal for Minnow to make the cover for his knife. The tanners had given him a couple of off cuts which were just the right size for his needs. His Mama had bought him some leather laces and his Grandpapa gave him the loan of a metal spike to make holes in the leather. Minnow was pleased with the result, the birch bark had done well but was starting to dry and crack. The bramble stem binding was also shredding.

When there was no work on their plot of land there were still things to be done. Mama dyed and spun wool, Papa wove the wool into blankets. These winter activities kept them busy and brought in an income after they'd purchased the wool.

The dyes were from the plants Mama had gathered during the summer and Grandpapa cooked up the mixtures. There were days when he struggled with his breathing, the heat of the fire eased his problem. Minnow was careful to always select dry, well seasoned wood that produced little smoke. Charcoal would have been the best fuel but it was expensive.

Minnow started to use his knife to whittle little useful items for his Mama. When she cooked things in the shallow pan she needed a food turner. Minnow selected a beech log, split it with the axe and split off a wide, thin length. He made it flat with a smooth handle and was pleased to see it used to turn over a cooked egg.

He produced tight fitting lids for clay pots but his challenge was a wooden spoon. The outside shape wasn't a problem, scooping out the bowl was a learning experience. It was then he started to fully appreciate the grain of wood. Inside the bowl it needed to be cut a little at a time at each end to produce the hollowed shape.

Minnow improved his technique and was soon producing a spoon or a couple of food turners a day. His Mama suggested he took some to a trader who ran a stall. The trader was happy to buy them and asked if he could make more.

Minnow soon ran out of beech wood so had to go searching the forest for dead branches as part of his daily wood collection. The blade started to become less sharp and Grandpapa helped him sharpen it using a stone he had from his days working at the farm.

Daylight started to lengthen and the weather improved. The cook and the king's men returned to Top Meadow. Deliveries were started again and included sets of carved stone shapes. These were the pieces of the arches that would sit on the pillars and rest on the wooden support Papa had constructed. The wooden support would only be needed while the mortar set.

There were so many pieces that it took quite a time for the king's men to lay out the shape on the ground. Papa's wooden frame was brought in to check against the stones. The frame was perfect and hadn't changed while stored at the farm over the winter.

Scaffolding was now needed to support the frame and provide platforms for the men. Some new poles were required which gave Papa additional work. It was a couple of weeks before there was anything for Minnow and the rest of the men to do.

One of the king's men had started to learn English from the cook over the winter months at Sunning. He gave simple instructions to the group on how the work would proceed. Minnow questioned the guidance with some additional words for clarity. Despite a few sniggers from some of the men he felt they would not have fully understood, just hearing the king's man.

The arch would be built, starting at each end at the same time and meet at the top on the wooden frame. Mortar would be applied to the block that was in place and then the next block added. The arch would need to set for several days before the supporting frame was removed.

Minnow and the men didn't believe the stone arch would stay in place. They could imagine it collapsing without the wooden support. No one wished to be underneath when the frame was removed and the arch fell down.

Minnow was back on mixing mortar. The bags of lime were fresh. The old lime that had been left at the end of the summer had been spread on a field to add something to the soil. Minnow didn't have time to talk with the cook about what was added to the soil but the farm manager was happy with it being used in that way.

Papa was already constructing a second wooden arch support with the help of the dark skinned king's man. They seemed to work well as a team despite the difference in language. It helped that Papa had already made one frame. The king's man was still needed for supplying the measurements.

The first stone arch was completed and left to set. Work on erecting the next assembly of scaffolding was well under way and the new arch frame put into place. The blocks for the new arch had been laid out on the ground in the correct order. The second arch was started next to the first.

More frames, more scaffolding, more arch blocks and more mortar kept the whole team busy. The build looked much like a leafless forest of bare timber with scaffolding everywhere. Ladders that had been made at the farm seemed to reach to the sky. Minnow had never seen ladders as long and it was then he started to understand how tall the church was eventually going to be. There were no dwellings that tall in the village.

His Papa had been correct. There was an even more obvious need for ropes now. The rope walk, where rope and cord was produced in the village, had taken on an extra boy. There was an increase in demand mostly from the build. Flax and hemp was having to be brought in from the Reading area. The family crop had produced a good price. Others in the village were wishing they'd planted more flax or hemp last year.

There had always been a steady demand for cord connected with weaving but the new demand for rope was exceptional. Minnow found he was collecting up the rope trimmings at the end of each day. He sold the very short lengths by the sackful back to the ropemaker which he would incorporate into new lengths of rope.

Once the stone arches had been set into place, walls were built upwards between them to eventually support the roof. One huge arch had been built at The Clearing end of the build along with the foundations for the tower. There was another large arch built at the end where the sun rose.

The outside walls had large gaps where windows were to be included. The stone for the windows would not be needed until next summer. There was enough work to keep everyone busy for the rest of this year.

Papa was constantly adding to and adjusting the scaffolding for those laying the blocks higher and higher each day. The church was taking shape. A small building was being added beyond the sunrise arch.

The cook told Minnow it was to be an area called the chancel, where the priest would conduct the services. It would be the most holy part of the church. Within would be the church altar. It was a special table that symbolised a table used by Jesus when all his disciples ate at their last supper together.

A start had also been made on a small doorway with a little arch leading out under a corner of the bell tower. At the far end of the Chancel, a window would also have an arched top.

Minnow now used the visits by the cook on a Sunday to learn more about the last supper and the disciples. He'd been to the small chapel-of-ease a few times at Christmas and Easter where he'd seen the priest behind the altar lifting a plate and a beaker. As the priest spoke in Latin he'd not understood what was happening and found it all very boring. He did like some of the stories the priest told using English but they didn't explain what had been happening at the altar.

One Sunday afternoon the cook took Minnow to a service at the chapel-of-ease. Minnow had a clean set of clothes to wear and looked tidy. The cook whispered what was happening at each part of the service and why it was included each week. Words were read from a book called the Bible which he didn't understand as it was also in Latin.

Minnow found the prayers quite interesting. There were instructions to remember the King, the Archbishop of Canterbury, the lords of the area and their knights. There were prayers to remember the ill and some were named, Minnow didn't know any of them. Thanks were given to the king's men who were building the new church. Minnow thought this was odd because it was the team of men who were doing the building.

Parts of the service were said in a singsong voice. Minnow had to resist having a giggle as it sounded so strange. The cook added that when the monks from the abbey sang they made a very special sound and it was particularly musical. While they all sang at the same time each monk had their own tune. When the voices were sung together they had a special affect on those listening, even if you didn't understand the words.

It sounded very different to hearing the minstrel at the alehouse. It sounded similar, suggested the cook, to the singing at the mummers plays which Minnow always thought magical. There was a lot to discuss about the service over the next few Sundays when the cook came to visit.

Chapter Twenty-Nine – Going Up in Circles

The tower of the church, at the village end of the build, offered some different building challenges. There was to be an upper floor and a system for hanging a bell. A spiral stairway was to be attached to the outside of the tower to reach the upper floor and spiral all the way to the roof.

Minnow had never seen a circular stairway and was curious about the triangular blocks of stone that were delivered to the site.

The foundation was similar to that of a pillar only a lot larger across and not quite as deep. The first block was set on the foundation a little way inside the small doorway. A low circular wall was built around and included the wide end of the first triangular block as part of the circle.

The second triangular step was placed on the circular wall, the thin end of the triangle placed on top of the narrow part of the first step. The circular wall was raised by a single block in height ready for the third step. The pattern continued until the steps came back to be quite a bit above the small doorway.

Up and up, beyond the top of the doorway arch, the triangular steps continued to be placed above the first set. There was enough height for a big man to stand on each step and not hit their head on the step above. Each wide end of a step was part of the circular wall, the centre looked like a small pillar but each step was part of that pillar.

Minnow could not have started to imagine how anyone could have thought of such a simple but effective way to build a stairway. Ladders were much easier to make but you did need to hold on to the sides when using them. The stairway could be used without holding the sides, items carried up or down much easier than using a ladder.

The tower was going to be even taller than the roof of the church. More scaffolding for Papa to construct and increase in height as the walls grew taller. There was to be a window above the main door arch and smaller openings higher again so that the sound of the bell could be heard when rung by the priest. Evening light would enter the tower and go directly into the main part of the church. It was going to be one of many windows all around the building letting in plenty of light.

News came through in July 1189 that King Henry had died. His eldest surviving son Richard was the new King. It was well known that Richard's plan had always been to lead a crusade to the Holy Land. He'd already started to gather funds and an army to go with him. There was one farm worker Minnow knew who would expect to go with the King.

Richard had appointed a Hubert Walter as the Bishop of Salisbury. The bishop asked that the knight should continue overseeing the Deanery of Sunning. Fortunately this included the building of the church at Wocca's Hamlet.

Hubert Walter had been a financial administrator, diplomat and judicial guide to the old King Henry. King Richard knew he could rely on his financial skills as well as be the local bishop.

The funding of the crusade was restricting some of the money for the build. The king's men had met frequently with the knight and they'd come out of the meetings looking quite gloomy.

Minnow and the rest of the men continued with their tasks as instructed. The main difference was the cut back in stock being held. Many items were delivered just in time but for some things there was a delay and men moved to farm tasks.

The two youngest men were told to return to full time farm work, replacing two who had left to join the King's crusade. Pay was sometimes a week late. Minnow was thankful his Mama knew how to keep coins hidden away safely and not spend all of them each week.

It was harvest time again and work slowed on the build to enable work on home plots and in the fields. Things were being finished off ready to be left over the winter months. There were some of the window structures now in place. Spur blocks, jutting out just above the pillars, were ready for the roof timbers of the side aisles.

There were a lot of things about the build that made Minnow marvel at the planning the king's men had to consider. Incidentals that needed to be included in the construction and would have been difficult to add later. He'd also learnt skills he could never have imagined a few years ago. Would he ever get to use them again?

He could not imagine building himself a dwelling of stone but maybe the farm would need some stone buildings. There could even be a manor house built if the village grew much larger.

The winter months flew by and the family were grateful for the payment from the ropemaker for their crop. Everyone was busy with their winter tasks and Minnow continued producing his wooden implements which were now being taken for sale as far as Reading by the traders.

There was talk in the alehouse that requests were being made to the new Bishop of Salisbury to grant permission for a regular market. Minnow thought it was a good idea but a new bishop would have lots of other things to sort before Wocca's Hamlet would be granted such status. Having a collection of stalls seemed enough for the needs of the village. The established traders were well used and trusted. If money was short they'd consider a trade of goods as part payment. A market would raise trading to be purely money transactions, in spring that could be difficult for many.

As normal, Papa was one of the first to be called back to work on the build. All the ropes on the scaffolding had to all be checked. Some of the winter winds had brought down parts of the platform support. A team of three were busy rebuilding and checking the structures for safety.

Fresh deliveries greeted the rest of the team when they returned. Window frames, stone blocks and fresh sacks of lime all required sorting. The most recent deliveries were wooden lintels that would sit above the inner part of the windows. Additionally there were long stone beams that would sit above the outside of the windows. Minnow was soon back to preparing the mortar mixes as the walls reached their final height.

Up at the farm, teams had been cutting and preparing the timbers for the roof. Papa was concerned the timber wasn't fully seasoned and could still twist and warp once in place. The dark skinned king's man had reassured the knight the timber would be ready to be used. Papa considered the drying methods used over the Narrow Sea may have worked there but he still thought in England it should have had more time.

Papa was positioning even more scaffolding to enable work on the roof timbers. One of the happiest people was the ropemaker, growing wealthy with the trade the build was bringing him. He already had a plan for the used rope that would come back to him after the build. Even if he had to buy it back, there would still be a market for rope at the farms.

He'd recently been able to purchase a horse and cart so would be able to travel with his rope to many places around Wocca's Hamlet. Farmers would buy from his cart. It would save the busy land managers having to travel themselves to make a purchase at a market. A cart was always useful and there would be few occasions when it would sit idle.

Minnow wondered what he'd be asked to do when no more mortar was required. He could whittle wood but wasn't a skilled carpenter like the other men who had been brought up to work with large pieces of timber. He could not imagine himself hauling the timbers up the scaffold. Soon he discovered his next challenge after seeing an unusual delivery.

There were several rolls of grey coloured metal that Minnow did recognise as lead. This was shaped like a ribbon, a bit more than a finger in width and thin. Also delivered were some sacks containing boards, thick wool blankets and flat pieces of clear material laid between the blankets. It was glass for the windows.

One of the king's men called Minnow to a trestle. He watched him mark out a section of a window shape on a large piece of parchment, using a thin stick of charcoal. After putting on a pair of leather gloves he then laid out pieces of glass to fit into the shape he'd drawn.

Some pieces were too large and needed some glass removed to fit the shape. The king's man took a ring off his finger and with the stone made a scratch along the piece of glass above the line on the parchment. With a little tap, using a small metal hammer, the excess glass fell off leaving the correct shape sitting over the piece of parchment. There was a little gap between each piece of glass and soon the whole shape had been filled.

The king's man handed the ring for Minnow to examine. There was a small, bright, clear stone in the middle of the ring. It looked like a small piece of pointed glass but it also had a lot of sparkle. It was the point that was used to scratch the glass. A long scratch and a tap with the hammer was all that was required to crack off the excess glass.

The king's man handed Minnow another pair of leather gloves and made him put them on. He then took one of the small pieces of glass and used the edge to cut a corner off the piece of parchment. He then produced a thin piece of leather and with the same edge of the glass, sliced it into two pieces.

Finally he waved his hand at Minnow and made to cut into his hand with the piece of glass before saying "Non, non, non". Minnow understood the edges of the glass would easily cut his hand and fingers. The point was well made despite the language difficulties.

Minnow was shown how to edge each piece of glass with the lead ribbon, wrapping it evenly to be equal on each side. At the corners he had to use scissors on the ribbon to avoid any overlap caused by the turn of direction. He had to be particularly careful not to cut away too much, there should be no gap or overlap.

Every single piece of glass had to have its edges wrapped and then be placed back inside the charcoal line in the correct position. If Minnow managed to turn a piece back to front it would not fit which at first confused him. He soon had the pieces back in place with their edges neatly covered by lead ribbon.

While he'd been working the cook had set up and lit a small brazier near the trestle. Again Minnow was confused as it wasn't a cold day. The charcoal was soon giving off a steady heat. A metal rod, with a triangular block on one end and a wooden handle on the other, had been put in the brazier to heat.

The king's man had brought a pot that looked as if it contained a dark fat. Minnow had to use a small brush to apply a layer of the soft fat where the lead ribbon was sitting adjacent to another ribbon between the sheets of glass.

A roll of flexible lead wire was laid out on the trestle and the heated rod removed from the brazier. The end of the rod was obviously hot but hadn't changed colour. The king's man dipped it in the fat. Some smoke was given off and there was some spluttering as if there were drops of water in the mixture.

The end of the lead wire was touched to one face of the hot triangular block. The wire melted and made the surface of the hot iron shiny like silver. All three faces were treated the same and the rod put back on the brazier to keep warm.

The tricky part was to stop the two pieces of glass moving while the hot rod and the roll of wire was moved along the join. The wire melted and became part of the lead ribbon. It was a slow job and any gaps had to be filled by going over it again without leaving lumps of melted wire. The gaps, that had been cut with the scissors, also had melted lead applied.

Minnow soon learnt to fix one end of a join with a small blob and then the other end. It was easy then to make the whole length of the join. The rod needed frequent re-heating but Minnow soon became skilled and enjoyed seeing the collection of pieces become one complete shape.

Time must have flown by as the call was made for a lunch break. The king's man was happy with the finished shape that was still within the charcoal boundary on the parchment.

Minnow didn't realise how how much he must have been concentrating until he yawned and took in a huge lungful of air. He shook his head and had a good long swig of cyder. The lunch of bread and cheese, was very welcome as was a short chat with the cook. Assembling glass windows was new to the cook and he'd spent a little time watching Minnow.

"The knight has told me you're very quick to learn things and from what I have seen he's correct. You only needed showing once and you almost became an expert," observed the cook.

"The king's man is the expert and made sure I understood what I had to do. There looks to be magic involved. That fat must be the real magic ingredient."

"I knew that lead could melt if heated. Getting edges to melt and join to other lead I couldn't do at home. The bits just fell apart when I tried a few years ago. Grandpapa showed me how small bits could be melted into a large blob. It could then be flattened and made into shapes or even a small dish. Joining is magic, and now I can do it, if I have that paste."

"Don't ask me what it is," said the cook, "I'm just as impressed as you are."

"This must be a first," said Minnow, "I can do something you've never done."

"The other bit of magic," added Minnow, "was the stone in his finger ring. It looked like a small piece of glass. I don't understand how it could make a scratch on the glass. I tried to make a piece of glass scratch some other glass but it would not make a mark."

"I do know the answer to that," said the cook. "It's a valuable stone called a diamond, one of the hardest stones there is, harder than flint and you know how hard that is I'm sure."

"A diamond, I've never heard of or seen one before. It must be special," observed Minnow.

"Very special and they can cost a lot of money," commented the cook. "If you're given it to use you will need to look after it. Looks as if you're needed back at the trestle."

"Thanks for lunch," added Minnow.

The king's man was waiting at the trestle. He indicated they needed to put another trestle board on top of the glass they'd been working on. A blanket was placed over the assembly, then the board was laid on top. The two boards were lifted together and turned top to bottom, while preventing the glass falling out. The old board, which was now on the top, was taken off.

The king's man took away the parchment. Minnow immediately understood that the edges needed to be joined with melted lead on this other side of the collection of pieces. He was a lot quicker doing this other side as there was little chance of any pieces moving.

Minnow was soon starting on a second collection of pieces of glass that was shaped the same as the first. The king's man was drawing up a new shape on another piece of parchment. Minnow was given the ring which the king's man had put on a length of cord and hung it around his neck.

It took two weeks to complete all the shapes that were needed for the first window. More lead was used to hold the window into the stone frame and the hot iron joined the window to the stone. The knight suggested that the fit would be so good as to keep out rain water falling on the glass. The inside of the church would stay dry. Each evening Minnow handed back the ring to the king's man.

The next week Minnow was instructing two others in the assembly of the glass for the windows. The king's man kept an overview and handed out the freshly drawn parchment patterns. The ring was shared between the trestles after Minnow was sure the new workers understood how it was used.

As the shapes were finished it was Minnow who had to fix them into place in the stone frames using scraps of lead to wedge the shapes in place. Any gaps were then filled with lengths of molten lead strip. Minnow used his own knife to trim off any excess pieces. Finally the edges were fused with the fat mixture and the hot rod.

All the while the work with the roof timbers was closing in the whole structure. Big rolls of lead sheet were being used to cover the timber planking and make it waterproof. The weight of each roll took two big men to carry and lift it to the roof. One of the king's men gave a demonstration of how the edges were joined to keep out the water. A wooden mallet was all that was needed to make the join.

Minnow's Papa was pleased to be just working with wood, rope and poles, materials he knew and understood. However he wasn't used to working at such a height above the ground. Each morning he checked all the scaffolding and only allowed parts to be used that he knew were secure. No one took any risks so high above the ground. Team work was required at all times. A lot of friendships had developed over the years of the build and everyone looked out for each other.

Chapter Thirty – The Bishop's Man

Work on the windows seemed unending. There was so much to do that it continued after harvest when there was enough light. The roof was in place and most of the scaffolding inside had gone but there was a lot of glass still needed to fill all the windows. The supply amount was difficult to calculate due to a lot of faults in some sheets of glass.

The tower window was particularly large and required many sections. There were a lot of finishing touches that needed to be done before the worst of the winter. Draining away water from the roof required stone block channels leading to shallow ditches around the building. There was no wish for the foundations to be undermined or washed away.

A most recent delivery had been carts filled with small white pieces of stone that had been spread all over the dirt floor inside the building. Heavy poles had been used to push them into the dirt and more layers had been added on top, each being crushed on top of the previous layer. Oak boards had been used with the heavy poles to give a flat surface.

Eventually the whole floor was gleaming white with the crushed limestone. Minnow was asked to walk barefoot over it to identify where extra work was require to smooth the surface. Minnow could not have imagined that a crushed stone covering would have made such a difference to the overall splendour and inner glow of the build.

With just a few days notice, Bishop Hubert Walter arrived on the first of November. He declared the building officially a church. This was despite there still being a lot of bits to finish. Minnow and his team still had several windows that were open to the weather.

The Abbot and some monks from Reading Abbey came with him, as did the curate from the chapel-of-ease. It was All Saints Day so the building was dedicated to All Saints. The monks sang and Minnow was astounded by the sound they made within the building. He couldn't understand what they were singing but the blend of high and low voices was an exceptional type of magic which was enhanced by the building.

Most of the village, including Grandpapa, gathered in the almost completed church building. The Bishop announced that he was to join King Richard on his crusade to the Holy Land. They were to depart this next week. He praised the team who had worked on the building and then appointed his priest for the village.

The old curate was to stay and would administer the few chapels-of-ease under the guidance of their new priest. The Bishop suggested that the village was now of a size to be considered a small town, it was becoming too large to be considered a village.

He indicated the size of the crowd within the building and declared Wocca's Hamlet the largest development in the Sunning Deanery. The knight, who had worked so well supporting the build, would continue to administer the lands of Sunning while he was away on the crusade with his majesty the King.

The new priest was shown around the build by the king's men. He asked a lot of questions in their language and after some time he came to talk with the build team. The first he spoke with was the cook.

They spent a lot of time laughing. It turned out that they knew each other from the time of the cook's crusade. One by one the rest of the team met the priest. Minnow was estimating how much longer the glazing would take to finish when the priest came and spoke with him.

"You're not very big young man. Did you dig foundations and move blocks of stone like the others I've been talking to?" he asked.

Minnow wasn't sure how to answer the question. He felt he'd played his part in the build and this person was suggesting he wasn't up to the job. A feeling of disquiet towards this priest was developing. The cook had heard the question and introduced Minnow.

"This is one of the team who has become invaluable as a skilled craftsman in many parts of the build. Let me introduce Minnow. His Papa is the constructor of the scaffolding, looking after the safety of the platforms. You can only imagine how the build looked as the roof went on, there was scaffolding everywhere."

"Minnow is now our chief glazier and keeper of the diamond by instruction of the king's men. He learns very quickly and is not usually stuck to answer a question, in fact it is he who is usually asking questions. We have been very lucky that he joined the team, one of the king's men spotted him as a quick learner while the foundations were being dug."

"Pleased to meet you, Minnow. Sorry but I thought you were still a child who was just helping out. Now I'm making it worse. It's unusual to meet an adult who is so small," struggled the priest.

"While working on the build my size has not been an issue. I have been accepted as myself and been one of the team. The king's men seem to have been happy with everything they have asked me to do."

"This build has been the best thing in my life, being accepted and learning so much. One of the best teachers has been the cook. Not that he has taught me any cooking skills. He has had experience of a life beyond Wocca's Hamlet. His stories have been the best education. Are you going to live in a tent like the king's men?"

"I told you he was the one who asks the questions," said the cook quickly.

"I'm based at the farm for a short while. Our knight is looking to find me a dwelling close to the church if possible. He did say that I may have a building made for me but it would have to wait until after the winter."

"Where were you a priest before coming here?" asked Minnow.

"I have been a curate near Salisbury. Bishop Walter knew my family and suggested I should have my own parish. I'm looking forward to gathering a regular congregation and organising activities to make use of the building. I think it would be a way of bringing people in who don't regularly worship."

"Activities will make the building less of a mystery, make it a place where people feel comfortable. What sort of activity would you like to see happening in this magnificent building young Minnow?"

"Singing would be good," suggested Minnow. "Some monks from Reading sang today and the sound within the building was magic. Mummers plays would be more comfortable protected from the weather. I would like to hear from people who have been places and can tell me about other lands."

"The cook has told me about harvest suppers that some places have to celebrate the end of bringing in the harvest. More should be made of Christmas and Easter. The women like to talk with each other while doing their laundry, a dry place to meet during the winter would be good for them."

"Whoa, Minnow, slow down a bit. Where did all that come from?" asked the priest. "I'll have other duties around the parish in addition to Sunday services. I shall need a second curate to help me at this rate!"

"I've been thinking about how the church could be used for some time," explained Minnow. "It will be such a useful building for Wocca's Hamlet. I couldn't bear to think of it being locked after matins all week and only used on Sundays or special Church days."

"The chapel-of-ease is too small to be of much use beyond a place for the prayers of a few people. This church is a natural gathering space and most of the village, sorry town, can fit in easily. It would be a waste of our efforts building it, if it's not going to be used frequently."

"There are things as the parish priest I must do in the church. There will be Matins and Evensong each day. Yes, during the main part of the day there will be times when some other things could take place."

"As I get to know the people of the town I intend ask them what would interest them if the building was open during the day. The Bishop has told me there's a request for a weekly market. He has not been able to approach King Richard due to all the plans for his crusade. I could perhaps invite people to come once a week and exchange items that they have as surplus from their plots of land."

"I do agree this magnificent building does need to be used. Thanks for your ideas Minnow. I must introduce myself and talk with some of the others before they drift away."

"Well done Minnow," said the cook. "He didn't speak to you very well at the start. You showed your maturity and he seemed to listen, maybe he'll respect your ideas. Hopefully he has learnt a lesson in how to approach people."

"I'm not sure he will restore my faith in the thinking of the Church after my experiences," added the cook. "He did start to sound as if he had a care for people. That could make all the difference towards gathering support. We will have to ask your Grandpapa what he thinks about him."

"That will be interesting," added Minnow. "Since his son was killed he has not had much time for 'authority'. He accepted he had a boss while a worker and knew where he stood, usually in a pit full of wood dust! His illness took any further chance of work away from him and he does feel he's now useless as a person. As family, he's important to us and does skilled things with us. To me he's a good teacher and a friend that I can talk to. Just like you, I hope I can call you a friend."

"I hope you can, your family have all become my friends since I came here. I have started to look at life differently here in Wocca's Hamlet. There's a good atmosphere about the place, the team have worked well together. The king's men have told the knight it has been the best build they have ever worked on."

"I'm starting to feel part of the community, a bit like I felt after a few years as a young monk. As the build comes to an end we all need to think what we will do next. I'm not sure there's a need for a cook here after the build."

"As I said before you would make a good tutor. I'm not sure there would be anyone wealthy enough here to be able to pay you. There may be a rich family in Reading."

"I'm thinking 'who is the adult here?' and then I remembered you're no longer the youngster with no experiences", added the cook. "You've grown in understanding and skills very quickly in these few years. You should feel proud and confident with what you've achieved. Speaking to the priest as you did, put him in his place and demonstrated he should not judge by looks. You've become a teacher in your own little way, sorry I didn't mean it as a comment on your size."

"You're forgiven, I knew you were being nice to me. Let me help you clear up after feeding the crowd. Half of them only turned up because there was food, they didn't leave much did they?"

"I dislike waste so I'm pleased if they felt they ate well. I wasn't sure how they'd take to the soft cheese that came from across the Narrow Sea. Even that went down well along with the pickles and green olives in oil. I think the children were the most adventurous with tasting, maybe its just they were very hungry."

"Hungry," commented Minnow, "I recall how I used to be hungry quite often as a child. Things have certainly changed thanks to the build. Shall we tip the crumbs into the hedge?"

"Let's put away the useable bits into the store first. Certainly a couple of the boards will need a wash off."

There were still too many people standing and talking for Minnow to resume work on the windows so he busied himself with helping the cook. This included stirring the pot as it simmered and cooked the evening meal for the king's men. He recalled the early days, when the cook with the rest of the managers had arrived on Top Meadow, his scheming to bring kindling in return for bread, his question about foundations. How things had developed.

The cook busied himself with sorting the store that was now a lot smaller since needing fewer items to finish the build. He was going to miss his relaxed life, following a simple routine of providing meals. Again he had no idea where or what he'd be doing in a month when the king's men were due to move back over the Narrow Sea.

They may invite him to join them on their next project. However, King Richard was more interested in funding his crusade than building. He was leaving the country to the barons. They all had secure castles from which to govern their parts of the land. Who would need a travelling cook?

It would be good to have his own place where he could settle down. Perhaps he could find a role on the farm or as Minnow suggested look at moving to Reading. There should be some sort of job for him there. It was a busy place being nestled between two rivers.

He decided initially he'd talk with the farm manager. Minnow brought him out of his thoughts when he said he was off home. He added that the pot would need some attention as it was getting quite thick.

On arriving home Minnow found his Mama in quite a state. Grandpapa wasn't well. He'd walked slowly back from the church celebration and was breathless as usual.

Now he'd chest pains and a pain down his left arm. Mama had given him a warm drink but he was still in a lot of pain. The herb woman had been called and she'd given him some powder but the pain was getting worse. Minnow didn't like the change of colour in Grandpapa's face, he was very pale. Despite lying down he was unable to rest because of the pain. Minnow saw tears in his eyes as he gasped for air.

Mama sent Minnow off to sort the meal. He and Papa ate in silence after he'd taken some food through to his Mama and Grandpapa. They felt so useless. Mama said she'd stay with Grandpapa through the night. Minnow was vaguely aware of her returning at some stage in the darkness and then settling down to sleep. He guessed Grandpapa would also be sleeping, the pain must have eased.

Chapter Thirty-One – Memories

The priest arrived mid morning, having been alerted by the cook. He said some prayers over the body of Grandpapa and spoke for a time with Minnow's Mama. He told her that they should use the church for the funeral and he'd make all the arrangements. Later in the morning the midwife arrived to tidy up Grandpapa's body and wrap it in a woollen cloth.

Minnow had been persuaded earlier to go and work on the windows as normal, there was nothing he could do at home. He'd wept as he looked at Grandpapa who was no longer in pain and then made his way to Top Meadow.

He still needed to concentrate. The last few bits were very individual and involved a lot of cutting to shape. He was very much on his own now, the rest of the team having moved back to work on the farm. Just one other person was helping the king's men collect together left over materials and sending them off by cart to Reading.

As Minnow arrived, he did register the priest talking with the cook for a short time and then going away. He could not help thinking about his Grandpapa. We all die, he knew it was all part of the cycle of life. Grandpapa had played a major part in Minnow's childhood, taught him many things, been a friend and good father to his Mama.

It was good he was no longer in pain, that had been the worst part. Concentrate, think about what needs to be done. He went to find the cook to borrow his sharpening stone and put the edge back on his knife.

"Yes Minnow, what do you need" asked the cook.

"Can I use the sharpening stone?" requested Minnow, "I need my knife sharp for the fiddly bits."

"I'll have to get it, everything is in a bit of a muddle with the king's men still deciding what can be sold back to the abbey at Reading. The knight needs to recover as much money as possible to help contribute towards the crusade."

Being able to work with his own knife had added pride to the skills he'd developed. His thoughts started to drift to what he could do in the future.

The cook returned with the stone and Minnow set about putting an edge on his blade.

"I should have done this using Grandpapa's stone."

Grandpapa. No more chats, advice, suggestions, company. Minnow froze with his thoughts. The cook put an arm around his shoulder and asked if there was anything he could do? Minnow shrugged and shook his head. He just wanted to cry but had learnt not to, other than in private now.

He took a deep breath, shook his head again, told the cook Grandpapa had died and finished putting the edge on his blade.

Having a task to complete helped him focus and think less about his loss. Lunch was eaten in silence as he kept control of his emotions. He still had quite a bit to finish and didn't need to be distracted.

Would he ever use these skills again? He knew nothing of the sourcing of the materials, the glass, lead, solder fat or even a diamond. He just knew how to assemble the parts. Perhaps he could become an apprentice in a large town where stone buildings and glass windows were beginning to be regularly needed.

It would be a risk moving away and hoping to be taken on, he did have a little savings from his regular wage. What would happen to Grandpapa's dwelling? Keep your mind on the work, he told himself. This muddle of thoughts wasn't helping.

When he returned home much of Grandpapa's few belongings had been moved into their dwelling. Mama had found a pot of nails and asked Minnow to use them to hang the bags of seeds in the rafters just like Grandpapa had done.

His cooking pots and storage jars were stacked in a corner, the trestle was stood flat against the wall, his stool added to the collection around their trestle. There was no room for Grandpapa's pallet so that had been left with his wrapped body still on it.

The priest had suggested he could be buried alongside the new church building. He would hold the service in the church tomorrow afternoon. He'd already been around the town passing on the information and inviting people to join the service for Grandpapa. The farm manager was going to be there along with Mama's sisters and their families. They would have a very early start the next morning.

The following day Minnow went off to work as usual. The cook met him before he started and told him he'd have a few things for people to eat after the service in the church. It had been suggested by the priest and the farm manager had agreed to supply the items.

Minnow was absorbed in his work and was surprised when it was lunch time. For several weeks they'd taken their meal within the building. Today the cook had set up some extra trestles and started to prepare food to be eaten after the funeral service. This was unheard of within the former village. Funeral services were normally held out of doors at the chapel-of-ease. There was never food and only the curate involved. It had been just a way of disposing of the body without too much fuss.

Minnow returned to his work. A little later he was told by the cook to make his way outside and saw a cart carrying the wrapped body of his Grandpapa on a trestle board. Following were his parents, the other members of the extended family, the farm manager with some farm workers and quite a large number of people from the town.

The body was carried into the church by the farm workers and placed on a couple of trestles in the chancel area. The priest explained what would be happening and thanked everyone for coming to remember the life of William who had been a sawyer at the farm.

The funeral was mostly prayers for the departed, a short story of how Jesus rose from being dead having been crucified by the Roman soldiers and then a blessing.

Some of the farm workers carried the wrapped body outside where a grave had been dug. The body was handed down into the ground and the priest said a couple more prayers. The family were asked to put some soil over the top and then everyone was invited back into the church for some food. A couple of farm workers completed the filling in of the grave plot.

The group, who had been so quiet, softly started to chat amongst themselves. They asked each other how they were keeping, what the children were doing and commented on the size of the church. Most said how lucky they were to have such a building.

The cook removed the cloth covers from the food and people started to help themselves. There was cyder to drink and soon people were starting to chat with Minnow's parents and share their memories of Minnow's Grandpapa. Minnow listened as he learned more about life lived in Wocca's Hamlet and the part everyone played supporting each other.

There were funny stories, sad ones and even unbelievable ones told that involved his Grandpapa. Minnow thought he knew most of Grandpapa's past, things Grandpapa had told him. There was so much more he discovered and understood by the end of that afternoon. He felt his spirits lifted after the sad start to the day. He'd miss his Grandpapa but he felt happy that so many people had good memories of him as a person.

Minnow hadn't seen Mary but she also didn't know his Grandpapa. He considered she would be busy back at the farm with her chores. Slowly people drifted back to their dwellings leaving just the family, the cook and the priest.

Mama and Papa thanked the priest and asked if they needed to pay anything towards the cost of the food. He explained the farm manager had provided the food and drink as a memory to one of his valued workers.

Minnow thanked the cook for his work setting up the refreshments. The priest was thanked for arranging to have Grandpapa buried beside the church.

The priest in return said that when the grave had settled the family could mark the place with a wooden cross. Papa suggested he'd make the cross from some oak and Minnow said he'd carve Grandpapa's name on it after he'd asked the cook how to form the letters.

Making their way back to their dwelling there was a lot of talk amongst themselves about the memories that had been shared with them through the afternoon. There was still some sadness at the back of their minds but they knew that the funeral had been a happy occasion thanks to the arrangements made by the priest. Mama was very impressed by his manner of care and considered he'd be a benefit to the town.

Minnow shared his first encounter of the priest with his parents and how he managed to rise above the implied rudeness by finally impressing him with suggestions for making good use of the church building. Papa called him a cheeky young cur but smiled knowing that Minnow could stand up for himself. The last few years had been quite a journey for the whole family.

Minnow was back at work the next morning. There was just one complex window that needed to be completed. As he worked he struggled to see where he'd be and what he'd be doing in a couple of weeks time.

He could glaze windows but it worried him that he'd no idea where all the required materials had come from. An apprentice would have been given those secrets. He could mix mortar but again he'd no idea how to obtain lime. The carter just collected the items delivered by boat. Where did they come from?

Two of the king's men were no longer on site. All the surplus materials had been taken away. Minnow was left with the items for glazing and bags of limestone pieces. The cook was packing up cooking implements and pots, scrubbing boards and packing away the tents. The canvas had been dried in the building overnight.

The night watch hadn't been needed once the doors could be locked, he and his huge dog had moved on. It was now the priest's church despite requiring Minnow's finishing touches. He guessed the remaining king's man was waiting for the return of the diamond as soon as the final window was completed.

This king's man was the one who had started to learn English. Perhaps he could tell him where to source glazing and mortar items. This was something to discuss with the cook and try and obtain his help with communicating.

The priest came in and asked, "How are things at home?"

"Fine thank you," Minnow replied.

"Were you happy with the funeral?"

"It was sad to have to say goodbye to Grandpapa. Having people stay around afterwards made it a good day. We went home with a lot of happy memories thanks to the other people who knew Grandpapa. Can I ask you to help me?"

"What can I do?" asked the priest.

Minnow explained how much he'd learnt and could do since starting to build parts of the church. He said how he was unsure how to move on as he'd no idea of how to obtain materials. He needed the help of the king's man but could not speak his language.

"I have some of their language. The knight confidently uses their language with them and is the expert but he's also a busy person. I could give it a try."

"I was going to tell you earlier that I'm to set up my home next to your family, in what was your Grandpapa's dwelling. Sunning Deanery are to build me a new dwelling but that will take some time. Perhaps you will be involved in the build. I'll talk to the knight who will still be in charge of Sunning while the bishop is away on the crusade."

"Would the knight be able to speak with me? I know I'm not an important person but I do owe him my thanks for making me part of the build."

Minnow was now thinking fast. He'd get the knight to obtain details for sourcing the materials, give him the details and a job helping build the priest's home. Then who knows what could develop after that.

The cook had his own news to share with Minnow. While they chatted over their lunch the cook told Minnow that the farm manager had suggested he could have a job initially at the farm as the baker. The farm cook had found the extra work too much over the last few years and she wasn't getting any younger.

They are looking to set up a bakery in the town which would take pressure off the work at the farm kitchen. It would involve building ovens at a dwelling when one became available. Grandpapa's old dwelling was going to the priest.

Minnow found some difficulty concentrating for the rest of the day. His thoughts were buzzing, imagining a future for himself. It was a couple of days later when the knight approached Minnow and said he'd been told he wished to speak with him.

Minnow made his thanks for all the things he learnt on the build. He then asked if there were any projects he could be involved with in the future. He explained he'd never had a job on the farm to go back to and it would be a waste not to use the skills he'd learnt. The knight said he'd give it some thought and was about to go when Minnow made his planned suggestion.

"The king's man has the knowledge of where to source all the materials. Once he has gone he will take all that information with him. Do you have plans for other stone builds? Would you find it difficult to source things? Would sourcing make any build longer to achieve?"

"I could tell you the things that would be needed but I do not know who can supply them. The king's man has the answers and he's only here a few more days." Minnow waited while the knight considered what he'd heard.

"The king's man was right about you. You're a bright lad and deserve the chance of a future. I do have a couple of projects being planned and hadn't even considered how they could be achieved. Thank you for your thoughts and suggestions. You will have to excuse me as I now have some urgent work to do before I return to Sunning."

"Thank you again for the experience of work on this beautiful church," added Minnow as the knight moved off to find the king's man.

There was little more he could do other than finish the window. At least the cook would still be around as the baker at the farm. Minnow wondered if Mary would ever speak to the cook when he worked in the farm kitchen.

Chapter Thirty-Two – Uncertain Future

Ridding the church of the last two pigeons once the windows were finished wasn't easy. Firstly it was important there was no food for them. The cook had moved to the farm and had started to learn the craft of baker. Mama had seen him a couple of times when she went for bread. For several days there had been no food for the birds.

The priest asked Minnow for his help. The plan was to light a brazier early one evening, generate some smoke with some green wood and open the large double west doors where the evening light would be brightest. The hope was that the birds would head for the light and escape from the smoke. The pigeons did as expected but chose the large west window and kept banging against the glass.

As the smoke density increased they flew lower but still headed for the glass. Minnow volunteered to climb the tower steps and flap a cloth on a pole to try and drive the pigeons down to the open doors.

As he moved out onto the upper floor platform he started to cough as the smoke hit his lungs. The pigeons were still trying to pass through the glass. Minnow managed to catch one with the edge of the cloth and direct it downwards towards the ground floor. The open door was its target and it flew free of the building.

The last one was so determined to fly through the glass it knocked itself silly and floundered on the floor at Minnow's feet. He gathered it up in the cloth and took it down the spiral stair, out of the west door and released it to join its mate. Grandpapa would have wrung its neck and prepared it for the cook pot. Minnow wasn't sure the priest would have approved of treating one of God's distressed creatures in such a way within the church building.

Minnow helped the priest to carry out the brazier using two long metal poles, pushed through the fire basket. They stayed cool enough as they moved the brazier outside. Minnow flicked off the sticks that were giving off so much smoke and they smouldered safely on the damp ground.

"One good thing about a stone built church is that the only wooden parts are the roof timbers. Being so high up they'd be difficult to set alight," said the priest. "Thanks for your help Minnow. Shall I see you in church on Sunday morning?"

"If I could understand what was going on you would," said Minnow, "but so much is in a strange language that makes no sense to me, I see no point. I understand Easter and Christmas. Those stories are an important part of the history of the Church. I have heard some of the stories of the things Jesus did, mostly by watching mummers plays. Why can the Church not give us these stories in a language we can understand?"

"You're not the first to make that point with me. I'm planning to explain parts of the service before I use the language the Church insists I use. The important part is to learn about God's love for us and how to give him thanks through prayers. Please come and tell me afterwards what more you need to know and what still confuses you."

Minnow and Mama made their way to church on Sunday when they heard the priest ringing the bell in the tower. Papa felt he needed to work on their plot of land. The priest had left his dwelling early as usual, to say Matins, and was at the church door to welcome the people from Wocca's Hamlet for the mid-morning service.

There was a lot of chatter between neighbours until the priest placed himself at the front on the step that led into the chancel. People nudged each other and a silence gradually descended on the group standing in front of the chancel.

"Welcome to All Saints church and our service to thank God for his blessings to us and our community. I plan to explain the various parts of our worship as most of you will be new to services. Do not worry about the language, the Church uses it to speak with one voice to God."

"There will be parts of the service where you can learn to take part as I ask you to repeat the words you hear. Today it will be the special Lord's prayer. I'll say a few words and you try to say what you hear. I hope over the weeks you will start to understand how we can together give thanks to God for His love."

Minnow concentrated hard to follow the service and enjoyed echoing the words of the Lord's prayer. He knew it would take a few weeks to learn it fully but felt it was a start. As people left the church the priest thanked them for attending and hoped they'd say if they'd found it difficult and where he could help further.

Most people took a walk around the outside of the building. Some stopped by Grandpapa's grave for a few minutes. It would take a time for the ground to settle. Papa had already made a start on the oak wooden cross.

The cook had sent Minnow a small piece of parchment with 'WILLIAM' and the word 'SAWYER' written on it. Minnow had asked the priest how each of the letters sounded. Even when given each sound it was difficult to make the letters flow into the word.

He'd practised the letter shapes in the soil with a stick and was improving slowly. The straight down lines were easy but even then it was difficult to keep them the correct length and make them look even. A couple of guide lines for the top and the base improved his layout. He knew it would take a lot more practise before he would make a start on the carving with his knife.

The priest had just finished talking with the last group to leave. Minnow had been checking the surface of the floor and found a couple of weak places where there were depressions. He'd add more limestone on Monday and pack it down. It would take some time for the floor to become stable and stay flat. The entrance was showing the largest area of sinking and his plan was to raise it above the surrounding floor level and rely on the footfall to bring it down to the same level.

"So young Minnow, did you manage to follow the service?" It must have been a question he'd repeated many times that morning.

"What did others say when you asked the same thing?" asked Minnow. "There were a lot of people here, you must have been pleased." Minnow then told him about the areas of the floor that needed repair and his plans for solving the problem.

"Most people found my guidance helpful and did say they'd come again next Sunday. Hopefully you feel the same. Thanks for looking at the floor surface. Buildings can take a time to settle and I guess I'll be busy with little repairs for quite some time."

"You should have finished the floor", continued the priest, "and working in the church by the end of next week. What will you be doing after that? I know the knight will only be paying you until Saturday. Have you any plans beyond then?"

"There are no jobs at the farm with the rest of the build team that are returning there. I shall work at my cooking tools. They are being requested by some of the stall holders. My tools are taken to hamlets and villages around the area, some end up being sold in Reading."

"The biggest problem is sourcing the wood. I have bought some wood from the farm and have my own saw to make cutting lengths easier. I'm fortunate that I can recognise types of timber from the bark. Some woods make better cooking tools than others. Maybe that is why there's such a demand for them, people recognise that the equipment is of good quality and the best materials."

"I shall see you tomorrow Minnow, just after I have said Matins. Think about how the Sunday service could be more helpful. Thoughts are better from your point of view, you and the rest that are new to worship see things with fresh eyes."

On his way home Minnow thought a lot about Grandpapa, his life and how long he might spend in purgatory. No one had been able to tell him how long he'd have to recall his life here on earth, everything that he'd endured and experienced. Would having lost his son shorten his time there or could having bad thoughts about the King extend his time?

His own thoughts went to himself having spent time helping to build a church. Would that excuse him from having to serve time in purgatory? He felt he was being drawn into a whole religious scene that he'd have known nothing about without the build. This construction that had taught him so many practical skills but also raised complex thoughts.

What did Grandpapa do in his life that made God happy? Why was Grandpapa born? Why are any of us born?

These thoughts reminded him of the cook who was once an active member of the Church. Life experiences took away his faith in the ways of religion. Did he still believe God has a purpose for him?

He played an important part in my life so far, passing on skills and knowledge. Is that what life is about, helping people to be helpful to other people? That was Grandpapa. He not only did a full time skilled job but passed on other skills and knowledge to those around him.

How else would I know about trees, gathering seeds and planting. Add all that to the skills passed on by the king's men. Yes, they were only doing their job and used me to achieve their task. Now I have all this knowledge and where will it take me? Does God have a purpose for me?

When he arrived home there was work to be done on their plot of land. Papa had been busy collecting seeds and had started to bury the withered plants in a wide trench. Even when dead the plants would give back to the structure of the soil, help retain moisture and be a base for new growth in the spring.

Minnow started to dig another trench alongside the first, using the dug soil to cover the bottom of the plant waste trench. Mama was still chatting with some neighbours who had also been to church and between them were finding something to laugh about. Minnow couldn't recall anything about the service that was funny, they must be on another subject.

The group moved on and Mama soon appeared with some bread, cheese and cyder. They sat on the long seat that had been moved from the outside of Grandpapa's dwelling and enjoyed the weak sunshine. It was still just about warm enough without an extra layer of clothing but they all knew winter was on its way. Would life be any different this next year? What would the Church be offering that would make it memorable?

Chapter Thirty-Three – What Next?

Monday morning and after he'd lit the brazier, Minnow was busy adding bags of limestone to areas of the church floor. He pounded it down as well as he could then left it to settle. He'd go over the top with boards later.

On Sunday he'd noticed some gaps around the glass were needing his attention. The brazier was burning well and he set the melting iron to heat. He remembered he still had the diamond on its cord around his neck. Soon he was trimming the lead to fill gaps around the window frames.

There was no sign of the priest which Minnow found unusual. He'd been able to walk into the church and found there was no one keeping an eye on the pieces of equipment he still needed to complete the windows. Lots of people had been fascinated by the pieces of glass sheet and some had taken bits of scrap. They liked the idea that the glass would cut as well as a knife.

Minnow had to warn them that, like a knife, glass could cut their hands just as easily. It was difficult to make a handle for glass and it would shatter very easily. Most who took bits saw it as a novelty and wanted to share it with their families as the new material.

Minnow didn't tell them that glass had been used for hundreds of years and people over the Narrow Sea used it for storing wine. Being able to make it almost flat made it ideal for sealing openings without blocking the light. Shutters closed out the light in all the dwellings around Wocca's Hamlet.

Minnow had been busy for some time before the priest made his appearance. The farm manager had kept him longer than expected. He'd been offered Mary as a wife which had been quite a shock for him.

He'd never considered being married he told Minnow. He thought Mary was still quite young, very attractive and would make someone a suitable wife but she came with no dowry. He'd heard that the cook for the king's men had also been offered Mary as his wife but he didn't wish to burden a young girl with an old man like himself. There were expenses in taking a wife and being a priest gave him little income.

He added he was going to need a pony to reach the surrounding villages and hamlets. He would need to talk with the knight about stabling, feeding and harnessing and see if the deanery would fund that. He added that as a curate at Salisbury, should he have needed the use of a pony, he'd have used the priests'. Only one of them would have needed to travel outside the immediate parish at any one time.

Minnow didn't know how to respond. He'd thought often of Mary but she didn't deliver to Top Meadow any more. He'd not seen her at the Sunday service and had no way of contacting her.

Mama had said she'd seen her a few times when she'd been to the farm for items of food but had never had a look from her. Mary was always busy with tasks and avoided eye contact with anyone. Minnow had the feeling she was a slave with no chance of freedom.

If there was no dowry there was little chance either of escape from her routine life. The farm manager may have hoped for a rich person to make an offer for her as a wife and save him the cost of feeding her. Offering her to the priest and the cook sounded as if he was getting desperate to be rid of her. He hoped she would be found a good husband.

She'd have a young woman's appetite. Minnow knew he'd not have an income soon to support a wife. The farm manager would have to do his best for her. As far as Minnow knew she had no skills that would bring in an income. It looked as if she was stuck as a servant.

Minnow explained to the priest what he'd done with the limestone pieces and said he expected to level it on Saturday as his last job. He did say he thought more limestone pieces would still be needed in the future as the floor settled.

The priest excused himself again and said he'd be back to lock up after evensong. He gave the key to the tower to Minnow so that he could secure his equipment and spare glass behind the door and not have to wait for him to return.

Minnow was told to put the key on the floor behind the altar by one of the legs so that the bell could be rung for the evening service. The priest checked there wasn't anything else that he needed and left him to his work.

Minnow found he was thinking repeatedly of Mary and her situation. This would have been a time when talking with Grandpapa may have helped. Even the cook was beyond offering advice. He only occasionally saw him when he visited on a Sunday afternoon with his own news about learning to bake.

He didn't feel he was ready yet to talk with the priest who was too new to understand the relationship with the farm, its manager and how Mary was seen by the workers. She didn't attend church on a Sunday either which made it more difficult to know how she was. He would have to talk to Mama and see what she had as ideas to help Mary.

Saturday, and Minnow was adding more limestone to areas of the floor. Raised areas were pounded down, with the help of the boards, to give a smooth surface. He had finished the windows on Friday. Using a candle he had checked all the others for any signs of a draught that may suggest an area that could leak.

The king's man appeared and he also did a check of the windows. He looked pleased and said with a foreign accent, "Well done, Minnow."

"Thank you," Minnow replied as he handed back the diamond that he'd kept around his neck. He was going to miss the feel of the cord and the small weight of the stone set into the ring.

"You keep," said the king's man. "Thank you, you good work." He handed him his pay for the week and patted him on the shoulder. Minnow didn't know what to say. He'd not expected to be left with such an important and expensive tool.

"Are you sure?" asked Minnow.

"I not know 'sure', ring is Minnow ring."

"Thank you sir." He held out his hand to shake the hand of the king's man. They both shook hands and smiled.

Minnow tucked the ring with its diamond back under his shirt. He had no idea how he'd use it in the future but he appreciated the gift from the man who came from across the Narrow Sea.

The knight appeared and the two men started chatting. They took a walk around the inside of the building and checked all the work that had been done.

Minnow returned to pounding the board and flattening the limestone. He could see there would be more work needed in several areas in the future as the ground dried out and the limestone settled. He assumed workers from the farm would be called in to carry out future maintenance.

He'd have his own work creating cooking tools, involved with the dyeing and weaving of the wool, helping with their plot of land and the crop strip. He was still going to be busy but his life would be less interesting with no new skills to learn, that part he was going to miss.

The knight came to where he was working having said a long farewell to the king's man.

"You're still finding things to do here then Minnow. I understand you've been gifted the ring with its diamond. The king's man thought highly of you."

"Yes sir," he replied surprised the knight called him by his name. "The floor will need extra limestone for some time as people move back and forth over it. There's just dirt under the limestone and as it dries out the limestone will settle. Even if there was money for a mortar covering it would soon crack and fall apart until the whole under layer has finally settled. That will take several years."

"Perhaps the people of Wocca's Hamlet by then will be wealthy enough to pay for it to be done. The people have started to see how important this building is going to be to them. With the help of the priest it is bringing the people together. Sorry sir, I do tend to talk too much."

"For someone your age you've a good understanding of how things work. We have all been impressed by your ability to learn quickly and your attention to detail. This brings me on to what I needed to tell you. On Monday you're to report to the farm manager."

Minnow was shocked. He'd not expected a job on the farm. He knew a couple had signed up to join the crusade but their places had been filled, one had been his Papa who now had a regular job there.

"Will I be working with animals?" Minnow asked.

"Nothing like that," replied the knight, "the farm manager will give you the details on Monday. I must go, I still have things to do before I return to Sunning. Well done for completing the build for us. I'm sure I'll see you again." With that he left, again Minnow was full of unanswered questions.

The floor still needed his attention but with so many thoughts rolling around in his head he found it difficult to concentrate. What work would he have on the farm? He'd not have the arm reach to be a sawyer like his Grandpapa, he'd be lost in a ditch if involved in digging. It was clear he'd not be working with animals so that removed ploughing or harrowing or being a stable lad. He could think of no other farm work that he could be asked to do. He'd just have to wait until Monday.

He'd foolishly stopped moving to think and out the corner of his eye he saw a pigeon ambling in through the wide open doors. Returning to flattening the limestone produced enough noise to see it off. It must have been one that had been difficult to remove recently. It was likely looking for a sheltered place to see out the coming winter months. He'd have to warn the priest to not leave the doors open when the building was unattended.

Back at home Minnow shared his news with his parents and neither of them could suggest any farm jobs he could do on a regular basis. Men were not normally given jobs in a kitchen and not being involved with animals ruled out even being a butcher. They were just as mystified as himself but pleased that he'd be offered something now that the build has finished.

The priest looked in after the evening service to thank Minnow for leaving the key. Even he had no idea what Minnow would be asked to do at the farm on Monday.

After the service on Sunday Minnow met up with the baker. He had slipped into the service late and explained he would give God another chance to direct what he should become. He was content to be a baker, that should see him out for the rest of his days.

Wocca's Hamlet was a developing area and the bishop had vaguely suggested he'd establish a regular market when he returned from the crusade. If he returned from the crusade were his actual words.

Minnow asked the baker if he knew why he was to report to the farm on Monday. The baker knew nothing that would help solve the mystery either.

He went on to describe how the art of baking was very different to cooking on an open fire. There were extra processes involved that needed starting the day before baking, temperature was very important and so was time for the products to cook and cool. With fire cooking, people required the meal to be hot or at best warm. Baked products were mostly consumed cool or cold but he admitted warm bread did give off a special smell.

The old farm cook was very pleased to pass on her knowledge to him and have one less thing to manage in her busy kitchen. The place did become very crowded at times but they were managing. He sometimes persuaded Mary to help him, she was slowly starting to relax in his company and just occasionally had a short conversation with him. She's still very afraid of the farm manager and the cook would still not teach her any cooking skills.

Minnow's face lit up at Mary's name and he wondered if he'd catch a glimpse of her on Monday. He wasn't sure where on the farm he was supposed to meet the farm manager so he'd report to the farm yard and be directed from there. He was aware of having had a restless night's sleep on Saturday and could imagine it being no better on Sunday night.

As he left the church on Sunday he could not help but study the floor just inside the entrance and was pleased to see there was no obvious sign of any sinking. Give it a few weeks and he felt sure someone from the farm will be asked to add more stone to the depressions that he expected to have appeared. Maybe that might be one of his farm jobs. The knight didn't say who would be paying him either. That would be another question for Monday.

Chapter Thirty-Four – New Challenges

Minnow and his Papa left to walk to the farm together a little after daybreak. The air was cool and the sky thick with cloud that threatened to make any dawdlers wet. Both were prepared for rain and had their well greased top layers around their shoulders.

Minnow's Papa knew he was to be involved in moving cattle up from the ground that could sometimes flood, the part that always became very wet over the winter months. With Top Meadow taken by the church building, the farm manager had one less area to use.

Papa had been busy felling timber in a poor part of the forest that would eventually become added to the supply of pasture. The pigs were already in amongst the roots of the felled trees. In the spring the oxen would start to drag out the roots to clear the ground ready for its first planting.

At the farm yard Minnow was told to wait by the door to the kitchen. The farm manager organised the teams of workers and gave them their tasks for the morning. Minnow was surprised at the number of people the farm needed to work at the various jobs.

He did notice that a couple of men from the build were not in the yard and guessed they were the ones who had gone to be part of the crusade. A couple of women carrying buckets of milk came past him and made their way into the kitchen. Both gave him a studied look and then giggled to each other once they were past him.

He could not hear their comments but knew it would be something about his height. The farm manager finished giving his specific instructions to the last group. He then indicated that Minnow should follow him through the kitchen area.

The baker had been correct, the kitchen was a busy, crowded and noisy space as there was quite a bit of shouting. Minnow followed the farm manager into the next room that had a large table in the centre surrounded by many chairs. At one end of the table were stacks of parchment, each stack held in place by a large smooth stone.

"What is your given name boy?" asked the farm manager.

"Will", answered Minnow.

"And you prefer to be known as Minnow?"

"Yes master. If you ask for Minnow everyone knows it is me you're looking for."

"Have you been told what you'll be doing?"

"No master. It was the knight who told me to be here this morning but he didn't have time to explain why. The only thing he did say is that I would not be working with animals."

"We have a construction project for you but it will not be a dwelling. You will have noticed that the kitchen is a bit busy but it is not going to be made any larger. There's increasing demand for bread and as you're aware the cook from the build is now our baker. He needs his own ovens but away from our kitchen."

"The knight has confidence in you. He considers you will be able to build me new ovens. You will be taking over a dwelling up in The Clearing and building two ovens with a chimney."

"The first thing you will need to do is study the design and construction of my kitchen oven and produce your ideas. You will talk with the baker who will explain how the ovens work. You will tell me the materials you will require and how you intend to complete the job."

"The winter is a good time to do this as you will be working within the protection of a dwelling. You can request help occasionally but the farm work will have priority."

"You can start by going outside and studying the outside of the oven and the chimney. Once you've some idea of their method of assembly you can then talk with the baker who should have finished the main batch of bread by then. Any questions?"

Minnow was speechless and in a state of shock. Never would he have guessed he'd be faced with such a challenge. How did they know he could even make a start on putting together a thing he'd never been near or seen being used? When he was being told what to do he didn't have a problem. The other person was the expert, he just followed instructions. This was a whole new experience that involved the unknown.

"I'll go and study the outside of the oven and then talk with the cook, sorry the baker."

"He should be able to answer most of your questions. I'll talk with you again tomorrow. I have a busy day today."

Minnow was ushered back through the chaotic kitchen and out into the yard area. He went to the far side of the yard and studied the chimneys that rose above the roof of the farm dwelling.

Adjacent to the door of the kitchen he focussed on a particularly large bulge that narrowed to become a tall chimney. It appeared to be a deliberate addition to the rectangular shape of the dwelling. The build material wasn't obvious. To obtain such a curve he thought it would have to be shaped from a mould filled with limecrete or maybe using clay.

Minnow felt the outside surface and was aware of a gentle, even, warmth on all sides above his chest height. The curve was more than two times his extended arm lengths, but the lower part was cold to the touch. As he reached up higher the warmth was just as evenly spread all around the bulge.

The whole length at the end of the building and up to the top of the bulge, had been covered by a lean-to roof. It extended over the kitchen doorway and against the curve were stacked many lengths of firewood.

He found a ladder to climb and checked the heat at a higher point just below the lean-to roof. It was still warm there. Above the lean-to roof the shape became an obvious rectangular chimney set against the outside wall of the dwelling. With some difficulty he struggled onto the roof and felt the chimney. He was surprised that there was no heat at this point and there was no smoke emerging from the top of the chimney. There was heat coming from the bulge with no sign of fire.

Someone had thought to use the warmth to dry lengths of firewood so he concluded it didn't become so hot as to set it alight. He returned the ladder to the far side of the yard.

It was then that Mary appeared with a basket of laundry and started to drape the items over the stacked firewood surrounding the bulge. She didn't notice Minnow.

"Hello Mary", said Minnow quietly as he crept up behind her. She spun round and hit him hard across the face.

"Leave me alone", she shouted, "get on with your own work and let me do mine. Go away, you shouldn't be hanging around here." It was only at this stage that she recognised Minnow and added with less volume, "Sorry, I didn't expect there to be anyone out here. I shouldn't be talking to you, I'll be in trouble."

One of the kitchen girls looked out to see what Mary had been shouting about. Spotting Minnow, who she'd seen earlier with the farm manager, commented, "Oh Mary, were you lucky enough to be touched?"

Mary flapped a piece of wet washing at her and drove her back inside. This brought out more girls to study the scene of Mary with a stranger. Mary's face was starting to colour up, she grabbed the basket of washing and fled inside pushing past the small crowd of girls who were having a fine giggle.

"So which one of us do you fancy then," called one of the group who were now studying Minnow closely. "I'm quite short, Mary is too tall for you," she added mockingly. Minnow was saved by the elderly cook appearing and chiding them all back inside to get on with their work. Mary re-appeared to continue draping her washing over the firewood surrounding the sides of the bulge. She didn't look at Minnow.

"Do the clothes dry better there?" he asked from a short distance.

"This time of year they do," replied Mary cautiously, "it is the back of the bread oven and always has some warmth. The bit of roof gives some shelter if it does start to rain but any wind will blow the drips back on to the laundry. I have to keep an eye on the weather. Sorry, I hope I didn't hurt you too much. What are you doing here?"

"You did give me a hefty wallop, it shows you can look after yourself. My work on the church has finished and I have been told to study the build of the oven. I'm expected to be able to make a new one. To be honest I don't know where to start from just looking at the outside shape, even that looks like a bit of a challenge. I'm waiting for the baker to finish and then I can have a look inside."

"He has just put in the last batch so you will have some time to wait. I'm just about to clear up his work area".

"I'll see you later, I expect, when I'm allowed inside. Nice to see you again Mary".

"Bye Minnow".

Mary went back into the kitchen while Minnow gave more thought to how the shape could have been constructed. There was no heat below his chest height, the curve shape must be important, fire wasn't involved all the time but the oven had to be heated somehow. He still had no clue as to where a plan could start.

While he was waiting for the baker he took a look around the farm yard. There were a couple of dog kennels that had long chains attached. The chains were just short of meeting, it suggested each dog could guard their half without meeting and fighting.

He never had much time for dogs, you could not read their mood or tell when they might turn on you. Once he'd been jumped by a dog while walking and gnawing on a cooked chicken bone. He always gave them a wide path since.

There were several doors around the yard and most had locks or chains to secure them. There was one that wasn't secured. As he was wondering what could be left unlocked a farm worker appeared and went in, closing the door firmly behind him. From the sounds that came through the door he knew at once what it was used for.

In a short time the man emerged, adjusted his clothing and went off to his task. Minnow followed the man for a short distance and noticed at the back of the unlocked latrine was a pig enjoying the gift left by the farm worker. So nothing goes to waste on a farm. Beside the pig pen there was a heap of waste floor rushes and straw. This he did know was taken to be put on the land before it was ploughed, to add back things that the planting had taken out.

Minnow heard his name being called and he recognised it was the baker calling him. He made his way back to the yard.

"So do you know what you're to be doing young Minnow?"

"The farm manager has told me but not how I'm to do it. He said he wants me to tell him how I'll be making him two ovens to be built in a dwelling on The Clearing."

"Well, I'm quite excited," suggested the baker, "two ovens and space to move. Once you see inside the oven I think you will soon form an idea of how to construct them. Let's go in and take a look. I'll explain the baking process as well so that you've the full picture."

It was hot in the kitchen despite the coolness of the day outside. It was also busy with every girl concentrating on each of their tasks. There was no sign of Mary, no doubt she was working in another part of the farm dwelling.

Minnow studied the front of the oven and saw only a blackened opening with an open store for kindling underneath. Sticking out into the kitchen above the oven was a curved metal hood that he assumed led up to the chimney.

Looking into the oven he could still feel a lot of heat but could see no other opening. The roof inside was curved all round like the inside of a very large upturned clay mixing bowl. How was he supposed to build anything like that? It would just fall in on itself and yet this oven was still solid.

"Let me explain how it is used," suggested the baker. "Lots of kindling size sticks are used to heat the inside, logs don't seem to do the same job. As you can see from the black around the opening the smoke comes out and then is caught by the hood and sent up the chimney."

"I often bundle the sticks into tightly bound faggots, put one each side and put a couple right at the back. Once they are ash I scrape out the bits then use a damp cloth on the end of a stick to mop and clean the floor. I'm then ready to bake. When the bread dough is in I put the wooden door across the opening to prevent too much heat being lost."

"Depending on the size of the loaves it doesn't take too long to cook and then more can be cooked. This oven is used several times, once it has been heated. A good oven keeps its heat so the construction uses a lot of material that releases the heat slowly. This oven has been made from clay bricks. Look closely inside and you can see the edges."

Minnow studied the inside more closely with the aid of a lit candle and made out the brick edges just about visible through the soot. He recalled the arches that were constructed in the church that they all felt would fall down once the timber supports were removed.

This was quite a small space and building a timber support would be difficult to remove. He'd have to think of some other method to provide support while it was being built, something easily removable but also able to keep the bricks in place as the mortar dried.

Wocca's Hamlet had clay pits and they made bricks so that would be no problem. Clay could also be used between the layers of bricks if it would help store the heat. He'd tried making a clay pot at home and knew the clay would crack if it was dried too quickly. More clay would easily fill the cracks and could make the end item stronger if it was slowly baked.

The base was also going to be tricky. This oven had a space under it for firewood storage. He could see the need to build another supporting dome that then would become the flat surface for the oven floor.

He'd been told there were going to be two ovens. Were they needed side by side, one above the other, back to back or two completely separate ovens? Would the base be stone blocks or expensive bricks? The blacksmith should be able to make another hood to collect the woodsmoke.

An oven would be a source of heat for a dwelling in winter but would it be too much in the warmth of the summer? The dwelling would need extra openings to keep the inside cool in the summer.

Dwellings had dry thatched roofs so there would have to be a good height chimney to carry away any sparks that came from heating the oven. Positioning the ovens in the centre of the dwelling would give the maximum distance to the inside of the thatch. Here, this kitchen had a second floor above so there was no thatch to catch any sparks or flames.

Minnow outlined his thinking to the baker who could find no fault with any of his conclusions.

"You also have a good list of options," he added, "the farm manager will know you've taken this seriously. How would a curved pile of damp sand work as a support for the dome shape? It could easily be removed once the mortar and the clay had set between the bricks."

"Brilliant idea," said Minnow with a huge grin over his face, "I can see we will make a good team with this challenge."

"Don't count on me being able to do much to help. My baking takes most of my time. I'll soon have to start preparing the bread mixture for tomorrow and I still need to order bags of flour from the miller for next week."

"Then I need to see the boy who collects the kindling. He has been selling some of the wood he has been collecting for me so I have to issue a severe warning. He does know I can find a replacement boy very easily, he will have to work twice as hard for me for the rest of the week."

Minnow fleetingly recalled when he first met the cook and helped gather firewood. So much had happened over those years and he was now being considered as a person of knowledge and skill.

He was still not sure he fully knew what he'd discuss with the farm manager in the morning. There were enough ideas to make a start. That in itself gave him some confidence.

Minnow let the baker continue with his work and he studied the lower area of the oven. He could see that the baker would need to work at waist height, able to bend just enough to check on the loaves and remove them easily. He thought the work area outside the oven could be larger so that the bread could be moved out and pushed to the side before being moved away completely to cool.

It would need extra materials but with two ovens to manage every bit of extra surface space would help. The under space was also topped off inside with a dome shape. Here he could build a wooden platform, put the pile of sand on that, before adding the bricks and mortar. A flat double layer of heat bricks should form a good base for the ovens.

Minnow was now becoming quite excited by the challenge and was sorry he'd have to wait until the morning to discuss it with the farm manager. The only other thing to include was the chimney which again would need to be made from bricks.

As far as he knew bricks didn't split and shatter like stones did when heated. Bricks would also separate the heat from the thatch. At home they'd a good layer of clay over the hearth stones but some stones would occasionally crack with a loud bang. Bricks and clay would have to be the main materials for the oven construction.

Minnow was ready to share his concluding ideas with the baker who looked as if he'd finished the dough preparation. He'd covered it with a cloth while it lay in the simple wooden trough.

"Do you've a few minutes for me to talk through my final ideas? I promise I'll be quick," added Minnow.

The baker listened and replied, "It sounds good to me. All you've to do now is convince the farm manager. When do you have to see him?"

"In the morning. It will give me time to think of anything that I have forgotten. Thanks for listening."

"Come and see me early tomorrow and I'll also think about anything you may have missed. You will have to try and make yourself invisible in the kitchen when you come in. It is a very busy place in the mornings."

"Thanks," said Minnow, "I understand what you're saying. I'll let you get on now while I have another look outside and see if I have overlooked anything."

Chapter Thirty-Five – Room to Move

Back at home Minnow put together his plans in his head and only added a foundation to his construction details. He talked it over with his Mama and Papa before they settled for the night.

Papa added that he could not have come up with such a comprehensive scheme and he felt proud of having a son who could look at things in such detail. Mama said she knew he'd make a success of it, his Grandmama had been a skilful planner. He must be following her as a thinker. Minnow went off to sleep easily and happy with his ideas.

In the morning there wasn't anything that the baker could add. Minnow was able to be in and out of the kitchen very quickly, even before the cook even registered he was there. He again checked the heat on the outside of the ovens. It was similar to the day before when he'd studied it, much later in the day.

The farm workers were gathered waiting for the farm manager to issue their instructions. Some recognised Minnow and asked what he'd be doing on the farm. Minnow just said he was here to see the farm manager who may have a job for him. They speculated on which team he could join but dismissed most work areas due to his size.

Minnow wasn't upset and just smiled at their list of rejections. The farm manager appeared and quickly sent off the teams. When it was just Minnow left standing in the yard he told him to follow him through the kitchen into the room with the big table.

There was still evidence of breakfast which Mary was clearing.

"Hurry up girl, this should have been finished by now. I've never known such an idle wench. Move, get on with it. Tell cook I do not wish to be disturbed. Don't just stand there. Do as you're told, and do it now!"

Minnow didn't like to hear Mary being treated in such a way but knew better than make it obvious he was concerned. He looked around the room so as not to make eye contact with either of them. He only looked at the farm manager when he said, "Well then, what have you for me?"

Minnow had practised this in his head and soon had his plans explained in detail. "Any questions?" he asked the farm manager.

"Considering that you've only had a day to put together your ideas I think you've come up with a workable plan. You've added some good ideas to the basic request that make a lot of sense. Did the baker suggest the extra work area in front of the oven opening?"

"I just watched him working and thought that would be what I would need if I was doing the job. I also thought I would build in grooves to slide the wooden doors into place."

"You planned all this from just studying my bread oven being used?"

"I hope the plans meet your requirements. The ovens should fit into a dwelling but a double dwelling would make more sense. Ovens give up their heat slowly. In the winter there would be left over heat to warm a two dwelling space. The baker would need a work, storage and selling space as well as a living area. Storage would include space for lots of kindling wood as well as a raised area for bags of flour," added Minnow.

"You're correct about the size needed for the dwelling and you've thought deeper about the project than I would have expected to come from someone who has never undertaken such a task before. Now let me see if you've plans for the first step," challenged the farm manager.

Minnow took a short time to gather his thoughts before replying. "I would like to see the pair of dwellings that will be used and then obtain an idea of how large I could make the ovens. I need to visit the brick maker and see the size of the bricks he produces before I start to work out roughly how many bricks could be required. I have no knowledge of bricks other than they are made from clay dug from the ground and set to dry."

"I have seen the blacksmith has used special bricks for his forge that can become very hot. They do not crack and shatter like stone would. I'll need dry lime and sand to be ordered. I'll need some tools, a water barrel along with boards that the mortar will be mixed on."

"The dwelling should be able to keep the sacks of lime dry, stacked on more boards once it is delivered and should be secure when I'm not working there. Later I'll require a platform to stand on that can be raised as work is done on the chimney. I think those are the main things for the moment."

"You've a plan and I have confidence in you, Minnow." He shouted for the cook who shuffled into the room.

"This is Minnow, he's working for me and will be entitled to midday food along with the other farm workers. He has a special project so may not always be eating here with the others so you're to ensure he is fed. Sometimes it may need to be delivered. I hope you understand."

"Yes master," answered the cook having taken a deep breath before answering. Yet another mouth to feed and still no space to move she thought.

"Bring us a drink, nothing too strong. It has been a while since breakfast."

"Could I have a drink of milk if possible please?" requested Minnow.

"That we have plenty of," suggested the cook, "watered wine for you master?"

"That will do."

"If you've any problems with her or anyone else let me know and I'll sort it out. We are not used to taking on new people and they'll need time to get used to you being around. You know the baker so if you talk with him when I'm not around he will pass on a message."

"After something to eat with the others the baker will take you to look at the dwelling we are going to use. It is mid way along The Clearing and still needs stripping out. That will be your first task while I arrange for us to visit the brick maker."

The cook arrived with the drinks which the farm manager drank swiftly.

"I have to walk around the fields and check on the workers," explained the farm manager. "You can watch the baker, especially how he manages the oven. You may get some more ideas."

With that he stood up and left Minnow finishing his milk. Minnow gathered the two tankards and took them to the kitchen.

"Where would you like these?" he asked the cook.

"That's the girl's job, you should have left them on the table. You can take them over to the girl through there," she said indicating an opening beyond the huge fireplace with its several simmering pots hanging from chains.

"Hello Mary," he said before he was even through the doorway. He was stood back far enough not to be hit again. Mary turned around slowly and then returned to her pot cleaning.

"What are you doing here?" she whispered without looking at him.

"I have brought you a couple of tankards to clean. I have been given a job by the farm manager but it is not on the land or with any of the animals."

"You working here in the kitchen? We don't have space for any more, we're falling over each other as it is, especially now the baker has his job here."

It was relatively quiet in the scullery area so Minnow was able to tell Mary what he was being asked to do without being obviously in the way of others. He was given a hard stare when a girl brought in another pot for Mary to clean and he was aware of chatter amongst the girls describing what had just been witnessed. Mary just kept scrubbing at the pots and listened as Minnow chatted.

"Do you really know what you're doing? An oven is very different to a church. Have you been taught anything about building ovens?" Mary asked sounding concerned.

"I just know I can do it. The farm manager likes my plans and I'm off with the baker to see the dwelling that will become the bakery after we have had some food here with the rest of you. Do you have your food with everyone else?" Minnow asked. He was unsure having seen how she'd been treated earlier.

"I have to wait my turn which is near the end, after the men have gone, then all the girls get to have what is left. You will be gone by then. I have to get these pots to dry off outside, you need to stand to one side and no please don't try and help me. I'll never hear the end of it from the other girls."

Minnow moved aside and noticed food being taken through to the large table in the next room. He joined the baker and they both went through to start eating. Quickly more men joined them and the level of talk increased to such a level it was difficult to hear what was being said by the person next to you.

The baker indicated that they should make a move to go up to The Clearing and inspect the empty dwelling. Minnow grabbed a last hunk of the freshly baked bread and followed back through the kitchen where he gave Mary a nod and then kept moving. She looked away very quickly but Minnow thought he saw the signs of a blush starting to spread over her face.

It was good to get outside into the cool of the afternoon. The kitchen hadn't only been busy but the surrounding heat was something Minnow wasn't used to experiencing. He understood direct heat from a hearth where you had to turn your body to warm the other side. Being in an area where you could only escape the heat by going outside was a completely new experience.

Minnow used the walk to explain to the baker some of the additional thoughts he had about the design that the farm manager had accepted. The baker confirmed he could not wait to be out of the confined kitchen and start using the new ovens.

The inside of the chosen dwelling was almost falling in. It had obviously been used by travellers as a shelter for sleeping and leaving their mess. The first task would be to make it secure. Board up all the openings, have just one door that could be locked and then work on removing the partition between the two dwellings.

There would be a lot of work before any oven building could start. Minnow made himself a list in his head of materials he'd need from the farm. The baker said he'd report back to the farm manager with Minnow's list and suggest that a cart would be needed to make the delivery. While that was being arranged Minnow would set about cleaning out some of the debris.

There wasn't anything of value left as people had helped themselves to everything that had some use. That was why there were no doors, even the hearth stones had been taken away. There were holes in the partition between the dwellings as if someone was going to return and take away the timbers that made up the frame. Minnow decided he'd use most of these timbers to close up the various openings and some could be used towards constructing a door. The few remaining timbers that had divided off each of the animal areas were holding up the roof, thankfully they'd not been taken.

He was going to need the few tools that he had at his own dwelling, the saw, axe, rake and hammer. They didn't have many tools but they'd be a start before asking for additional items from the farm.

The next morning his Mama helped to carry his bedding so he could spend the night guarding the dwelling. She promised to bring him some food before dark.

Minnow set about raking out the rubbish from the two dwellings to make a heap at the back where there was little left of any planting. It had been 'help yourself' to the produce that was once a reasonably productive piece of land.

The area was starting to be very overgrown with weeds and brambles. It was too late in the season to find any blackberries but there could be a good crop next year if the weeds didn't choke them.

The partition timbers had been well constructed and it took a lot of hard effort to locate the wooden pegs and knock them out to release each piece. In amongst the rubbish he raked out he'd found an old solid pot handle that was slightly smaller across than a wooden peg. He'd used this to help hammer the wooden fastenings clear.

A few crucial timbers were left to hold up the roof. The rest he sorted into their various sizes and started to wedge some into the numerous openings that would need boards to fully close them off.

The farm manager arrived late morning with Mary beside him. She was carrying a basket of food for Minnow. She put down the basket and made her way back to the farm without saying a word. The farm manager had a look around, asked Minnow what was needed urgently and how long he'd need to make the dwellings secure.

Minnow explained about needing some planking to cover openings and to be able to construct a door. Some iron nails would be needed along with some hinges and a door lock.

Minnow said he'd spend the night at the dwelling to prevent any further items being taken away now that he'd stacked the partition timbers. He would include some of those as part of the door. At this stage he'd continue salvaging materials and perform a good clean round.

By the end of the next day he hoped the dwelling would be secure. The farm manager agreed to send up some planks and the other bits by mid afternoon. The hinges and a door lock could take a bit longer.

Minnow was surprised that all the requested items arrived a bit later accompanied by the baker who led the pony and light cart.

"I can't stay long," explained the baker, "I have dough to prepare but I can give you a hand to unload. The farm manager hopes the hinges and lock are suitable."

Once all the items had been moved into the dwelling Minnow asked if the baker had any further thoughts about the design ideas. Minnow suggested that the oven openings should face the track. If the baker was on his own he'd then not be hidden behind the ovens where he may not be aware of people coming in to buy.

The baker agreed with his thinking and added he'd like a living area with a securable door out to the back of the dwelling. It would not need a lock, a simple bar system would be fine. Minnow asked if the baker would be keeping any animals that would need some space as he didn't think it could be fitted within even a double dwelling that had two ovens, a preparation area, storage, a hearth, a trading top and all the equipment that went with being a baker. The baker agreed that if animals were required at a later time he'd request an outbuilding.

Minnow chose the door frame closest to the Reading track end of The Clearing to become the main door. Using the saw he cut planks that would become the door that opened outwards. A 'Z' shape structure, that would take a top and bottom hinge, was soon cut to size and the planks were quickly secured in place. The iron nails were long enough to bend over on the inside and prevent the planks being wrenched off from the outside.

The lock was going to be a bit more of a problem. He could secure it to the door but it needed a hole cut for the key through the edge plank.

Fortunately with the door opening outwards there was no need to cut or build a socket for the lock bolt that appeared when the key was turned.

Minnow remembered he'd a good knife that had lasted well since he had the help of the cook to attach the handle. He'd replaced the leather binding just once but the blade held its edge well. He was soon attacking the plank with his knife and quickly had a key shaped hole.

The lock was attached and the nails made secure by again being bent over. Minnow used the key from both sides then closed the door and checked it was secure first on the inside and finally from the outside. He found he'd an audience of small children who laughed and clapped when he locked the door and then could not force his way back in until he'd used the key successfully. Minnow gave a huge smile and promptly disappeared from view by locking himself inside.

There were a lot of openings still to secure that he would complete the next day. Collecting together the offcuts from making the door he moved them closer to where there would be least work in putting them in place. Darkness prevented further work so he settled to a restless sleep.

The following day the building was secure and he could spend the night at home. He was looking forward to having a hot meal and a good night's sleep. He was surprised to find the priest had been invited to have a meal with them and he'd brought a skin of wine to share.

There had occasionally been some wine at the build but often just the leftovers from the king's men. Minnow had previously only had small amounts but this evening there was quite a bit for each of them. He quickly became light headed and giggly. He was also hungry after his two days away and the food was still being cooked.

The wine had a sharp taste but with several fruit aromas. Mama prevented him from having more drink after seeing his change of behaviour and insisted he had some bread before eating the cooked meal.

He tucked in greedily and was soon belching from having eaten too quickly.

The priest talked a lot about his former life but Minnow was only half listening. He was so tired and was finding it difficult to stay awake. Once he'd eaten he made his way quietly to his pallet and immediately fell asleep. He woke well after light and was desperate for a drink. His head ached as never before and he felt very unwell.

Chapter Thirty-Six - Plans

"It's time you'd started work," said Mama. "Papa went to the farm ages ago. Did you have too much wine last evening?"

"I don't feel well, could it be the wine?" he asked groggily.

"Drink some milk, I have just bought some so it is fresh. You had better grab some bread and go to your job. I've never known you be so late up of a morning. Perhaps you need to avoid wine in the future or just take less of it on an empty stomach. Off you go, move."

Minnow grabbed the milk and a crust and staggered out of the dwelling. The key was still in his shoulder bag and the tools he needed would be in the bakery shell. He was due to visit the brick maker sometime today and he hoped the farm manager wasn't waiting for him. He unlocked the door and had started to mark out the hearth area and the oven bases with grooves in the dirt floor when the farm manager arrived.

"Show me where you plan to put things Minnow," he demanded. Minnow tried hard to concentrate and make the picture complete.

"Sounds good to me and the dwelling is secure."

After locking the door they made their way to Clay Lane and the brick maker. The farm manager introduced Minnow and explained that he'd the authority to place orders for bricks. He'd be needing construction bricks and some hearth bricks to make into an oven. The hearth bricks needed to be of the type used by the blacksmith that could withstand heat without cracking.

There would also be a need for fresh clay at different times. Minnow and the brick maker would keep a tally separately of how many bricks were supplied and there should be an agreement at the end. He warned Minnow he could make a rough count of bricks used and didn't expect to be sold more bricks than had been used. He made sure the brick maker heard every word.

It would take several weeks for hearth bricks to be made as they were only provided by special request. Minnow would need to estimate the number required before anything else.

Construction bricks could be delivered whenever he needed them along with clay. Minnow asked to take away a sample brick so he could calculate the number he'd need to be able to make a start.

He would have time to make a count of the number of bricks needed for the base of the ovens plus a few spare that would later be part of the chimney. He could easily do this before the cart arrived the next afternoon with his first supply of lime and sand along with a water barrel. There would also be a couple of boards, one for the mixing and the other to help keep the bags off any dampness in the ground.

Minnow finished the marking out which was now more accurate thanks to the sample brick. The foundation would be solid and four brick layers deep. Estimating the number to support the floor of the ovens and their front shelves would be a little more of a guess. For the oven floor, two layers would have to be the special bricks.

Once he'd marked out the base he could easily calculate the heat bricks needed for the ovens as they'd be a similar shape, just with extra layers to hold the heat along with lots of clay that would need slow drying and lots of crack filling.

Minnow dug out the pit for the foundation, to include some extra space for the mortar, double checked the brick count, locked up and went to the clay pits to place his first brick order.

The brick maker promised delivery first thing in the morning. With nothing else to do he went home and promised himself an early night. His head still throbbed, he wasn't interested in having wine again.

Well rested the next morning he arrived and unlocked at the same time as the cart delivering the construction bricks drew to a stop. The carter unhitched the pony and tipped the bricks onto the track. Minnow selected the broken bricks and put them back onto the cart as quickly as he could. The farm manager was only buying whole bricks and the carter could explain how the bricks became broken to the brick maker.

As he stacked the bricks inside the dwelling he counted them and wrote the number with a burnt stick on the inside of the far end wall. While waiting for the other supplies Minnow fetched a couple of buckets of water. He was sure the barrel would arrive empty and that would delay his start with mixing the mortar.

While he waited he took a wander around the patch of land that went with the dwellings and discovered a few root vegetables that had been overlooked. There were no apples left on the trees, most were rotting on the ground. The edge bushes were ragged but there were no gaps that needed layering to close them. He could bring in their pig to churn the ground, perhaps the baker would let someone make good use of the land. He'd have little time to do much himself, baking for the expanding town.

The next few days went very smoothly for Minnow. Mama had been around to gather the root vegetables. Papa delivered the pig and checked it could not escape, not that it needed to as there was so much for it to feed on. Minnow worked until it was dark and slept at the dwelling. Mary brought his lunch each midday and took messages back to the farm manager.

Each day he managed to get her to stay a short while by describing what he was doing and answering her questions. He was surprised at how quickly she understood and often added more searching questions about the methods he was employing. Minnow looked forward to her arrival each day but understood why she needed to hasten back to the farm.

The only breaks he'd had were to gather water and place orders with the brick maker. Mama supplied his evening meal and checked he'd enough for the start of the day. He was quite enjoying his style of living despite it being surrounded by his work. The lower storage domes worked perfectly on their mound of damp sand supported by their wooden table. Things were going well.

The special bricks were due for delivery and arrived as promised. This time they'd be taken off individually, they were too expensive to be broken by a careless carter. Minnow was surprised how light they felt compared with the construction bricks. Some still had a warmth to them. Minnow added the count to a separate wall.

When Mary arrived she announced that the farm manager would be there after his lunch to check on progress so she'd better not stay and chat. They must have passed each other as he arrived very soon after she left.

He studied Minnow's work and was pleased with the neatness and attention to detail. He handled one of the special bricks and commented on the weight. When he caught sight of the pig on the back patch of land he asked where it had come from. Minnow explained and was praised for his thinking.

"Can I ask you something that is not to do with the ovens?" enquired Minnow. "I know you're always busy but it is just a thought I've had and you will need some time to think about my idea."

"You're in luck today, I have an assistant who I wish to leave in charge without me being around. So, what is your question?"

"Can my parents talk with you about me marrying Mary?"

The question was met with stunned silence and the farm manager just stared at Minnow. There was no clue to the thoughts that may have been going through his mind, but it was obvious he was struggling to make a response.

"I hope you've not touched her, or brought shame on her. I've done my best to protect her and bring her up to be worthy for marriage. I shall not be giving her away but be aware she comes with no dowry. She's my ward and has cost me to raise her since her mother died. I will talk with your parents, I doubt you will be able to pay me her worth. They can call on me this evening."

"Thank you," was all that Minnow needed to say. That she was treated as a slave, didn't need payment other than feeding and providing with shelter were just the start. With her having no dowry, that two others had rejected her when offered in marriage, no family would consider Mary suitable for a son were thoughts he didn't voice.

"I shall require more sand and lime at the start of next week," Minnow added diplomatically as a return to the subject of oven construction.

"You're a bright lad, I like you and your skills impress me. Your question was quite unexpected and I need time to think about your suggestion. Yes, sand and lime can be with you by Monday afternoon. I'll expect your parents later today."

Minnow was surprised at his own boldness and struggled to control the small shakes that came with his excitement. Something had come over him and used his voice. They were words he wished to say but hadn't rehearsed or even planned them. This wasn't the first time his words had seemed to come from nowhere. One day such an outflow would give him trouble. Maybe this would be the time. How would his parents react?

The farm manager took a final look around without further comment and left Minnow to consider the implications of what he'd put in motion. Now he needed to talk with his Mama and prepare her. He decided he'd finish up early and make his way home before his Papa arrived in from his work.

Look around you, he told himself, there's work to be done. Minnow set about laying down mortar for the two layers of heat bricks to form the base to the ovens on top of the supporting structure. He ensured each brick was laid over the join of the under layer. It was done almost without thinking until he recalled having first seen the technique used for the lower wall on the foundations of the church all those years ago.

Here he was now, considering the ultimate role of being a man and sharing his life in marriage. The two layers would need time to set so it would be a good time to finish early and discover the reaction of his Mama.

Minnow's arrival at the dwelling was unexpected but welcome. Mama had finished turning the damp clothes on the bushes to catch the last of the afternoon sun and was stirring the pot that was simmering over the fire.

"There was an ox tail that no one wanted at the farm today and the butcher took off the skin for me," Mama announced as Minnow stepped through the door. "It's been in the pot since mid morning so it will add some good flavour to our meal. Have you come to eat or is there a problem?"

"I think I may have caused you and Papa a bit of a problem. I wish to have Mary as my wife, if she'd consider me suitable. I have dared to mention it to the farm manager who says he can talk with you both this evening."

"He mentioned that he didn't think we could afford her despite her having no dowry. You did tell me that you could find no family that would consider me as a husband for a daughter. I talk often with Mary and we like each other. It's my hope that this would be a suitable arrangement that you both could agree to happening. I'm not sure what he meant by being able to afford her."

"I must admit it has not come as a complete shock to me. I have noticed the two of you have chatted. It may come as a shock to your Papa however. You can go and meet him from the farm and tell him as you walk back together." Mama returned to checking the contents of the pot as Minnow set off towards the farm.

Papa had just started on his walk home and was surprised to see Minnow.

"Not working, we hardly see you from one day to the next?" said Papa. Minnow explained the reason he needed to talk with him and Papa quickly understood why he should be involved.

"I agree it seems strange that we may not be able to afford her if she has no dowry to bring. It's not as if he's given her any particular skills, he treats her badly and I often see her in tears. Does she have feelings for you Minnow?"

"That could be a problem. I don't want to ask her before you both have talked with the farm manager. I would not wish to say anything that may never happen. First I would need your agreement, then the agreement of the farm manager and the terms he'd put in place. Only then should I speak with Mary and see if she was agreeable." Minnow saw problems which ever way he approached the situation.

Mama had the bowls of stew set on the trestle for them as they walked in the dwelling. Bread had been torn into pieces and they all sat to eat as quickly as possible.

"We will just have to see what the farm manager says," commented Papa. "He may have had time to see this as a solution that saves him having to pay for Mary's keep."

At the farm they were kept waiting while a meal was finished and they were then shown into the cleared room. The farm manager sat at the end of the long table and indicated the chairs either side of him for

Minnow's parents. Minnow took the chair at the far end of the table facing the farm manager.

"Our son has asked our permission to talk with Mary about marriage," said Papa. "We would be happy that they married but she's your ward and you would need to also agree."

"She is my ward and a very attractive young woman who is deserving of a good arrangement. She has been protected from any male attention and is in perfect condition. My plans are for a match with a person of status. There were some young squires with the king's men who could be suitable. They are due to return for some of their training."

"Because I protect her and keep her busy they'll not have had opportunity to meet her yet but it is still within my long term plan. Mary is not available for marriage at the present time." The farm manager sat back and gave Minnow a strange smile.

Mama gave a slight tap on the trestle and obtained the farm manager's attention.

"You suggested to Minnow that Mary had no dowry. Would any young squire be interested in a woman who came with no dowry and no parents to have given her guidance? Has she had any training in the duties of a wife, has she had charge of young children, can she cook, what skills does she have to bring to a marriage?"

The farm manager started to look a little uneasy, he wasn't used to talking with such a forthright woman. She was correct but he was reluctant to agree. He needed to turn this to his advantage. He recalled he'd suggested to Minnow that he may not be able to afford her, perhaps he could still profit from the situation.

"I may consider selling my wardship to you, she has cost me over the years to keep, feed and clothe. This is what I needed to explain to you both and why I asked you to come and see me. There are two of you earning so you must have put aside some coin."

Papa started to fidget on his seat and looked across at Mama. She'd a fixed stare on the farm manager and didn't see the look from his Papa. Minnow felt for the ring he always carried around his neck and started to consider how much it may be worth. Before he even opened his mouth his Mama started her response.

"I can see we are wasting your time. You've plans in place to sell her as you would one of your farm animals as breeding stock. We came here to consider the future for two young people, we as parents and you as a guardian. We can see that you can only operate as a farmer, which I suppose comes most naturally to you. Investments are made and you expect a return for your capital which is understandable."

"You're investing in Minnow's skills to bring a steady return from bread sales and you provide similarly for the community in many ways. We wish you good fortune in persuading a young squire to acquire Mary and accept her without you providing skills or a dowry. We had better not take any more of your time, thank you for meeting with us."

Minnow's mouth was operating like the gills of a gasping fish but was unable to form words to follow Mama's summation. The farm manager was unable to respond either. He stood and moved to the door, opening it to allow them to make their way home as night fell around them.

"I hope he feels ashamed of his attitude towards Mary," whispered Mama. "It's no wonder he has the reputation for being astute but mean."

"Mama, you forget I have a valuable ring given to me by one of the king's men," said Minnow quietly. "I was going to offer it as the payment he was demanding."

"Don't you even consider it, young man. There's no way even the simplest thinking young squire would be allowed to consider Mary despite her good looks. Squires are answerable to a knight or lord and they'd quickly dismiss a girl with Mary's background. I'm not saying you would not suit each other but your circumstances are very different to that of a squire. I believe you would be a good match. He will have to think long and hard on what we have said. I consider he will agree to the match if we are patient."

Papa said nothing more than that he agreed and added, "you were most impressive in your dealings with him."

"Years of experience bartering prices for provisions from him. Sometimes he needs time to think and other times I can confuse him by changing offers I make for a combination of items. I have learnt to have a quick tongue and the more I mix the items I have interest in, offer to take more of one than another and then change back to other combinations he starts to become flustered. Before he can think about how much he eventually charges me I start to ask about other items he has for sale, when will be the next time he expects an item to be available along with other bits of gossip and distraction."

"I have bagged up my purchases, handed over my coins and left before he can calculate what I have paid for. I don't cheat him, he has a fair price for his products but I'll not let him overcharge me like he does to some others."

"I knew I married you for a reason," said Papa smiling to himself in the dark. Minnow remained confused, there were times when she was too quick for him as well.

Chapter Thirty-Seven – A Special Christmas

Minnow returned to the oven construction after a bite to eat the next morning. The days were becoming shorter and he needed what little daylight that crept into the dwelling to be able to concentrate on the dome that would hold the heat and bake the bread.

He'd be using the damp clay along with the fire bricks but could only build up a first layer. It would then need at least a week to dry enough before he gave it some gentle heat from some hot ash to help cure the clay, bind the bricks and reduce any cracking to the minimum. At least there were two ovens so he could let one dry a bit while he worked on the other.

He could also work on the hearth with some of the fire bricks and clay so there was plenty to do. He planned the hearth close to the ovens so that its smoke could also be directed towards the chimney. He had yet to submit his chimney hoods designs to the blacksmith but knew that a wide rectangle could be produced that would taper up to a simple square that he'd incorporate into the brick chimney.

No smoky dwelling for the baker but he'd need to be aware of the air flow and sometimes juggle with three fires. A thought occurred to him to extend the working surface at one end of the ovens to enable the baker to sweep the hot ash sideways from inside the ovens directly onto the hearth.

A shadow filled the doorway and took away some of the daylight. Minnow looked around and saw Mary in the door frame.

"Come in Mary, it's good to see you. Have you a message for me?"

"Hello Minnow," she said quietly. "The farm manager will be here this afternoon with the blacksmith to talk about your fire hood plans. Were you at the farm last evening with your parents? I heard your voice along with a man and a woman talking with the farm manager. I couldn't make out what you were saying but you were not there that long if it was you."

Minnow gave a little thought about what he should say next. He decided to tell Mary a little of what was said.

"My parents were asking for his permission to let me marry you Mary."

"Why would you consider marrying me?" she gasped. "I'm but a serving girl with no chance of a dowry and no taught skills. I have been offered to at least two others who declined to consider me as a wife. I would never have thought that you may have feelings for me as a potential wife. I know we are no longer children, are we of an age to marry?"

Minnow smiled, nodded and asked, "Would you consider being my wife Mary? I don't know how it could be arranged, the farm manager says he has plans for you but it may be a ploy to try and turn the situation to his advantage. It would be good to know if you would consider me as suitable."

"Minnow, you're the only person I can relax with and talk to without feeling trapped or bullied. I would like to get to know you better and I think we could make a relationship. What you've told me has come as a shock, a shock in a pleasurable way. I thought I was to be a farm serving girl all my life. You're given me the possibility of a future."

"We will have to wait to see what the farm manager has in the way of plans for me," Mary continued. "I only heard I had been offered to other men from gossip from the other girls who then walked away with a snigger."

"Give it some thought Mary but don't get your hopes too high. Thanks for the message about the blacksmith. You had best get back quickly or you may be asked what has taken you so long. Hope you get sent with more messages, I do enjoy seeing you."

Mary slipped out through the doorway and set off at a trot back to the farm. Minnow had to bring his thoughts back onto his work. There had been a good response from Mary but still no obvious solution to the problem of the farm manager.

That afternoon the farm manager arrived before the blacksmith. He gave Minnow's work a quick glance, was impressed by the domed areas under the oven floors and asked how the ovens were progressing. Minnow suggested all was going well and he thanked him for sending Mary with the message.

"Ah, yes, Mary," he said slowly, "does she know you're attracted to her?"

"She does now," said Minnow, "and has not rejected the idea. Have you given any more thought to the discussion from last evening?"

"I have given it some thought but it will have to wait. I see the blacksmith approaching, we have work to discuss."

The blacksmith soon understood Minnow's plans, suggested building in some lengths of metal rod as support in addition to the brick walls that were planned. He gave the farm manager a price for the work and agreed a date by which it should all be ready.

Minnow was pleased it would be after Christmas as he still had a lot of slow curing of clay to manage. The blacksmith had many farm implements to repair before the spring so the timing suited them both. The farm manager was less pleased as the baker would still be needing kitchen space over the busy Christmas but he could now see an end in sight.

The blacksmith took away his measurements marked on some wooden rods, promising Minnow he'd cut lengths of wooden rods later that he could use for planning.

Minnow was pleased with the progress of his construction. Lighting small fires within the ovens helped with the drying. So far there were no signs of cracks. The real test would be when he was brave enough to bring the ovens up to their working heat but that would be several weeks yet. There were still layers to build and then he could concentrate on the chimney.

The metal rods had been delivered and they were a perfect fit as support for the open part where the smoke would be collected.

Without warning, Mary had been given permission to visit him for a short time in the middle of the afternoon, once a week. Minnow considered this was a good sign that the farm manager might agree to their having a relationship.

One day the farm manager had turned up a little after Mary had arrived and found Minnow still working as well as being able to chat with Mary. They were told quite forcefully that they were on trust and Minnow was expected to continue working, he wasn't being paid to stop and chat or make Mary feel awkward.

Minnow knew that Mary would not visit him if he made her feel uncomfortable. He'd have liked to see Mary more often and preferably during the evening but that was when she had her duties at the farm.

He would have to persuade his parents to visit the farm manager again and discuss his agreeing to a marriage. Perhaps just after Christmas when he could be in a good mood and full of festive drink. It would be dependent on whether the festivities had cost him too much.

As the days grew even shorter the progress slowed. The ovens were not a task to rush. Being able to leave a small fire within the ovens at the end of the day, giving time for them to cool overnight, suited Minnow. He was pleased to find a trace of heat in the ovens when he returned each morning which encouraged him that the ovens would retain their heat. There was even a trace of warmth within the dwelling so the baker should be the most comfortable habitant in Wocca's Hamlet.

The hearth was complete with its clay and fire brick base. The chimney was progressing well leading up from the large metal hood that would collect the smoke and soon he'd be breaking through the roof. He'd take the chimney high enough to take all sparks clear of the thatch.

Too many dwellings had been reduced to ash when hearth fires had gone out of control and sent sparks into the thatch. Roasting fatty meats were the most dangerous, when the melted fat dripped into the flames and on to the hot logs. It made the logs explode, sending sparks high into the reeds.

Even after heavy rains the underside of a good roof would still be dry enough to catch fire. The metal hood and chimney would take care of any sparks. Perhaps one day all dwellings would have such a system.

Christmas took on a new aspect with the town being able to gather together within the new church building. Some charcoal braziers gave their smokeless heat while everyone contributed food and drink. Once the priest had blessed the food and the gathering, everyone shared each other's company and were surprisingly moderate with their consumption.

Minnow concluded that they should have built a latrine. He hoped the outside walls would not suffer too much from the men who kept popping out to be hidden alongside a buttress. The women made their way beyond the hedges before returning looking more comfortable.

Mary was at the church with everyone else from the farm and it gave his Mama and Papa chance to talk with her. She'd developed more confidence talking with people over the last couple of months and Minnow was pleased to see how she'd changed.

The farm manager also seemed relaxed, not having to host the usual gathering at the farm. If it had been summer the barn would have been available but at this time of year it was full of the harvest, another reason the farm manager was happy. The space within the church building was ideal, people were being measured with their amount of drink and the talk wasn't as crude as it would have been at the farm or alehouse. It all combined to encouraged the folk of the town to relax and enjoy themselves.

The dancing and other entertainments were being relished more than usual as everyone felt they could participate without raucous comment or ridicule. The whole atmosphere was easy and very social. The braziers had no need of being re-fuelled, the crowd was generating warmth by their activities.

Lanterns had been hung between the pillars, their soft light reflecting from the white chalk surfaces. There was ample food as no one wished to look mean by their contributions and Christ's birthday was looking and feeling like a version of Heaven. Exhausted children were sleeping in their woollen blankets close to the walls while their parents considered this the best Christmas ever thanks to the Church, Henry II and the building.

Minnow spent the whole of the evening in the company of Mary, dancing, eating, drinking, singing and applauding the other entertainments. It was the first time they'd been so close to each other and able to share the warmth that each generated.

Mama had brought them to the attention of the farm manager who smiled while recognising how they obviously felt about each other. It was very soon after he sought out Papa and agreed to their being joined in marriage. He'd thought through all the alternatives and Minnow was obviously keen to be responsible for her care.

The only thing he'd offer as a dowry was the linen coffer she'd have inherited from her own Mama. He'd claimed he had never looked through the contents and it had been stored within the rafters of an outbuilding. He did hold the key but suspected there were few items of interest within. Mary's Mama didn't come from a wealthy family and her Papa was just a farm labourer come common soldier. He'd leave the arrangements for Minnow's parents to organise. His parting comment was that she had a healthy appetite.

"Mary would be one less mouth for him to feed," Papa confided to Mama.

Mary was given a short time every early afternoon to meet with Minnow's Mama and make preparations for the wedding. She welcomed the prospect of a future with Minnow. Somehow, she thought, his parents had managed to persuade the farm manager to release her as his ward. Mama reassured her that the family would be there to offer support.

Mary had anxieties as well as excitement about the future. Anxieties included how she would be accepted by the community, the farm girls had never been kind to her. The excitement was being away from the farm environment and starting a new way of life.

The farm manager and his wife delivered the linen coffer along with the key. They handed it to Papa on the morning of the wedding. Mary found little of significance among the linens other than a small child's bonnet with a fine lace brim. Mary thanked the pair for the care they had shown her and for giving her the prospect of being a parent herself.

The wedding was conducted by the priest in the church and attended by many from the town. They all stayed, having contributed food, to help celebrate. Mary and Minnow used the new bakery as their home while he completed the work. It was a basic existence for a few weeks and then a dwelling became available that they could call their home.

Mary quickly learnt to manage the plot of land. Mama gave her instructions for preparing meals and Minnow provided everything they required to stay fit, healthy and reasonably clothed.

The baker soon had a thriving business. He employed Mary to look after the customers each morning. It was a small income for her but, added with Minnow's, made them comfortable.

Minnow had been given his new task by the knight. The deanery was having a brick and timber dwelling built for the priest, opposite the church, at the end of The Clearing. It was just within the deanery of Sunning and on the very edge of the town.

It was unusual in that there would be no plot of land attached. However, it was designed to be a fine building, with an upper floor and Minnow would manage that. He'd no plans for chalk pillars, but, there would be a solid foundation, brick and timber walls, chimneys and windows.

Appendix

I'm grateful to have read the novels of **Elizabeth Chadwick**, where she provides a glimpse into the lives of ordinary people, in addition to the nobility, around the reign of Henry II. Her meticulous medieval period research gave me confidence to include details for the time span covered by this novel.

The **Scouting** movement provided me with many basic survival skills that would have been a natural way of life for medieval folk. It is concerning that many of these skills are still essential in many parts of the world today especially where there is conflict.

I was further inspired by the 800^+ year history of the Grade 2* listed **All Saints Church in Wokingham,** particularly by the survival of their chalk pillars, and their foundations, throughout its long life as a place of worship, along with being a community building. The roof and its timbers continue to be a challenge, especially with our expectation of being infrequently in a warm place and that heat rises to constantly affect the roof structure timbers.

Please visit All Saints Wokingham web site for more information about the historic building and the plans for the future of the building.
www.allsaintswokingham.org.uk
Follow the drop down menu to see the work of the **Community Church 2020** group for progress and detailed plans.

My thanks go to my sister and Su McArthur for their suggestions and corrections.

A time line of the period covered by this novel.

1135	Henry I buried in front of the altar of the incomplete Reading Abbey which he founded
1135	Stephen usurped the throne from Henry's daughter, Empress Matilda
1153	Eustace, son of Stephen dies
1154	Stephen dies leaving no male heir
1154	Henry II, son of Empress Matilda and grandson of Henry I, started his reign
1155	Henry II made Thomas a Becket his chancellor
1162	Henry II made Thomas a Becket Archbishop of Canterbury. Thomas resigned as chancellor being unable to serve two masters
1169	Henry had his eldest son crowned Young King Henry by the Bishop of York, Thomas a Becket having fled to France, but Henry II gave the Young King no authority
1170	29th Dec. Murder of Thomas a Becket, Archbishop of Canterbury by four of Henry's knights
1173	Pope declares Becket a Saint following reports of some pilgrims to his tomb being healed
1174	Henry II agreed to be whipped by monks of Canterbury as penance for any part he may have played in the death of Becket
1174	Queen Eleanor placed under house arrest in Salisbury for conspiring with her sons and rising against Henry
1183	The Young King Henry dies from dysentery in France, aged 28

1184	Bishop of Salisbury, Josceline de Bohon, resigned and became a monk at Forde Abbey in Dorset
1184	Post of Bishop of Salisbury vacant to prevent Queen Eleanor having a religious spy. Henry took tithes directly from Wiltshire and the associated Sonning Deanery
1186	Geoffrey, third son of Henry II, dies after being trampled by a horse, aged 28. Only Richard and John remained as male heirs
1189	Henry II dies
1189	Start of reign of Richard I
1189	Bishop Hubert Walter appointed Bishop of Salisbury which included the Sonning Deanery
1189 ~1193	Between these dates Bishop Hubert Walter dedicated the church at Wokingham to All Saints
1190	Bishop Hubert Walter joined the Third Crusade, also known as the King's crusade, with Richard I and Philip II of France
1193	Bishop Hubert Walter became Archbishop of Canterbury
1199	Richard I dies